Alone with   e
situation you're _____, _____ ___ _____ ___ _____ of
someone you loved so many years after it happened. I'm
sorry to say it so awkwardly."

He acknowledged her apology with a nod. "It's been
a shock. I thought Krystal left me and didn't want to be
found."

"Joni told me someone killed her. Is that possible?
Couldn't it have been an accident?"

"At first that's what I assumed, but apparently,
somebody hit her on the head and left her in a gully. In
the national forest beyond the lodge. The police seem to
think I could be capable of doing that." He cleared his
throat. "It's good you came, but I don't want you
burdened with my problem."

"It's Joni's problem, too. She sounded frantic when
she called."

"That's because of the rumors that I'm some sort of
monster."

He put his hands on her shoulders, locking eyes with
her. His grip felt so tight that she winced. "Look, I didn't
kill Krystal. Joni believes me. But we can kiss goodbye
to paying guests if people worry they're not safe under
this roof."

She stepped back to free herself from those hands.

"Sorry." He led her out of the lodge and down the
front steps, their hiking boots thudding on the wood.

Praise for *The First Fiancée*

"Rita A. Popp's debut delivers a brilliant whodunit set in the winter-chilled New Mexico mountains. Cozy up to the fireplace with a cup of hot chocolate and a copy of *The First Fiancée* for a delightful read. Highly recommended!"
~ *Margaret Mizushima, author of the award-winning Timber Creek K-9 Mysteries*

"Rita A. Popp's sleuth, Bethany Jarviss, is clever, determined, and fearless. In her well-paced novel, Popp takes us on a search for the killer of The First Fiancée to help her sister, Joni, who's walking a tightrope as the second fiancée. An excellent series debut."
~ *Patricia Stoltey, author of mysteries and frontier fiction from Five Star/Cengage*

"Bethany Jarviss heads for the New Mexico mountains when the body of The First Fiancée turns up in the woods seven years after her unexplained disappearance. Armed with the doggedness of Jessica Fletcher and the plunk of Nancy Drew, she is determined to clear her sister's fiancé, Matt, of murder charges or expose him before the second fiancée meets the same end. Filled with suspicious characters, each with something to hide, Ms. Popp has written a whodunit that intrigues and surprises. Just when you think you know who—you don't. A great read."
~ *Terry Korth Fischer, author of The Rory Naysmith Mysteries*

The First Fiancée

by

Rita A. Popp

A Bethany Jarviss Mystery

The First Fiancée: A Bethany Jarviss Mystery

COPYRIGHT © 2022 by Rita A. Popp

Cover Art by *Kim Mendoza*

The Wild Rose Press, Inc.
PO Box 708
Adams Basin, NY 14410-0708
Visit us at www.thewildrosepress.com

Publishing History
First Edition, 2022
Trade Paperback ISBN 978-1-5092-4542-0
Digital ISBN 978-1-5092-4543-7

The First Fiancée: A Bethany Jarviss Mystery
Published in the United States of America

Dedication

To Tony, for asking me to dance

Acknowledgements

Writing is a solitary business for the most part, helped along by those who take more than a casual interest in a writer's dream of publication.

My husband Tony Popp has never wavered in encouraging my journey from journalist to fiction writer. Retired publisher Linda Harris and former writing group partner Jim Earley have been steadfast friends during the ups and downs of this writer's life. My editor at The Wild Rose Press, Melanie Billings, guided the manuscript from submission to final product with an incredible level of skill and encouragement. The Colorado Chapter of Sisters in Crime welcomed me into their ranks when Tony and I moved to Colorado a few years ago. My special thanks goes to the SinC-Colorado Book Club for the lively discussions and camaraderie.

Prologue

Panting in the thin air, Jason trailed Cory along a ridge thick with pines, junipers, and gnarled oaks shedding dry, brown leaves. Jason's lungs ached, but what a relief to escape Sorrel, that nowhere New Mexico town, at least for a while. It had little to offer thirteen-year-old guys stuck with two sets of parents for a whole weekend. They'd begged off Sunday lunch at the motel's café, tossed granola bars and water bottles into their daypacks, and promised to be gone an hour max. They kept secret their plan to get off the beaten path they'd hiked with the grownups the day before.

Half an hour out, Jason, his chest heaving, called a halt to their march. "We ought to turn back." He imagined the mothers packing up everybody's stuff, the dads settling the bill. The parents wanted to get down the bad part of the mountain road to La Plata in full daylight so they could relax the rest of the way home to El Paso.

"Let's go a little bit farther," Cory said. "To that pine with two tops." He didn't wait for an answer.

Jason, trudging on, felt his boot catch on something—an exposed tree root that he saw too late as he slid down a ravine, yelling as his hands scraped against jagged rocks and prickly cactus. He landed with his backpack bunched under his neck and heard Cory's hoot of laughter. Mindful of last winter's skiing lessons, he rolled to his side to get up and let out a shriek. Inches from his face, a creepy skeletal hand thrust up from the ravine's rocky floor—a left hand with a dirt-encrusted diamond-and-ruby ring encircling the fleshless third finger.

Chapter 1

Bethany Jarviss hated to admit it, but the ascent to Sorrel had her spooked. Narrow and bumpy usually didn't faze her—a New Mexican born and raised, she could handle rural roads—but these particular switchbacks made her teeth ache. *Get a grip*, she ordered her panicky self. *Joni needs you to be the strong big sister. Almost there now.*

Bethany tightened her hold on the SUV's steering wheel. At a particularly harrowing blind curve, she held her breath and hugged the inside of the road so closely the passenger doors rasped against scrub oaks sticking out of the crumbling mountainside. Beyond the curve, as a pickup aimed straight at her—its cowboy-hatted driver raising his hand in a customary back-country salute—she thought her heart would stop.

Actually, there had been a good inch of clearance between the two vehicles, Bethany told herself as she pulled off at a railed overlook and got out of the car. She tried to relax her jaw, which throbbed from the last, scary twenty minutes. A sheer drop-off beyond the railing set her heart racing again, as did the sight, on the inside of the road, of boulders positioned to fall on her head. High above, pine trees brushed a cloudless sky. At their base, she detected movement—a lone hiker aiming binoculars at the view. He saw her and waved. *Don't fall off the edge,* she wanted to cry out but merely called hello.

She checked her watch. Almost noon. She'd made good time taking back roads south from Las Cuevas. She resumed the drive, bracing herself for more close squeaks, but didn't meet any other vehicles. The road widened and flattened, *thank goddess*, as Joni would say in a nod to the divine feminine. In a couple of minutes, the gravel turned to weathered pavement at a sign, *Welcome to Sorrel. Alt. 7,886*. A considerable rise above the valley floor of 3,800 feet, no wonder she felt light-headed. On the right sat a clapboard building labeled *MUSEUM*. A guy stood pumping gas outside *Ernie's Mercantile*, a building topped by a false Western front strung with holiday lights. A few people strolled past gift shops and a tavern on a covered boardwalk. At the far end of town, Bethany got a quick look at a café, motel, and redbrick schoolhouse—no, the library, by its sign.

The pavement ended, but the SUV rumbled sure-footedly over a narrow forest road. Bethany took the turnoff Joni had said to expect and saw, at the top of a wooded slope, the hunting lodge Matt and Joni planned to open before Christmas as a bed and breakfast. Its log sides appeared freshly stained, and the window frames freshly painted a greenish turquoise, a color choice Joni said she'd agonized over.

When no one answered her knock, Bethany let herself into a large lobby and said "Wow" out loud at the massive stone fireplace and wagon-wheel chandeliers hanging from a beamed, cathedral ceiling. Joni's flare for set design showed in the Southwestern wood-framed furniture, bright Mexican rugs, and nineteenth-century pictures of miners with pickaxes, cowboys on horses, and studio portraits of solemn-faced men, women, and children.

Bethany peered into the rooms surrounding the lobby: an enclosed porch piled with sealed cardboard boxes, the office, and the kitchen where a dishwasher and new cabinets waited to be installed. As she decided to investigate the upper floors for signs of life, Joni ran down the stairs. "I saw your car. You made it!"

As always, Bethany keenly felt the five-year gap between herself and her younger sister. Joni, at twenty-seven, resembled a rebellious kid with spiky hair dyed a whitish blonde. People who didn't know she'd been adopted assumed she took after their petite mother. A head shorter than Bethany, she was tiny in every respect, from her elfin face to her feet.

Hugging Joni felt like holding a quivering butterfly. Her delicate frame seemed thinner than ever. *Is she not eating? Best not ask now.* "The lodge looks terrific. Even better than in your pictures."

Joni's blue eyes, artistically made up, looked huge, sad, and scared. "It's Matt's dream project," she said. "Mine, too, now. It's so close to happening, but it won't if Matt is arrested for something he didn't do."

Joni had bitten her nails to the quick and left them unpolished for once. She wore rings on most of her fingers and a diamond stud in her right earlobe. Her embroidered silk shirt and red cowboy boots made Bethany aware of her own unglamorous black parka and black jeans, her scuffed hiking boots.

"Hey, don't worry." She made a wild promise. "Everything will work out."

"Says you." She took Bethany by the hand and pulled her onto a loveseat. "We're still in shock over Krystal Decker's bones turning up three weeks ago. After seven years! Why did it have to happen right after we got engaged? People are calling her the 'First Fiancée,' like an official title. Matt's been grilled by the sheriff's deputies and the state police. It's been horrible for him."

Bethany gave Joni's hand a light squeeze. "What has Matt been saying lately about Krystal?"

"Not much more than I already knew. Krystal with a K. A small-town star. Matt heard her sing at one of the festivals and asked her out. His job as a financial adviser must have impressed that gold digger! Once they got engaged, he found out how bad she wanted to get away from Sorrel. She never liked his plan to move down here from Santa Fe and run this place as a B&B, not just come for weekends. That's why when she disappeared, he thought she ran out on him."

She jumped up as Matt came down the stairs. "Look, Bethany's here!"

Matt's expression shifted from preoccupied to polite in an instant. He came across as Bethany remembered him—impressively tall and strong—with freckles that fit his last name, MacGregor. Today the freckles stood out on winter-pale skin. The man looked exhausted.

"Bethany. You made good time. You must have left Las Cuevas before dawn."

"At six. It's not that much farther than from Santa Fe." She moved to a chair on the far side of a rough-hewn coffee table so the couple could have the loveseat. "The road up the mountain must be a mess during a snowstorm."

"The last few miles for sure," Matt said. He gathered both of Joni's hands in his. "Let's hope the weather holds. Joni said she told you we have bookings for less than two weeks from now, all the way through Christmas and New Year's. But first, we're throwing a dinner for the locals—"

"Shop owners, people who've lived here forever, those types," Joni said, her voice upbeat.

"People we want on our side," Matt said. "On Friday, only five days from now. And an open house next Sunday."

He blinked and squeezed the bridge of his nose. Bethany guessed the contacts Joni had said he wore were bothering him.

"We're cutting it close to be ready to open," Joni said. "We're still painting and decorating."

"I can stay for a few days," Bethany said. "I came to help."

"I know you did." Joni slid closer to Matt. "And like I told you on the phone, we do have two employees who live with us. Matt, tell her about David and Gloria."

"David is a good friend," Matt said. "He's going to be the lodge's massage therapist and our handyman. Our housekeeper will cook breakfasts for the guests."

"Gloria," Joni said. "From La Plata. You'll like her. She works nights at the Black Bear, the bar. Around here, people do whatever jobs they can get. You'll like David, too. He teaches P.E. part-time at the elementary school. He's from Santa Fe, recovering from a divorce."

"Our guests will stay in rooms off the lobby," Matt said, gesturing to a hallway, "and on the second floor. Joni and I, plus David and Gloria are on the third floor."

"You'll be up there with us," Joni said. "Let's get you settled."

"Or maybe you'd like some lunch?" Matt asked.

"Sorry, I should have thought of that," Joni said. She drew down the corners of her mouth in her characteristic *whoops* gesture.

Food could be a touchy topic with Joni, so Bethany rushed to say, "I had a burger in La Plata. I'm fine."

"Okay," Matt said, "but raid the fridge any time you like. The kitchen's that way."

Bethany didn't bother to say she'd peeked into the kitchen. Matt insisted on helping fetch her luggage from the SUV, and Joni said she would head upstairs to turn on the heat. "It'll take a while for your room to warm up," she said. "Think rustic charm."

Alone with Matt, Bethany said, "It must be hard, the situation you're facing, finding out about the death of someone you loved so many years after it happened. I'm sorry to say it so awkwardly."

He acknowledged her apology with a nod. "It's been a shock. I thought Krystal left me and didn't want to be found."

"Joni told me someone killed her. Is that possible? Couldn't it have been an accident?"

"At first, that's what I assumed, but apparently, somebody hit her on the head and left her in a gully. In the national forest beyond the lodge. The police seem to think I could be capable of doing that." He cleared his throat. "It's good you came, but I don't want you burdened with my problem."

"It's Joni's problem, too. She sounded frantic when she called."

"That's because of the rumors that I'm some sort of monster."

He put his hands on her shoulders, locking eyes with her. His grip felt so tight that she winced. "Look, I didn't kill Krystal. Joni believes me. But we can kiss goodbye to paying guests if people worry they're not safe under this roof."

She stepped back to free herself from those hands.

"Sorry." He led her out of the lodge and down the front steps, their hiking boots thudding on the hard wood.

****

Unlocking the SUV, Bethany let Matt take charge of her duffel bag and a smaller holdall. She slipped her daypack over her shoulder and gathered up the pillow she toted on her business trips and the briefcase that held her laptop. She told Matt to leave the sleeping bag; she kept it in the car for emergencies.

"You could be glad you brought it." He made a short "huh" sound that might have been a laugh. "Heat is a scarce commodity on the top floor."

They climbed creaky, uncarpeted stairs to the second-floor lounge where Joni had upholstered the easy chairs in the same fresh fabric as below. An antique pot-bellied stove contrasted with a wall-mounted flat-screen television. "We've got satellite TV and Wi-Fi through a phone company's landline," Matt said proudly.

The third-floor lounge mimicked the one below in size, but no one had attended to the worn furniture, cracked stucco, and scratched wood floors. Joni had mentioned the lodge's origin as a nineteenth-century private home turned boarding house, unused for decades before Matt's uncle acquired it. The third floor certainly showed the building's age.

As if reading her thoughts, Matt said, "We're making do up here for now." He nodded toward a door. "Our bedroom is over there. Eventually, we'll build ourselves a decent-sized cabin behind the lodge, along with several guest cabins. We don't actually have many of our things here yet. They're still at the condo we're renting in Santa Fe."

Joni waited for them in a chilly room where a space heater going full blast supplemented a faint stream of warmth seeping from a floor vent. She smoothed a patchwork quilt as Bethany admired the light pine furniture and pictures of old-time scenes like the ones in the lobby.

"I love this room," Bethany said. "It's so homey."

"You'd enjoy the best feature in the summer," Joni said as Matt pulled open floor-length drapes to expose french doors to a private deck fitted with a rusting wrought-iron table and matching chairs.

The deck faced the forest behind the lodge and a range of craggy mountain peaks in the distance. *Gorgeous view.* Bethany didn't say it, realizing Krystal's bones had been found somewhere out there.

"I helped my uncle, my dad's brother, build the deck when I was a kid." Matt's voice softened. "He taught me how to do things right. Brought me here a few times a year to give my mom a break."

"You're the son he never had," Joni said. "That's why he willed you the lodge."

"I'd best get back to whipping it into shape." He flashed a smile and left them.

"Matt was barely ten when his dad died of a heart attack," Joni said. "But I think he took it harder when his uncle passed away eight years ago. He doesn't like to talk about it." She cleared her throat. "I'll let you settle in. I'm painting a guest room on the second floor. Come down in a while."

Chapter 2

It took all of five minutes to unpack. Bethany tossed
her pillow onto the bed and stowed her bags under it, and
set her briefcase on the desk, all the while thinking about
her sister. The family's free spirit, Joni had married at
nineteen, been divorced by twenty-one, and been in
several relationships before she met Matt less than a year
ago. She'd gotten engaged so fast! To a guy now
suspected of murder!

Bethany took her toothbrush next door to an
obviously shared bathroom. A crowded assortment of
towels hung on racks, and a variety of shampoo bottles
balanced on the wall side of a claw-footed tub.

The bathroom felt ice cold. As Bethany brushed her
teeth, she noticed an ancient electric heater built into the
wall. She hoped it would work when she needed it and
that there would be enough hot water for everyone living
here plus guests on the two floors below. In an email,
Joni had admitted worrying that the second and third
floors only had one bathroom each. Matt's inheritance
and savings wouldn't begin to cover a complete remodel
of the lodge, she'd confided.

If it weren't a conflict of interest, the Jarviss
Foundation might award a development grant for this
project. The lodge would be a boon to the Sorrel
economy. But as grants manager, Bethany knew full well
the Foundation couldn't support the projects of family

members. And Matt might soon become one.

Finished in the bathroom, she noticed a nearby door standing open. She stepped into a narrow space and saw a man stretched out on a massage table. Before she could back away, he yawned and sat up. "Whoa, didn't mean to fall asleep."

Bethany apologized for intruding and told him her name. "I'm Joni's sister."

"I heard you were coming down from Las Cuevas. I'm David Sudesky. Matt's friend. And Joni's. How do you like my massage room? It's an old linen closet. We had to take out the shelves, and it's kind of a tight squeeze, but it'll do."

The walls were a soft butter color. A lighted candle in an ornate sconce gave off a vanilla scent that almost disguised the smell of fresh paint. On the far wall of the windowless room, a print of two hands, the index fingers nearly touching, depicted Michelangelo's Sistine Chapel image of God creating Adam.

"First massage with my compliments," David said. "I've been testing my new table. I think it will do."

The man had kind eyes and well-tended hands. He looked to be about forty, but he hopped off the high table with the grace of a gymnast. "Where are Matt and Joni?" he asked.

"I'm not sure. Joni said she was going to do some painting. She and Matt met me when I arrived a while ago. They showed me to my room, the one with the deck."

"Right," David said. "Matt's favorite but too small for him and Joni. Matt's uncle had emphysema— breathed easier in the mountain air—and wouldn't let anybody smoke in the building. As a kid, Matt sneaked many a cigarette on that deck."

He blew out the vanilla candle. "I'd better go see what he needs done. Like I said, if you want a massage, let me know."

****

Bethany found Joni in a second-floor room rolling pale cream semi-gloss on a wall with fast, steady strokes. She had changed into old clothes and was humming along to a tune on her audio device. Bethany tapped her sister's shoulder to get her attention. Joni set the roller in a pan on the floor and took out her earbuds.

"I met David," Bethany said. "He seems like a good guy. I found him testing his massage table, but then he went to help Matt."

"Testing his table! Well, he deserves a break now and then."

"If you've got another roller, I can help paint," Bethany offered.

Joni gave her a serious look. "Sure, but there's something I'd rather have you do." She hesitated, then went on. "Matt and I have been avoiding Sorrel. People started giving us funny looks right after the gruesome discovery three weeks ago. But nobody knows you. You could go into town and find out all the gossip."

The idea of being a snoop did not appeal to her. "Joni, I don't think—"

"Listen, okay? You're good at talking to people and finding out things. Dad's always bragging about how well you investigate all those organizations in line for grants. I bet you could hear some interesting things about Krystal that Matt never knew. After all, you—not the cops—found out that girl in Albuquerque didn't trip on the stairs."

Suddenly Bethany got it. "You want me to get involved in this murder? That's why you begged me to come?" Her jaw clenched at the thought of her one brush with crime a few months before. What started out as a favor to the dead student's mother—to clean out the college girl's room in the house where she had boarded—ended with discovering the girl had been pushed to her death.

Joni planted her hands on her narrow hips. "You helped that mother. She didn't have to go on thinking her daughter accidentally caused her own death. That woman isn't even your friend. She's Mom's. Can't you talk to a few people in town for me, your sister? I'm dying to find out what they're saying about Krystal. And about Matt."

Matt had said people called him a monster. Had he been exaggerating, or could people really believe that? And assuming Matt hadn't killed his first fiancée, who had? Someone long gone or who still lived in Sorrel?

Gnawing on a cuticle, Joni watched with hope in those huge blue eyes.

"Tell you what," Bethany said. "Tomorrow, I'll go into town. I drove straight through it on the way here and barely got a look at it. Today, let me help you paint this room. But first, I'd better call the folks so they know I made it here safely. I'll use my cell phone."

"Cell phones don't work in the lodge and most places in Sorrel," Joni said. "Use the landline out there in the lounge. Tell the folks hi. I've been meaning to talk to Mom and Dad, but we've been so busy…"

Bethany dialed, dismayed at Joni's relationship with their parents. Busyness hadn't kept Joni from phoning; she could make the time. When Krystal's bones were discovered, Joni had called Bethany, imploring her, as usual, to be the bearer of bad news. Bethany had complied, stopping by the university where education students lined up outside her mother's door for help during office hours.

After hearing Bethany out, Eleanor said, "Joni's standing by her man, but is he worthy of her loyalty? You'd better do what she wants and drive down to Sorrel, set our minds at ease if at all possible about this Matt MacGregor."

Now, Bethany left her mother a brief message, then stood wondering why Joni could not discuss her problems with Eleanor the way students did, the way Bethany had done all her life. She often wondered the same thing about her sister and their father. She valued his advice; Joni avoided it.

The previous day, after listening to an update on a grant recipient's project, their father had asked, "What has Joni told you about the murder?" She hadn't phoned him, he said. No, he wouldn't contact her; she could call if she needed him. "At least she spoke to you and Don. She told your brother not to worry, to stay focused on his golf tournament. As if any of us could not worry about Joni."

****

In the morning, Bethany had dressed when Joni, in a fleece bathrobe and fluffy slippers, knocked on her door.

"If you don't need the bathroom, I'll grab a shower and get to work, Joni said. "Matt's already doing stuff in the office. And FYI, it's fend for yourself around here for breakfast." Joni yawned.

"No problem," Bethany said. The night before, at

dinner, she'd checked out the kitchen. "I know where the coffee pot is. I'll be fine."

Back in her room with toast in a napkin and fresh brew in her travel mug, Bethany turned on her laptop and got to work. A few days here didn't mean a break from reading grant proposals. But first, she'd email Don to say she'd arrived and find out how he'd fared in his practice rounds for an end-of-year match.

The time flew by. At noon, ready for a break, she went out to her room's private deck. The room below hers didn't have a deck, so she could see two floors down to the patio behind the kitchen. Matt and David sat there talking as smoke wafted up from Matt's cigarette. David wasn't smoking, but the massage therapist probably wasn't a smoker. Matt's bad habit worried Bethany, not only for his sake but for the effect of secondhand smoke on Joni's delicate health. But tobacco use had to be the least of Matt's troubling baggage.

David said something Bethany didn't catch, then, "You need a good lawyer."

Matt replied in a voice too low to hear.

"You'd make bail and be out right away, but it won't come to that," David said.

"Keep it down. Somebody'll hear."

By somebody, Matt probably meant her. He knew she had the room above them. But why would it matter if she overheard? Matt had confided to her about Krystal at the first opportunity. But maybe he didn't want her telling Joni he feared being arrested.

Bethany went back inside and resumed work, but she couldn't concentrate for long. She grabbed her parka and daypack. She would make good on her promise to Joni to go into Sorrel.

She found her sister, Matt, and David in the kitchen between a worn chopping block that dominated the room and new cabinets stacked two-high along a wall. The dishwasher sat with its hoses not yet hooked up to the water pipes.

"One of the top cabinets is missing," Matt said.

Joni ran her fingers through her spiky hair. "Oh goddess, we can't just run out to a big box store and solve this pronto. Either we drive down to La Plata or wait another week for a delivery." She looked at Bethany. "Sure, it's only an hour to La Plata, but you know what this end of the road's like."

"Brutal," Bethany agreed.

"The store messed up for the second time," Matt said, pounding a fist on the chopping block, sending a knife off the edge. "First, one of the bottom cabinets is the wrong oak color. Now this. What's the matter with those people?"

David picked up the knife and set it gently back into place.

Bethany listened as the others talked anxiously about pulling off the lodge's opening events. Would the Friday buffet dinner for the locals prove too ambitious for Gloria? Should they have hired a catering company from La Plata?

"Gloria insists she can handle the bulk of it, with a few things on order from the mercantile and pies from the café. Everyone knows I'm a hopeless cook," Joni said.

Matt put his arm around her shoulders. "That's well documented. Leave the cooking to Gloria."

Joni elbowed Matt lightly in the side, then relaxed against him. "Okay, but you guys better get the

17

dishwasher installed. Since I'm not cooking, I'll have to help Gloria clean up."

"Where is she anyway?" Matt asked.

"At the merc. She'll be back soon."

"Looks like she's got dinner in the crockpot," David said. He took a deep breath. "Oh, does that smell good!"

Minutes later Gloria, a slim, pretty girl introduced the night before, came into the kitchen through the back door, lugging four cloth tote bags filled with groceries. Cold air whooshed in with her. She kicked the door shut, thumped the bags on the floor, and unwound a long, mauve scarf from around her neck. Her denim jacket over a thin sweater didn't look heavy enough to keep out the cold. As she shrugged out of the jacket, her dark, messy ponytail swung and bobbed.

Deep into their project, Matt and David barely said hello. Gloria put away the groceries with help from Joni and Bethany, then lifted the crockpot lid and gave the contents a stir.

"What's that dish?" Bethany asked. "Something out of the ordinary by the aroma."

"Beef bourguignon with a handful of spices and the cheapest cut of meat I could find in La Plata," Gloria said. "I don't think it's horse meat." She giggled, a sound pegging her as more girl than grownup.

"You can't get everything at the mercantile in Sorrel," Joni said. "Gloria goes to La Plata every couple of weeks. It's a major shopping trip. Sometimes we go together."

"And hit the thrift shops," Gloria said. "And garage sales."

"We've found a lot of things for the lodge that way," Joni said. "Saved hundreds, maybe thousands."

"She's an amazing shopper and decorator," Gloria added.

"She is," Bethany agreed. It wasn't surprising, given Joni's degree in theater set design.

"Dad would say shopping is my only talent," Joni said. She fiddled with her hair, messing up the gelled spikes.

"No, he wouldn't." Bethany knew it was best to say nothing more. *Let's not go down that road*, their brother would have cautioned. Like Joni, Don was adopted, but he didn't share her sense of failing to measure up to some never-specified standard of success.

"Damn appliance," Matt said from the floor, giving no sign he'd heard Joni and Bethany. "Why is everything so fracking hard?"

Installing the dishwasher wasn't going well, it seemed.

"We can figure it out," David said. "But maybe we should take a break."

"Maybe you guys should read the instructions," Gloria suggested in a mock-serious tone. She looked at the two men sitting on the floor. "My dad always does that as a last resort."

"Where are the instructions?" David asked, playing along. "Tossed out with the packing materials?"

Matt forced a grin. "Probably. Let's keep at it."

Bethany pulled Joni aside. "Tell you what. I need some fresh air. I'll take a walk into town and get some lunch, okay?"

"And talk to people, right? Find out all the gossip."

Joni's face expressed such relief and hope, Bethany felt a pang of anxiety. "I can try."

"That's all I ask," Joni said. She trailed Bethany to

the lobby entrance. "What's your story going to be?" She came across like a kid planning some scheme to fool the folks.

Bethany put on her parka. "My story? The truth—that I'm your sister."

"You saw how edgy Matt got in the kitchen. He normally doesn't fly off the handle like that. I think he confides more in David, which hurts, you know? Shouldn't Matt talk to me? I'm his fiancée." Joni compressed her lips into a thin line.

"How long has he known David?"

"Quite a while. Since before David's divorce."

"Matt wants to be strong for you, but he probably doesn't have to act that way in front of David."

"I guess, but this is our first crisis as a couple. We should face it together." Joni raised her chin. Her eyes shone with unshed tears. "I believe in Matt completely. I'm going to go tell him again."

"Maybe you should let him be," Bethany suggested gently. "Let Matt and David finish with the dishwasher."

"I do have stuff to get on with," Joni admitted. "The last of the painting."

"Good idea. Keep busy. Joni, what are the locals like around here?"

"They're friendly, but most of them are really conservative, like Dad. They probably think I'm weird, but that's nothing new, is it? Matt's more like them, but he's still an outsider."

"Where should I get lunch?"

"Besides the bar, where you can only get pizza, there's the mercantile's deli and the Ponderosa Café. Try the Ponderosa. It's at this end of town."

"Okay. I saw it when I drove in."

As Bethany pulled on her gloves, Joni said, "When I first met Matt, he told me that after Krystal Decker left him, he realized she didn't live in the real world. Like a lot of actors, I told him. Maybe you can find out more about that." Her mood much improved, she smiled like a conspirator. "Have a nice lunch while I get high on paint fumes." She screwed in her earbuds.

Chapter 3

The solitary ten-minute walk into town gave Bethany time to wonder what chance the lodge had of making it, given its remote location. Southern New Mexico wasn't a tourist mecca like the northern part of the state. No pueblos down here, no legendary Southwestern cities, no resorts to attract tourists except one owned by the Mescalero Apaches near Ruidoso. But travelers seeking an off-the-beaten-path experience, having braved the road up to Sorrel, would appreciate the absence of stoplights. A rustic lodge would keep people in town overnight or longer. It would be a boon to the shops and other businesses.

At the edge of town, where *School Road* crossed *Main Street*, a sign pointed to an elementary school out of sight. On the corner, white paint flaked from the window frames of the weathered redbrick library. Maybe someday, the Jarviss Foundation could provide a grant for repairs to the aged building.

Bethany continued down Main to where the *Ponderosa Café and Motel* announced its dual purpose with a sign aptly but unnecessarily decorated with an image of a pine tree. Ironically, the motel and café shared a cramped, paved lot devoid of trees. To the rear, a hillside rose sharply. On it stood a few dwellings with smoke rising from the chimneys.

The café most likely had been a miner's cabin,

judging by its small size. Its empty, enclosed front porch, fitted with booths and decorated with yellowed newspaper articles and historical photos, felt chilly. Bethany passed through a low doorway, surmounted by a *Watch Your Head* sign, to the main dining room. Here, a Christmas tree blazed with lights, as did the antlers of a mounted deer head. Paintings of mountain vistas, ranchers herding cattle, adobe dwellings, and red chile ristras covered the walls. Bethany loved the place. *Vintage New Mexico.*

Two girls, who looked barely out of their teens, sipped sodas as they watched over three toddlers in booster seats. An old fellow chewed his hamburger as he did a newspaper crossword. He grunted a thanks as a young waitress refilled his coffee mug.

As she poured, the waitress, who wore a red sweater with appliqued snowmen, called, "Sit anywhere, miss. I'll bring you a menu."

The girls and toddlers paid no attention to Bethany, but the old guy nodded almost imperceptibly. When the waitress deposited the coffee carafe on a hotplate near the opening to the kitchen, Bethany saw a stocky, middle-aged woman in a stained, white apron—the cook probably—standing there.

"We still have some soup," the waitress said. "Beef barley. Good for a cold day, 'specially after a long drive."

Great! She wanted to talk. "Do I look road weary?"

Bethany meant it as a joke, but the waitress said hastily, "No, miss, I don't mean that. But you're not from around here, and you didn't stay at the motel last night, so you must've drove up today. I clean the rooms. There's plenty empty if you need a place for tonight."

Why not satisfy her curiosity? Bethany said she didn't need a room, that she had arrived yesterday to visit her sister and her sister's fiancé.

"You're staying at the old hunting lodge?"

"That's right. I'm Bethany, by the way."

"Trudy. Nice to meet you." She looked over her shoulder. "I better take your order. I'm not supposed to chat up people. Mrs. Callender don't like it."

Bethany ordered the soup, declined a sandwich or burger to go with it, but agreed to coffee. "Coming right up," Trudy said. "I'm real sorry about everything they're going through at the lodge." She made tracks for the kitchen without waiting for a reply. Soon, she returned with coffee and water. The old man finished his crossword, folded the newspaper carefully, put cash on the table, and left without waiting for change.

The other woman brought the soup, along with two dinner rolls, while Trudy bussed the tables. The woman, who had kind blue eyes, asked if Bethany needed anything else. Bethany cast around in her mind for a conversational opener, but the woman saved her from thinking of one. "Trudy says you're Joni Jarviss's sister."

"That's right. Bethany. Same last name."

"Lorene Callender. Just call me Lorene. This is my café and motel. Can I join you for a bit?"

"Sure."

Lorene took a seat. "Joni's a nice person, not that I know her well, but I can tell. And Matt's good people. It's nice he's back."

The woman had a comforting voice. Despite thick eyeliner and smoky shadow that gave her a hard appearance, she exuded a motherly warmth. "Joni must be glad to have you here," she continued. "But I have to say, you don't look a thing alike. Both of you pretty ones, if I may say so, but Joni's getting thin as a rail."

In silence, Bethany placed her napkin on her lap. She would not gossip about Joni's health. Fortunately, her silence served as a prompt. "Matt and her have got to know people are talking about the grim discovery," Lorene continued. "Krystal being dead all these years came as a real shock to everybody."

Bethany imagined the gossip mill regrinding every aspect of the story of Krystal and the man who loved her.

Lorene's blue eyes took on a faraway look, but then she snapped back to the present. "You're not eating your soup. Don't let it get cold, honey."

Bethany picked up her spoon. After a mouthful, she said, "This is delicious."

"Homemade by me," Lorene said. "Rolls, too. And you ought to try a piece of my pie."

"How do you manage to do all that cooking and baking?"

"I don't sleep a lot. And, to be fair, Trudy and another girl help me."

Bethany broke apart a crusty roll, realizing how hungry she felt. Lorene watched her butter it with the satisfied look of a nurturer.

"You said the death shocked people," Bethany prompted.

Lorene folded her hands across a plump middle. She had changed her stained apron for a fresh one to come out to talk. "They're dredging up what they said years ago. Awful things. That Krystal chased Matt for his money, that she aimed to get as much of it out of him as she could. Never intended to marry him at all. That might be she had a new lover, somebody she expected to run off with to a whole new life. A singer, she was, and an actress back in high school. Wanted to go live in L.A. with the stars, join a band, maybe get a part in a movie. Always in la-la land about her future."

"Did people think she had talent?" It seemed like an irrelevant question, but Bethany wanted to know.

"She had a voice like an angel. Sang any kind of song people wanted to hear. No idea if she could act. I never went to any of the school plays in the valley. We've only got an elementary in Sorrel. After that, the kids get bussed down to La Plata."

Lorene paused as if aware she had gotten off track. Bethany waited for her to go on, and sure enough, she continued: "I have to say Krystal was a looker. A natural blonde that stayed blonde from girl to woman, not like some of us bottle gals." Lorene patted her brassy hair. "You could say she had natural beauty and knew it. But fat lot of good it did her, come to find out. Gorgeous face and body, all the female assets, plus an eye to the main chance."

Lorene leaned toward Bethany. "You know what? Matt never could of kept hold of Krystal. He's too tame and respectable. Probably thought after they wed, she'd forget all about her silly notions. Didn't see Krystal for what she was, a dreamer and a schemer. That's what people are saying anyway."

Bethany had finished her soup and started picking apart the second dinner roll, reducing it to a pile of crumbs. Getting this woman to talk about a dead girl made her uneasy and a little ashamed. When she interviewed grants applicants, she had a right to their information. But if Lorene noticed her unease, she pretended not to.

When Trudy came over to freshen Bethany's coffee, Lorene said without making it sound like an order, "Might as well sweep the floor in the front room while nobody's in it, honey."

Lorene waited to say more until the waitress moved out of earshot. "How's Matt doing? He hasn't been in since the police showed up."

"He's busy working on the lodge."

"Good for him." Lorene's head bobbed like a dashboard hula dancer's. "The state police will sort it out. It's beyond those sheriff's deputies. State cops have been up and down the mountain for the last three weeks. They've eaten plenty of meals right here."

The café owner surveyed her small kingdom, then dropped her voice. "I've talked to the lot of them."

Bethany took that as her cue to ask, "What do they have to say?"

"Nothing except questions and more questions. Did I know the dead woman? Do I remember anything about the day she went missing, the days just before that? How long I knew her, how long I've lived here, and so on and so forth. And when they huddle together and eat, they talk so quiet you can't hear a thing unless it's about wives and kiddies. But they sure like my food. I hate to say it, but the murder has brought me extra business. Come to think of it, though, not for the last few days. I haven't seen any of them."

Lorene stopped talking. David from the lodge stood in the doorway between the two rooms. She called, "Hey, David, how's it going? Cup of coffee or still a tea totaler?" She cocked her head and winked at the deliberate misuse of teetotaler.

David came toward them and said affectionately,

27

"Chamomile if you have it. I already had too much caffeine at the lodge."

"Coming right up. Menu?"

"Just the tea, please."

Lorene waved a dismissive hand to Trudy, who watched them, clutching a broom. "I'll get this one. You finish your sweeping."

"May I?" David indicated a chair across from Bethany.

"Of course. Any luck with the dishwasher?"

He raised clenched hands in a victor's gesture. "The ceremonial first load is running as we speak. I came into town with these." He drew a stack of flyers from his coat pocket and pushed one across the table to Bethany as Lorene brought a cup of hot water and, on a matching saucer, a packet of chamomile tea. He handed Lorene a flyer and asked if she would put one up on the bulletin board.

"Sure thing. If my back keeps hurting like it's been in this cold weather, I'll give you a call. You don't do feet by any chance? Mine are plenty sore at the end of the day."

"I can help you with that. Come and see me."

"Glory be," Lorene said. "You'll have more customers than Crush, mark my words. Well then. Enjoy!" She headed for the kitchen.

"Crush?" Bethany asked.

He ripped open the packet and dropped the teabag into the water. "Crush Dobbs. He owns the Black Bear Bar. On the other side of Main Street, down a ways from here."

"I see. Where people normally go for R&R." She studied the flyer, which read *David Sudesky, Massage*

Therapist, Sorrel Lodge, and in smaller type *Swedish Massage. Hot Stone Therapy. Foot Reflexology. Cranial Sacral Therapy.*

"Are you booking massages already, even though the lodge isn't open?"

"Sure. Matt said to me, why wait?"

"You and he are good friends, aren't you?"

"The best." He lifted the teabag out of the golden brew, took a sip, and visibly relaxed. She glanced at his face: smooth but with faint age lines around the eyes. Probably an older man than she first guessed, closer to forty-five than forty.

Bethany drank some of her now-cold coffee and pushed the mug aside. "Did you guys meet in Santa Fe?"

"That's right. My wife and I hired him to manage our admittedly modest investments. He's still my financial adviser but not my ex's. I'm glad I made the move to Sorrel. I won't always live at the lodge. I own a cabin, a fixer-upper I plan to work on a little at a time. Santa Fe wasn't big enough for that woman and me." He shook his head at the pathetic attempt at humor.

Seeing the two young ladies across the room zipping the kids into puffy jackets, Bethany asked David if he had children. Twin daughters, he said. Nineteen-year-old college students. "They're spending Christmas with their mom," he added. "They're supposed to come stay with me after the first of the year before their spring semester starts. Matt has reserved them a room and insists on me not paying for it. For friends, his policy is like that hotel chain advertises: *Kids stay free.*"

"Matt and Joni must appreciate your handyman skills."

"I'm not that handy," he admitted. "I do it to help

Matt. And I teach physical education two days a week at the grade school. I taught full-time at the school in Santa Fe, where my ex still does. After the divorce, we kept bumping into each other in the teachers' lounge, so that didn't work. I moved here for a more peaceful life."

"But that's changed now, hasn't it, with Krystal's bones being found?"

His voice hardened. "It's incredible Krystal's been dead all these years. It's awful for Matt."

"For Joni, too," Bethany pointed out.

"Right," he said. "Awful for both of them."

He stared into his cup like a psychic reading tea leaves. He seemed to be a decent, caring person. Bethany wondered why his marriage had failed, what his ex-wife would say about him. Most of all, she wondered what he thought about Krystal. "Did you like Krystal? Or didn't you know her?"

"I met her a couple of times in Santa Fe and once in Sorrel. She was young. Too young for Matt, my ex thought. He's thirty-five now, just had his birthday, so he must have been nearly twenty-eight when she disappeared. Krystal was in her early twenties, but my wife said she seemed like a kid playing dress up."

"Dress up?"

"The times we met her, she wore long dresses and cowboy boots. Beads and fringe. My wife described her as a cross between a retro-hippie and a cowgirl wannabe. Said she clung to Matt's arm like a teenager to her first steady boyfriend."

"You remember that quite vividly."

"My wife made some pretty catty remarks." He took a drink of tea.

"But you didn't approve of Krystal either."

When he didn't immediately answer, Bethany feared she'd said too much. But then David said, "No, I guess not, but she'd had a hard life growing up. Where I taught before, I met a lot of kids like her. I can understand how her background affected her."

"Her background?"

"Matt told me she had a tough life in foster homes, along with her brother, before they came here. Their last foster mother, the librarian here in town, was a stabilizing influence. A long time after Matt thought Krystal left, he kept in touch with the last one, Barbara Ziggerton. He said Ms. Ziggerton believed Krystal would come back eventually."

"Why did Krystal get together with Matt in the first place?" Bethany asked. "What about him appealed to her?"

"Besides his good looks and great personality? A job as a financial manager impresses people. And Krystal met him after he inherited the lodge and twenty acres of land."

Bethany frowned. "Joni says Matt calls the lodge a sinkhole for capital. She says it's going to be more a labor of love than a big moneymaker."

"And you're wondering if Krystal realized that. Probably. When she disappeared, Matt suspected it might have been partly because she figured out he wasn't a millionaire."

"What did you think back then? About Krystal's disappearance?"

"Don't know. I guess that his fiancée ran off to become famous, and when that didn't happen, probably wound up in L.A. with some other guy paying the bills. Matt was inconsolable."

"He talked to you about it?"

"Actually, I was staying at the lodge for the first time, helping him caulk some leaky windows. Krystal hung around—not doing anything useful, underfoot as a matter of fact—then she was gone. It was bizarre."

"Who do you think killed her?"

He looked shocked at the direct question. "No idea. None at all. But Matt didn't do it. He loved Krystal unconditionally."

The *unconditionally* troubled Bethany. Unconditional love usually meant putting up with someone's bad behavior. But too much bad behavior by the beloved could trigger violence. The memory of Matt's fist hitting the butcher's block, the knife flying off it flashed through Bethany's mind, followed by the image of something she hadn't noticed at the time: Joni's look of alarm.

"Why did he love her? She sounds shallow and selfish."

"Beauty does strange things to a man." He said it without irony.

"David, do you think he loves my sister as much?"

He looked away as a couple came in, chose a table near the Christmas tree, and took menus from Trudy. He used the distraction to buy himself time to shape his thoughts, it seemed.

"Joni got Matt to come out of his shell," he said. "After Krystal disappeared, he went back to Santa Fe. He came down here once in a while to work on the lodge, but then he stopped. With Joni's help for the last six months, the place is almost ready to open. That means the world to Matt. And there's no question of her being after Matt's money."

"Right, but why do you know that about Joni?"

He looked embarrassed. "Surely, being a Jarviss…"

Light dawned. "The Foundation, you mean. Look, David, it's true my ancestors got lucky drilling for oil and set up a modest charitable fund, but we're not the Ewings of *Dallas*. We don't live off trust funds. I hope Matt doesn't think Joni has millions to spend on the lodge."

"No, I'm sure he doesn't. Sorry."

He hadn't answered her question directly. Maybe he didn't think Matt loved Joni as deeply as he had loved Krystal. Or maybe David didn't like Joni. What did it matter anyway? Unless David murdered Krystal and would murder any fiancée of Matt's that he didn't approve of.

Bethany didn't hear Lorene return to their table. The café owner, suddenly beside them, set down a glass carafe filled with hot water and a small plate with another teabag on it. "Extra chamomile on the house." Watching David make a second cup of tea, she asked, "How's it going at the lodge? Matt still planning to go ahead with the party and open house?"

"Things are on track." He dunked the teabag rhythmically.

Lorene persisted, "But Matt must be pretty upset."

David set the dripping teabag on the saucer next to the first one. "You have to remember Matt is engaged to Joni now, this lady's sister." He spoke gently. "He's turned a new corner in his life."

"That's right," Lorene said. "Matt's a lucky fellow. I'm sure Joni will stand by him if worse comes to worst."

David, who had picked up his cup, set it back on the saucer without drinking from it. "What do you mean?"

"If Matt gets arrested for Krystal's murder. Not that he did it, mind." She gave Bethany a guilty glance. Then, at the sight of Trudy seating a group of men in khaki work coats, she said, "I better get back to the kitchen, fry up some more burgers."

Bethany felt the tension in the air dissipate with Lorene's leaving. David drank tea and then said, "Lorene's a good woman, a widow. Her husband died in one of the town's tragedies."

"A tragedy? What happened?"

"Accident on the road outside of town. Could have happened to anybody. He lost control of their truck on a curve, and she couldn't do a thing to help."

Bethany flinched, recalling her anxious moments on the same road. "Was she injured?"

"Minor scrapes, I think. She and her husband came here from Texas to run the café and motel together, and she stuck to it without him."

"How long ago did the accident happen?"

"A couple months before Krystal went missing. Matt told me about it at the time. He went to the funeral. He and Lorene have had something in common all these years in a way, and now more than ever. Both lost loved ones. Only Lorene had closure, and Matt didn't—until now."

David took a last sip of tea. "I'd better get going." He tossed cash on the table and said he noticed Bethany had left her car at the lodge. He offered a ride after he finished handing out flyers. She thanked him but said she wanted to take her time checking out the town.

"Sure you want to walk back? It gets dark early up here and cold once the sun goes behind the mountain."

"Don't look so worried. That's hours from now. I'll

be fine."

Staying a while longer in the café to organize her thoughts, Bethany wondered if David had sought her out to make a case for Matt's innocence. He hadn't liked Krystal one bit. Nor had Lorene.

She signaled Trudy for her check. From her place in the kitchen doorway, Lorene called, "Thanks, honey. You come back now!" in her Texas accent toned down by years in New Mexico.

Outside, Bethany gazed in the direction of the lodge. In her immediate line of sight stood the public library, directed by Krystal's foster mother. No time like the present to stop by and ask to see her. *Barbara Zig something. Ziggleton? No, Ziggerton.*

Chapter 4

Bethany didn't bother to zip up her parka for so short a walk. She pulled open one of the library's double doors and saw an empty pair of comfortable-looking armchairs near an unattended checkout counter. Rows of book stacks lined the musty interior of what surely had been a schoolhouse. Bethany walked toward the sound of someone reading aloud. She came upon a group of older women, seated in a circle, listening to a scene from *A Christmas Carol*—Scrooge's rebuff of the men seeking donations for charity. The reader looked up at Bethany but didn't miss a word. The others noticed her, too.

One of them stood up. "May I help you?" She drew Bethany away from the group.

"I hope so. I'm looking for the director, Barbara Ziggerton."

"You've found her. Do you need something in particular? This is a small library, but with the Internet, we have access to the world." She said it with a touch of humor.

Bethany took a breath. "I'd like to talk to you about Krystal Decker."

"I'm not speaking to any more reporters." She was medium height, about as tall as Bethany, and thicker bodied but fit looking. Over her steel-gray bob, she wore a headband that on someone else might have seemed girlish. On this woman, it simply looked practical.

"I'm not a reporter," Bethany said, keeping her voice low. "I'm the sister of Joni Jarviss—"

"Matt MacGregor's new fiancée," the librarian finished. Her dark eyes became wary.

"Can we go somewhere so I can explain?" Bethany whispered. "Please?"

The reader had stopped, and the women frankly stared. The librarian gave a sigh of exasperation and exhaustion. She led Bethany to a private office, took a seat behind a metal desk, and gestured to a visitor's chair. "Please sit down. I can give you a few minutes, but then the book club will expect me to join them for refreshments."

"Ms. Ziggerton—"

"Barbara," the older woman said kindly enough.

"And I'm Bethany. I'm so sorry for your loss. I've been told Krystal Decker was your foster daughter and that you know Matt. You probably know that he and my sister Joni have been getting ready to open the lodge to the public. But it's a terrible time for Matt. For both of them. The whole community. I want to help." There, she'd blurted it out.

"Help how?"

Bethany drew her daypack from her shoulder and held it like a lapdog for comfort.

"By finding out as much as I can about Krystal. Maybe discovering something that can help the police determine what happened to her."

Barbara gave Bethany a penetrating yet sympathetic look. Bethany imagined this woman dealt with foster children with firm compassion. "Do you think the police need help?"

Bethany straightened her spine. "Matt says he's innocent. Joni asked me here because he might be arrested, and if that happens, somebody is going to have to prevent a miscarriage of justice."

"That sounds very melodramatic."

Silence settled between them.

The office's credenza held a computer monitor and keyboard at least twenty years old. Bethany made a mental note to tell the librarian about the Jarviss Foundation some time. She waited for Barbara to say something, anything.

Eventually Barbara asked, "Are you absolutely sure Matthew MacGregor isn't the person who caused my foster daughter's death?"

Bethany met a steely gaze and blinked first.

"You're not completely convinced of his innocence," Barbara said. "That's interesting. I'm sure Matt didn't kill Krystal. He's a genuinely good man. And he thought she deserted him, simply vanished from his life. Devastating for him, as you can imagine. I explained that's what Krystal did to people. He wasn't the first she'd left. As a girl, she ran away from several foster homes before she came to live with me. As a young woman, she dropped in and out of college. After she left college for good, she took off twice with no word to me with men she thought she loved. Each time she came home when things went badly. I told all this to Matt after Krystal left him."

"But she didn't leave," Bethany said as quietly as if they had stayed in the library's public area. "As I understand it, some boys found her body within walking distance of Sorrel."

"Her bones," Barbara said. She blinked back tears.

"And all that time, I thought she'd gone away because she'd done it several times before. The 'cry wolf' story. Now it appears she should have feared a big, bad wolf."

"You mean a man? A particular person you suspect killed her?"

"No, definitely not," Barbara said hastily. "I have no idea who hurt my girl." She turned her face to the office window.

The poor woman! How many times had she sat here over the past seven years wondering where her foster daughter might have been? How many times in the past three weeks had she stared out of this window, realizing Krystal's dead body had been in the forest all along?

Bethany pulled her attention back to what she needed from this woman. "You call her a girl. Did she seem young for her age?"

Barbara took a tissue from a box on the desk and blew her nose. "Here we go again. A sheriff's deputy asked me to describe her. As did a detective with the state police. Then the reporters from the *Albuquerque Journal* and *La Plata Citizen*, and three TV stations until I said *enough!* While I would still comment, I said Krystal was a lovely young woman, talented and beautiful. But because of your personal involvement, I'll say what I didn't tell any of them: My foster daughter's beauty may have been a curse. Can you understand that?"

Bethany took a stab at an answer. "Beautiful women get a lot of attention, not all of it welcome or beneficial."

Barbara nodded. "You must know that."

"Me? Not really. I have friends so gorgeous they attract a certain kind of attention I don't, from men especially. And from other women who want to be around them as if their beauty will rub off. Did that happen to Krystal?"

"Oh yes. And because of it, she had, as Dickens phrased it, great expectations. She expected to be discovered and made famous."

"By whom?"

"Ah, that's a good question. She didn't know. By some new band looking for a female lead singer. By a Hollywood producer seeking a fresh new face, and although she never said it, by a rich man looking for a bride, a twenty-first century Prince Charming in essence."

"She saw Matt as her prince?"

"I do think his money helped make him desirable in Krystal's eyes. In reality, I suppose he's merely comfortably middle class."

Bethany nodded. "It's been suggested Krystal may have become disillusioned with Matt, might have thought he'd sink whatever wealth he had into a losing proposition."

"People are still saying that," Barbara said with a slight smile. "I hope they're wrong, that the lodge will be a successful venture for him and your sister. But truly, I have no idea if Krystal worried about Matt losing money on the project. I do know she soon tired of the hands-on aspect of it. She wasn't a girl who liked physical labor."

Neither is my sister, but she's doing it for Matt's sake. With effort, Bethany pushed the thought aside as Barbara continued.

"One time, shortly before Krystal left—oh dear, I still have trouble realizing she didn't leave—she brought Matt to the house for dinner. Naturally, we talked about the lodge. She said the work was taking forever and that

Matt needed to hire a crew.

"They got into a little spat as they did the dishes. I was wiping off the dining room table and couldn't avoid hearing them. Matt didn't have the funds to hire anyone else. He said they had to put sweat equity—an unpleasant term, isn't it?—into the lodge. At the time, he intended to refinish the hardwood floors. He asked Krystal to help, but she flatly refused, saying the fumes would bother her eyes and throat and could damage her vocal cords. An exaggeration probably, an excuse to get out of the job."

"Did she have a good singing voice?"

"Lovely to hear. And not only do I say so, but so did the musician she ran off with in her junior year of high school, and her music professor at UNM who phoned me when she dropped out of college to go on the road for a short time with yet another band. That put an end to her second year at the university, to which she had a music scholarship. I'd filled out the college admissions forms and financed as much of her education as I could. It was a true disappointment when she never returned to her studies. Not that she did any substantial amount of studying. Dismal grades in every subject, even music. She wasn't a scholar, and I had to accept that. Oh, I am painting a dark picture. Not at all capturing the essence of Krystal for you. She deserves a better biography. I was actually very fond of her."

They sat quietly for a while, then Bethany asked, "Do you have a picture of her?"

"One that I haven't displayed for years." She bent over to rummage in a bottom desk drawer.

What a fine profile this woman has. What a firm chin for someone her age!

Barbara straightened up, holding a framed photo of

about five-by-seven inches. She studied it before handing it over. "Krystal's senior portrait."

In it, a girl posed before a wagon wheel, an obvious studio prop. She had a mass of golden hair and huge green eyes emphasized by heavily mascaraed lashes. She wore a white blouse with a ruffled collar, a full denim skirt, and Western boots. The hairstyle and clothes dated the picture but did not detract from the beauty of the girl, who smiled so naturally and radiantly at the camera that Bethany caught her breath. None of her beautiful friends compared to how stunning this girl had been at seventeen or eighteen. Her eyes, nose, lips, and oval face all approached perfection. She seemed innocently sexy. A knockout, men would have said of her. A princess, a diva, a star in the making.

"Wow," Bethany said. "She was gorgeous. Did she enjoy life?"

"No one has asked me that before." Barbara appeared to give the question serious thought. "She could be charming and entertaining. Sure of herself. Sure good things were right around the corner. Certain she'd meet someone who would determine her fate. Not willing to work hard for what she wanted. Always quitting or taking shortcuts, then dreaming some more. Not honest with herself about her shortcomings. No, not honest."

The librarian glanced at her wristwatch, a simple one on a leather strap. She wore only one piece of noteworthy jewelry, a stone pendant wrapped in a spiral of silver wire.

"I must rejoin the reading club. This is their holiday meeting, with homemade cookies." She said it with an ironic twinkle in her eye. "An obligation I enjoy." As she rose, the stone swung out and then settled against her upper chest.

"That's a lovely necklace," Bethany said to keep the woman a moment longer.

"My foster son makes them." Barbara's eyes shifted to a framed photo on her desk next to the tissue box. She turned the frame so Bethany could see a husky teenager in an awkward *Thinker* chin-on-fist pose. "This is from ages ago. Rusty is twenty-nine now."

"Krystal's brother!" David had mentioned a brother, but Bethany hadn't been quick enough to ask about him.

"Yes, that's right."

Bethany stood up and took a closer look at the pendant. "The stone is beautifully wrapped."

"Yes, it is."

"I should talk to him. He might know something useful. Can you give me his address and phone number?"

Barbara moved around the desk, but Bethany blocked her exit. "Please, it might be important."

They stood eye to eye, neither moving. Then Barbara relented. "Rusty still lives with me. He's a special-needs young man."

"Oh," Bethany said.

"A well-meaning but a negative term, isn't it? Rusty is not profoundly mentally handicapped. He functions well in this small community. His pendants are sold in an art gallery here," Barbara said. "He's very upset about Krystal's death. He never stopped waiting for her to come back. Excuse me." She deftly herded Bethany out of the office.

"May I come again if I have more questions?" She asked it as the librarian turned toward the women munching cookies and sipping from red plastic cups.

With a quick, backward glance, Barbara replied, "This is a public place. How could I stop you?" She excused herself and headed toward the reading group.

As Bethany passed the stacks, she noticed an elderly man in one of the rows and a woman with a small boy in another. Up front, as before, no one staffed the checkout counter. She sat down to collect her thoughts. What had she learned so far? That Krystal's foster mother appeared to be in deep grief. Bethany could only begin to imagine Barbara's sense of shock at the discovery of Krystal's bones. A shock no doubt shared by Krystal's brother. She would have to meet the brother. He might be a good source of information.

What else had she found out? Krystal had been beautiful in that senior photo. She had a voice "like an angel," according to Lorene, and dressed like a cross between a cowgirl wannabe and retro-hippie, a cutting description David attributed to his ex-wife. Krystal dreamed of becoming a singer or actress, left town with men who ultimately did not help her start a career, and came back to Sorrel when the relationships ended.

Then Krystal met Matt. Although he dedicated time to restoring the lodge, he lived primarily in Santa Fe. She might have imagined marriage to him as her ticket to an exciting life in the capital city. David had said something Barbara confided to Matt after Krystal disappeared, that she feared Krystal only wanted Matt for his money, consistent with what Barbara had said today. Joni said Matt once alluded to Krystal being "messed up." But he didn't go into details, and Joni hadn't pressed him to say more.

The overall picture of Krystal didn't flatter her. Krystal sounded like a woman who, at twenty-four, might have realized her girlish dreams were not going to come true and that Matt offered a financially secure life. But if she couldn't push those dreams down inside herself, if she still wanted out of Sorrel as Matt prepared to live at the lodge full-time, what might Krystal have done? Who might she have turned to? *No sense sitting in the library speculating. Meet more townspeople who remembered the dead woman.* Krystal's story had her hooked.

Chapter 5

Bethany stepped outside, glancing toward the forest. In the distance, snow dusted the mountaintops, but there had been none in the valley or La Plata since a storm in late November, Joni had said on the phone a couple of days earlier. Southern New Mexico had been in the grip of a drought for the past decade. Sorrel wasn't a tourist town that could count on a white Christmas, but if the white stuff fell, it would help the economy. People would come from the warmer, dryer flatlands to cross-country ski and make snowmen and snow angels. Bethany sniffed the air and thought she detected a hint of moisture. Of course, a winter storm could be a double-edged sword. It might block the road up to town.

At the corner, with the library behind her, she surveyed Main Street. The café and motel sat on her left, the mercantile beyond them. A wooden boardwalk and false fronts overhead connected a line of buildings. The street might have been a set for a classic cowboy film. A director could dress the locals in Western wear and stage a gunfight here.

Bethany crossed the street to the boardwalk's nearest shop, *The Treasure Box*, where huge Christmas ornaments and Styrofoam snowflakes dangled from the ceiling. She goggled at a maze of tourist souvenirs. Jewelry, T-shirts, postcards, jellies, and salsas mingled with wind chimes and dreamcatchers. Near the front door, a man stood behind a counter, a newspaper spread out before him. To his back were a coffee maker, espresso machine, and a glass case with a display of pastries. In a voice infused with warmth, he asked if he could help her.

For a moment, Bethany lost heart and almost said no, just browsing. But she remembered her mission for Joni. Hoping information might come with a small purchase, she ordered a coffee.

"Plain or something classier? A cappuccino or espresso? How about it, young lady? You only live once."

"A cappuccino then. Skinny."

"With skimmed milk. Coming right up." As he made the drink, he said, "It's my lucky day. Not every day a gal as pretty as you comes in here."

She took a stool and felt his eyes sweep from her face to her breasts hidden under the parka. His look, definitely sexual, should have been unwelcome from a man undoubtedly in his mid or late sixties—old enough to be her father. But he looked so openly appreciative that she didn't take offense.

As he set down her drink, she said, "I wonder if I could ask you some questions."

"TV reporter?"

"No, I'm not."

"Sorry, my mistake. We've had some local excitement, so I assumed you came about that. Don't get many females visiting Sorrel on their own, you see. The gals from out of town usually come in with their boyfriends or their hubbies and kids. And we get almost no traffic weekdays except in the summer. Anyway, what do you want to talk about?"

She sipped the cappuccino and patted her lips with the napkin he'd set near the cup and saucer. "Krystal Decker."

"I get it. Newspaper reporter, right?"

"I'm not with the media. My name is Bethany Jarviss, and my sister is—"

"That little Joni. Second girl Matt MacGregor has got himself engaged to."

"That's right. Sir, is this your shop?"

"Mine and the wife's." His hand shot out and enfolded hers, keeping the contact a beat too long. "Tom Whitney. From Illinois originally. The wife and I retired and then, fools that we are, tied ourselves to this place for better or worse."

He folded the newspaper and stuck it out of sight behind the counter. "Troublesome situation, a man's first fiancée turning up dead to haunt his dreams. Because something like that must, don't you think? Haunt a fella's dreams?"

"Mr. Whitney—"

"Just plain Tom."

"Tom. As you can imagine, I'm concerned about how Matt's situation affects my sister. I want to talk to people who knew Krystal Decker."

"Why, for heaven's sake?" He looked honestly perplexed.

"Not from idle curiosity. To find out anything that might help determine who killed her."

"Well, it wasn't me!"

"I'm not suggesting that, of course I'm not. But…"

"But somebody did kill her, that's what you mean. What are you, a lady Sherlock?"

"Would that bother you?"

48

He slapped the counter and guffawed. "Not at all. Ask me whatever you want, Miss Sherlock. I've got nothing to hide."

"Okay. What did you think of Krystal?"

"Very pretty girl." He said it without pausing for thought.

Bethany simply nodded, hoping he would say more without prompting.

"But maybe not as pretty on the inside. Your sister, now, there's a good-looking little gal who doesn't have a swelled head."

"You thought Krystal had an inflated ego?"

"Everybody will tell you she expected to be a big star. Singer or movie star, take your pick." He shook his head. "But she wasn't that special, let me tell you. Sneaky more like."

Now we're getting somewhere. "Sneaky, how?"

"She took things. Shoplifted. One time she stole a box of fancy stationery from the shop. I know she did because back then, The Treasure Box did business for the post office. Sold stamps, mailed letters and parcels, that kind of thing. Don't do it anymore. You have to go to La Plata. Back then, Krystal had a boyfriend in Albuquerque for a little while. She'd mail letters to him. My wife noticed the fancy envelopes, same as went missing from our shop. Oh, I suppose she could have got that stationery somewhere else, but the wife didn't think so. Too much of a coincidence that we missed one box of that paper, and Krystal Decker starts using the same kind. We should have called her on it, but we didn't. Gutless of us, especially since we knew in high school in La Plata, Krystal got in trouble for stealing stuff from other kids' lockers. Her foster mom had to drive down

49

the mountain to pick her up after detention a couple times." He shook his head. "Dishonest, that girl."

While he talked, a woman about his age came through a back door and worked her way through the obstacle course of display cases, listing to the side with each step. A woman with a bad hip.

"This is Flora, my wife, come to count the day's take," Tom said. "This here is Joni Jarviss's sister." He apparently couldn't recall her name.

"Bethany," she said.

"Nice to meet you. We appreciate Matt and Joni's business," Flora said. "Joni came in here the other day to buy a few things for the lodge. And Matt has sat right where you are, having coffee. How's the cappuccino, dear? The way you like it?"

"Yes, very good." Bethany took another sip.

"Tom can whip you up another one. How about a nice piece of pie?"

Before Bethany could decline, Tom said, "We're talking about Krystal."

"Oh?" Flora said.

"Bethany is concerned about the girl's death since her sister is marrying Matt. Not that Matt did anything wrong. She doesn't think that, and neither do we, right?"

Flora hoisted herself onto a stool, leaving an empty one next to Bethany. "Matt is a fine young man who had a bad shock when Krystal supposedly left. I imagine he had a much worse one when he found out she's been under a pile of rocks all the time he thought she went heaven knows where."

She shifted on the stool and gritted her teeth as if in pain. "It's such a shame, isn't it, that he no more gets himself engaged to a nice young woman, Krystal causes trouble from the grave. Not on purpose," she said quickly. "I don't mean she's a ghost haunting him. But I bet he can't get her out of his mind."

"Your husband mentioned the theft of a box of stationery." Bethany let the comment hang in the air.

Flora shot a disapproving look across the counter at Tom. "Did you have to bring that up?" To Bethany, she said, "Could have been Treasure Box stationery. I think so. But the girl had it hard as a little one, you have to remember. When Krystal and her brother first came to town, those kids pretty near dressed in rags. They'd been shunted from one foster home to another after their mother gave them up and not to good homes either. Lucky for them, they landed in a nice situation here with our librarian. November they came, and she bought them warm coats first thing."

"What age were they? Young kids?"

"No, Krystal had to be about thirteen or fourteen. Rusty, her brother—his given name is Russell—was only a couple years behind her but seemed a lot younger. Slow, if you know what I mean. In special-education classes. Those kids had been through a lot by the time Barbara took them. She made sure they saw school counselors. I doubt it helped, but Barbara did the best she could for them, that's for sure."

"I met her," Bethany admitted. "At the library before I stopped in here. I appreciated her talking to me, considering the pain she must be in at finding out her foster daughter is dead. She said the brother still lives with her."

"He's almost thirty but can't live on his own," Tom said. "Works at the mercantile but needs supervision."

"Makes nice jewelry," Flora said. "Got to give him

his due there. Necklaces out of natural stone. Sells them, too, not at our shop but the so-called 'fine-art shop' in town." She coughed as she eased her body off the stool.

"Where's that located?"

"The only place there's any shops in Sorrel. On Main Street." She turned her head. "Our side. Beyond the Black Bear and the Hike N Bike that's closed for the winter. Marcham's Fine Art. Ha!"

Tom chuckled. Bethany turned to him. "Is the merchandise overrated?"

Flora answered. "It's nice enough stuff. Jazz Marcham has good taste. But she has no call to act superior because she sells more expensive things than we do."

"That's right," Tom said. "Some people want a T-shirt or a shot glass that says New Mexico on it. They aren't in the market for an oil painting. Some are, I guess, and I have to say those necklaces Rusty Decker makes fit in at her shop. She's smart to carry them and good to Rusty, isn't she, dear?"

Flora exchanged glances with her husband. "That's true. Rusty makes some nice things, but he's not easy to get along with. Too loud. And he's either up or down. Too happy or too, I don't know what, gloomy or angry or whatever. And I mean before he found out about Krystal. He must be in a state now."

"Does he understand she's dead?"

Flora rocked her body to the front door and flipped over a sign to read *CLOSED* from the outside. "He understands, sure. He's slow, but he knows about life and death. Not that we've talked to him about Krystal's murder."

"Wouldn't know what to say to the young guy,"

Tom said. "But Flora called Barbara and expressed our condolences. We'll go to the funeral when she's allowed to have one. Body's still in Albuquerque, what there is of it. Could be months before she can bury the remains."

With a hand on her side, Flora moved to the end of the counter as Tom came out from behind it. She sprang open the cash drawer. "Time to count the day's takings."

Bethany took it as her cue to pay. Tom followed her to the door. "Come again, Miss Sherlock. Be careful, you hear. Seems impossible, but somebody did kill that beautiful young gal. He's probably long gone, but you never know."

****

Streetlights had come on while she talked to the Whitneys. Like their shop, other businesses must be closing for the day, except for the Black Bear, Bethany assumed. Two doors past it, she could see the shop Flora Whitney seemed jealous of, *Marcham's Fine Art*, where Krystal Decker's brother sold his beautifully wrapped stone pendants. She'd have to stop by to see them and perhaps find out more about both Deckers, the special-needs Rusty, and the late, pretty, thieving Krystal.

But that would have to wait for tomorrow. Still plenty of time today to check out the bar, where the lodge's cook and housekeeper, Gloria, also worked. What had David called the bar owner? Crash? No, Crush. That was it. Crush somebody. She couldn't recall the man's last name. She would have to do better than that, commit facts to memory, and take notes if she meant to be of any real help to Joni and Matt.

She passed through swinging doors reminiscent of the Old West. A compact entryway displayed realtors' listings, garage sale and bake sale notices, and odd-job advertisements, along with David's massage-therapy flyer tacked over older postings. An inner door flew open, and two men in cowboy hats squeezed past Bethany, one holding the door to let her through. He tipped his hat. "Ma'am."

It took a moment for her eyes to adjust to the tavern's gloom. A counter and line of stools filled a narrow space on the left. The bartender stood listening to a bald man nursing a beer. They didn't pay her any notice as she passed between the bar and a few tables to find the restrooms. Some guys playing pool, who looked too young to drink, barely noticed her; they flicked glances at her and refocused on the game. She made a beeline for the ladies' room, a priority after the double dose of coffee at the café and The Treasure Box.

Graffiti covered the rough pine paneling and the stall partitions. As she used the facilities and washed her hands, she read various messages of love and despair. One lipsticked scrawl warned of going with Karl. Below that, someone had responded in a different shade *too right! puny peenie!* At the washbasin, Bethany ignored her reflection. Tom Whitney considered her a pretty girl. At thirty-two, she might still seem girlish to a man in his sixties, but the young guys at the pool tables obviously considered her too old for them. *Kids! Pay no attention!* She ran a hand through her hair, let the thick mass settle on her shoulders, and set out to meet the bartender—for Joni's sake.

For the second time this afternoon, she took a stool, leaving plenty of space between herself and the bald man at the bar. She didn't look at him, hoping he would ignore her, too, and within moments, he put some bills on the counter and left. She took her phone from her daypack. No cell service; Joni had been right to warn her. Wishing she felt comfortable in a bar, that she had come in with a partner, she clutched her wallet and tried not to fidget.

"What's your pleasure?" the bartender asked. He gave her an amused look as she hesitated.

Could he tell she didn't drink much alcohol? She ordered a beer advertised on one of the lighted signs above his head.

"Bottle or tap?" he asked, cordially enough.

"Tap." A random choice.

"Coming right up." He pushed a bowl of shelled peanuts toward her and turned to pull the beer.

He exuded confident masculinity, this handsome, broad-shouldered guy. No gut hung over his belt, so he didn't overindulge in the booze or peanuts. He might have looked tough but for rimless eyeglasses like those of her high school chemistry teacher, who also coached football. But for bad eyes, he might have gone pro, he always claimed.

The bartender set down a coaster and a glass of beer in a practiced motion. She opened her wallet and considered handing over a credit card but decided on cash. Without saying a word, he took her ten and moved down the line to the register. The room smelled of beer and wood polish but no smoke since the law prohibited lighting up in taverns.

When the bartender came back with her change, she said to keep it.

"A bit generous." But he tucked the money behind his white apron into a pants pocket. He looked above the bar at a TV tuned to a soccer match.

"I wonder if I could ask you something," she said.

She aimed for light and friendly.

He turned his head but kept his body angled toward the TV and met her gaze. She would wait all day for him to reply, she realized, so she plunged on.

"I'm the sister of Joni Jarviss, the fiancée of Matt MacGregor. I'm staying with them at the lodge. Helping them get it ready to open to the public."

He still said nothing.

"And you're the owner here, I assume." Suddenly she remembered his last name. "Mr. Dobbs."

He nodded. "Crush to my customers."

"Bethany."

"I haven't heard a question." He turned back to the soccer match. He stood in profile to her, so she could see a corner of his mouth turn up. He enjoyed letting her flounder.

She took a steadying breath. "Okay, here's a question. Did you know Krystal Decker? What did you think of her?"

Finally, he gave her his full attention. "That's two. Two questions."

"Right." *Irritating fellow. A joker.*

"You're not drinking your beer."

She took a sip and tried not to make a face. Beer always tasted sour to her. This one tasted sour and weak. She pushed it away. "I'm not really thirsty. The thing is, I'm worried about my sister. I think the sooner the truth is known about Krystal Decker's death, the better."

"Better for who?"

"For Joni and Matt," she said. "And other people. For this town, don't you think?"

He said nothing to that. "Can I get you a soft drink or something? On the house?" His smile revealed an even set of teeth. In the dim tavern, she couldn't tell the color of his eyes, only that they conveyed sympathy. The man matched the bar's name in a way, but he seemed more teddy bear than black bear.

She declined a change of drink and thanked him but didn't take another sip of beer. "Did you know Krystal? Did you own this bar when she lived here?"

"Two questions again. You're acting like you don't know she worked here."

"She worked for you?" *Joni didn't mention that.* "Seriously, I didn't know. I know she was engaged to Matt. And she was the librarian's foster daughter. A beauty and a singer." She stopped short of mentioning the Whitneys' claims that Krystal shoplifted from them and stole from kids at school.

Crush folded his arms across his broad chest. "She sang like an angel drunk on mead. That girl had honey in her voice."

The poetic imagery made Bethany blink. The teddy bear was a romantic. "You heard her sing?"

"She sang right here. Open mike nights, I'd give her a break so she could join in. Those nights got to be real popular. Folks would come in to hear her."

Bethany leaned closer to the counter. *The girl had a following.* "Did she still work here when she died?"

"When people thought she left town. Just singing, but Matt didn't like it."

He grabbed a rag and wiped the counter with hard back-and-forth strokes.

"Matt didn't like her singing in a bar?"

"He was restoring the lodge back then, same as he's doing now. Krystal helped him some. But he wanted her there full-time, she said. I think so he could have her all to himself. But she defied him."

"She kept on singing for your customers?"

"Once in a while. She needed an audience. Deserved one."

He kept wiping the same clean spot. *This big guy had been in love with Krystal. You could bet money on it.*

"What did you think when she disappeared? Did she say anything to you about wanting to leave town?"

"Two more questions." He tossed the rag into a sink near the beer taps and focused on two men in faded denim who entered and headed straight past the bar. "Keep it down back there," he called good-naturedly. To Bethany he added, "More of our local pool sharks. Regulars after work."

"Did Krystal mention anything about leaving town?" Bethany persisted.

Crush crossed his arms again. She steadied her breathing. It wouldn't do to press him further. Behind those rimless glasses, his eyes met hers. *He's assessing me. Deciding if I'm worthy of confiding in.*

She must have passed some test because he said, "As far as I know, Krystal never planned to leave right then. She sure didn't say anything to me. That's what I told the cops back when she supposedly took off, and that's what I told the ones who came here asking questions recently. And now everybody knows she didn't go anywhere, did she? Somebody murdered that lovely, talented girl, but I sure as hell don't know who. Maybe you should talk to your future brother-in-law about what he knows. I heard the cops figure he's the one who did it."

"But he didn't. He's innocent."

"Because now it's your sister he's engaged to? Give that some thought, okay? Being his fiancée might not be good for Joni's health. How well do you know him anyway?"

Too many questions at once, questions she had thought of too. She pulled the beer toward her and took a sip. Sour, weak, and warm. She couldn't help but grimace.

Crush snorted. "You should have ordered what you wanted. It's okay by me to have something soft or a bottled water. No shame in not drinking alcohol. Not in my place."

Their eyes met again. Bethany felt a wave of some emotion coming from Crush, sympathy maybe with her need to know who ended Krystal's life. "Next time, it'll be a glass of wine, actually. Or sparkling water."

He nodded. "Good deal. Look, Bethany, is it? You need to talk to Matt MacGregor about Krystal. All I can say is one night she didn't show up for a singing gig. I figured he finally put his foot down and told her she couldn't come."

"Did you ask him?"

He turned his head away from her. "Not at first."

"What do you mean 'not at first?' Did you speak to him later?"

Crush didn't call her out on asking two questions. He turned back to her. "Yeah, when people started saying Krystal had left Matt all of a sudden and that he'd called the cops and filed a missing person report. He said his relationship with Krystal was none of my business. I've never liked Matt MacGregor. He didn't understand Krystal. He was holding her back from her destiny."

"Her destiny?"

"To be a star. That girl meant to go places. Someday people would say this is where she got her start, right here in the Black Bear."

"Do you still have live entertainment?"

He looked past the empty tables. "Nah, see that jukebox in the corner? That's where the stage used to be. Must have been the last place on earth Krystal sang. People around here imagined her someplace fancy. Some nightclub on the west coast. But she never went away and forgot us ordinary Sorrel folks."

The silent jukebox shared the corner space with a chainsaw sculpture, a carved wooden bear about four feet high. The crudely carved bear wore a Santa Claus hat, the full extent of the bar's holiday cheer. The rest of the place remained undecorated.

Chapter 6

On her way back to the lodge in the last light of day, Bethany wished David were around to give her a lift. She clipped along, considering what Crush had told her: Krystal sang like an angel drunk on mead, essentially the same thing as Lorene saying Krystal had a voice like an angel. Crush thought Matt had stopped her from becoming a star, that Matt might have killed her. *But surely not! For Joni's sake, let the murderer be anyone but Matt!*

Bethany had been walking without noticing her surroundings. Now she stopped at the entrance to the lodge where someone had installed a new hand-lettered sign—Joni's work, no doubt. The *S* and *L* of *Sorrel Lodge* curved gracefully. Nice to see Joni's skills used here, in partnership with her future husband, instead of in minimum-wage jobs at resale shops and hour after hour of free theater work. Not that community theater wasn't worthy of effort. But up to now, Joni's subsistence lifestyle had troubled the family as much as her failed relationships.

At the top of the driveway, strings of white icicle lights dangled over the entrance. The sight lifted Bethany's spirits and quickened her step. Indoors, she found Joni in the porch putting together a pewter floor lamp. Its empty box lay nearby, as did a second, identical, sealed one.

"I saw the new sign. Your lettering is beautiful. Hand-drawn, right?"

"Sure is. Matt likes the sign, too. He and I put it up together. It's real now, the lodge. People are actually going to stay here. They won't all cancel their reservations." Her voice quivered. "That's what we have to tell ourselves."

"It's all going to be okay, Little Bird," Bethany said, using the family's nickname for her sister. She watched Joni's deft assembly of the lamp. "Want some help?"

"Sure." Joni handed her a pocketknife. "Open the other box?"

Bethany shrugged off her parka and slit open the tape on one end of the box to reveal a flattened lampshade. "What do I do with this? Inflate it like a balloon?"

Joni rolled her eyes. "No, unfold it like an umbrella."

"I can do that. These are nice lamps. Expensive?"

"Not at two for one in La Plata. Bargains all over the place down there for Christmas. Gloria and I found great things for the lodge."

Joni had a flair for design and an eye for quality. On a mission to find props and costumes for theater productions, she had done it consistently and under budget. Obviously, she put those skills to good use at the lodge. The lamps fit beautifully with the other lodge décor. Bethany hoped Matt valued Joni's enterprise.

Bethany fiddled with a set of metal stays, trying to figure out how to fit them inside the shade to hold it open. Dealing with physical objects had never been her strong suit, so she always aspired to be the brains of the family.

"Are you going to keep me in suspense or tell me

what you did in town?" Joni asked.

"I went to quite a few places—the café, the library, that shop called The Treasure Box, and the bar."

Having put together the first lamp, Joni turned her attention to the other one, expertly sliding the poles together and into the lamp's base. "That's amazing! Who did you talk to? What did people have to say?"

"Did you know Krystal had a special-needs brother? Rusty. I found out he works at the mercantile, and he makes pendants out of stone."

Joni said she knew about the brother but hadn't thought to mention it. "I've noticed him stocking shelves in the merc. And I've seen his pendants in Marcham's gallery."

"You know the gallery owner?"

"Jazz. A little," Joni said. "We'll most likely buy our wedding bands from her shop. What about her?"

"The husband and wife at The Treasure Box consider her elitist," Bethany said.

"She has excellent taste in art. The Treasure Box carries ordinary tourist stuff. What do the Whitneys think, that Sorrel doesn't deserve a first-rate gallery?"

"I suppose they think their merchandise doesn't measure up."

"Why should it? It's not the same kind of thing. Maybe there's something else going on between those people." Joni stopped working and sat back on her heels.

"If so, it probably has nothing to do with Krystal," Bethany said. "And her brother and his pendants probably don't either."

"From what I've seen of him, he's a limited sort of fellow. But what did people say about Krystal? Besides her famous beauty and voice? I've heard enough about that." She removed a twist tie from a lamp cord and straightened the cord.

Bethany followed suit with the other lamp's cord. "The Treasure Box people said she stole things from other kids in school, and she might have stolen a box of stationery from their store sometime before she met Matt."

"A shoplifter? First I've heard of that. Matt probably never knew. Interesting, huh?"

That wasn't the most interesting thing she'd learned, Bethany said. "I met the bartender, Crush. He said Krystal worked and sang at the Black Bear. He seems to have had a thing for her. From the time she went missing, he never believed she intended to leave town."

"Awful, isn't it?" Joni said. "Like something you see on TV, but usually it's a child missing, and then pretty soon they say she's been found dead. Only this time it took seven years. Probably some pervert did it. A lot of oddballs live in these mountains in old cabins, people you never see. Matt says some are hermits who live entirely off the land, eating nuts and twigs. I told David he'd better not turn into one of them when he gets his cabin fixed up."

Joni continued talking about David's project while Bethany's thoughts strayed. She wouldn't mention that Matt hadn't liked Krystal working at the Black Bear, according to Crush, or that Matt denied arguing with Krystal. Those were things to ask Matt about. No need to tell Joni and get her upset.

"Do you have any light bulbs?" Bethany asked. "Let's see if these floor lamps work."

Joni went in search of the bulbs, giving Bethany time to consider her next moves. Visit the crime scene tomorrow to see the spot where a teenage boy had accidentally dislodged some rocks and found the remains of a human hand. In a long phone call at the end of which Bethany had committed to coming to Sorrel, Joni reported what the whole town knew. The boy and his friend moved more rocks, found a damaged skull, hot-footed it to Sorrel, and called 911.

With Krystal's bones, a forensic team discovered the scant remains of a daypack. Matt had been convinced, by its absence years before, that his fiancée had left him. It probably had been about the size of the one Bethany carried instead of a purse. It had contained the usual things: cash and plastic, some makeup. Krystal's engagement ring, which Matt assumed she had pawned for cash, had been found on her finger bone.

The poor girl, none of her dreams had come true. She hadn't become a bride or a star. For the first time, Bethany wanted to find her killer not only for Joni's sake but also for Krystal's.

****

At dinner, Matt and Joni both seemed on edge. David didn't join them, nor did Gloria, who dashed off to her shift at the Black Bear before anyone could praise her beef bourguignon. Bethany contributed wine she had brought in her duffle. Talk centered on the work still to be done on the lodge, primarily painting and decorating the third-floor lounge. Matt said flatly that they couldn't get everything done before the party and open house, especially since he wouldn't be around the next day.

"Matt has to go to La Plata. The police want to question him some more." Joni cast a sidelong glance at Matt's tense face. "I had to tell her, Matt. Bethany deserves to know what's up. And I'm going with you."

She shifted in her seat and said to Bethany, "Sorry to be leaving you alone tomorrow, but I'm going along to the station to support Matt."

Good for you, Little Bird.

Matt reached out a hand and covered Joni's much smaller one. She had painted her short nails a blackish purple in an effort to stop biting them; she couldn't stand gnawing on polish.

Bethany forced her mind back to the conversation as Joni said, "Matt, stop protesting. I'm going along." She raised her chin. "We'll pay Gloria to put in extra time painting the rooms. And David plans to help tomorrow."

"Why do the police want to see you again?" Bethany asked Matt.

Matt released Joni's hand. She stacked the dinner plates and took them to the sink, then at the sideboard, spooned out servings of apple crisp. Bethany resisted the urge to get up and assist. She waited for Matt's answer.

"I'm their only suspect. They don't have any evidence, so I bet they'll want to pressure me to see if I'll confess. Which I won't because I'm no murderer."

Joni set desserts before each of them. "This time, he's going to have an attorney there."

"You didn't when they questioned you before?" Bethany couldn't conceal her surprise. "How many times did they interview you? Who interviewed you, by the way? You haven't had counsel up to now?" Crush would have gone crazy at the barrage of questions.

No, Matt said, but up to now, he hadn't been practically forced to go down to La Plata. Sheriff's deputies, then a state police investigator, had taken his statements at the lodge. "My lawyer in Santa Fe recommended a defense attorney from up there and one in La Plata. The La Plata guy's going to meet me over breakfast tomorrow before I have to be at the station. If things get worse, I'll call the Santa Fe guy, but for now, a local is the way to go. I don't want to get so lawyered up I look guilty. And it's best if Joni stays here."

"No way," Joni said. "What do you think, Bethany?"

Hating to be put on the spot, she looked from her sister to Matt.

"Say what you think," Matt insisted, his voice dead calm.

"Stand by your man." As the words left her lips, she heard herself echo her mother's usual advice.

Matt seemed amused. His face lost some of its tension. "You could play that on the jukebox at the Black Bear."

Bethany gave Matt a look of gratitude for his willingness to help lighten the mood. She took a bite of apple crisp. "Praise be to Gloria."

Matt dug into his dessert, too, but Joni only moved her fork around, finally dropping it with a sharp clink on her plate.

"It's going to be okay," Matt said. "Really, it is."

"We had a couple cancellations," Joni said. "One by email and one phoned. They gave shifty excuses. What if we open and nobody comes?"

Matt swallowed the last bite of his dessert. "Joni, please, don't get spooked. We have two more openings now. Other guests will fill them. Don't worry. The murder might even be a draw. People will come to see where it happened. They'll want to lay their eyes on a suspected killer."

"Don't say that. That's appalling," Joni said.

"Human nature, right?" He glanced at Bethany for

moral support.

Bethany didn't disagree. "I guess."

Matt's comments fell flat. Both he and Joni looked so beat that Bethany offered to clean up, insisting she could do it alone. Matt poured each of them more wine, emptying the bottle before he and Joni headed upstairs, glasses in hand. Bethany loaded the dishwasher, tidied the kitchen, and took her wine to the lobby. The fireplace contained enough hot embers to get a blaze going with only an additional log and a few pumps of a hand bellows.

The burning pine smelled like Christmas; she didn't care about its effect on her lungs. Was Joni's relationship with Matt like that, irresistible but ultimately a bad choice? Joni's two-year marriage had been a disaster. After the divorce, for five years, she ran through a succession of lovers, then swore off men entirely until she met Matt eight months ago. Their engagement, announced two months later, had worried Bethany as much as it did the rest of the Jarvisses. Most of what they learned since then came in the form of Joni's brief emails from Sorrel. She insisted Matt could handle most of his financial management responsibilities from here, via the phone and Internet.

Only after she became engaged to Matt did Joni mention that his first fiancée had left him high and dry. Bethany found out her father hired a private investigator who vetted Matt as squeaky clean—respected and well-liked by the clients whose money he managed. After Krystal's disappearance he had dated a few women but none seriously until Joni. He had been the much loved, only nephew of the uncle from whom he inherited the lodge. His plans for it made sense. So Joni never saw the detective's report.

Had Dad ever checked up on her own lovers? Bethany wondered. She had never given her parents cause for serious alarm, not like Joni. Now, under extreme stress, would Joni neglect to eat, become anorexic again? Tonight she had managed only a small portion of the beef dish and had played with her dessert.

Bethany sat staring at the fire, missing her snug home in Las Cuevas. When the fire burned down, she added another log, emptied her wine glass, and settled deeper into her chair. She and Joni were so different, but then they weren't related by birth. Compared to Joni's string of men, she could count her adult romantic relationships on one hand. She missed her current lover, Nathan Fuller, an all-around good guy.

"You're still awake," Joni said.

"You too." Bethany hadn't heard her come down the stairs in her bedroom slippers and robe. She carried the two now-empty wine glasses.

"Matt zoned out, but I couldn't. What you thinking about?" She set down the glasses and took a seat.

"At the moment, Nathan."

"You miss him. Bet you wish he'd phone."

"Sure, but I don't expect him to. Days can go by when we're not in touch. We suit each other. We're both independent types."

Joni folded herself into a small package—arms around her legs, chin on her knees. "You don't even have a goldfish to tie you down."

"I have my house."

Joni raised her head. "You walk away from it in a flash when Dad has you travel for the Foundation. You're married to that job."

The comment surprised Bethany. Normally, Joni didn't speak so bluntly. "I'm busy, that's all. We've been flooded with grant proposals right at the end of the year."

Joni yawned. "And you've got to tell Dad which ones to fund. Sounds thrilling. I'm getting a splash more wine so I can sleep."

"We finished the bottle, remember?"

Joni picked up Bethany's stemmed glass and the other two. "Don't look so alarmed. I'll make it milk then."

Bethany closed her eyes and tried not to worry about Joni or yearn for Nathan or think about the professional tasks she couldn't put on the back burner for long.

Chapter 7

She awoke to the lobby door's squeaky groan as Gloria returned from her bar shift. Seeing the fire had turned to ashes, Gloria asked, "Want me to put another log on?"

Bethany rubbed her eyes. "What time is it?"

"After eleven. The Bear's so dead, Crush let me leave early." She proceeded to build a new fire, starting with newspaper and kindling, coaxing a flame to grow, adding a log. She didn't use the bellows. Tonight she wore her hair loose instead of in a ponytail, so she seemed less girlish. Shedding her jeans jacket and scarf, she plopped down across from Bethany. "How did dinner turn out? Everything taste okay?"

"More than okay," Bethany said. "Your beef bourguignon? Perfect! The apple crisp, too."

"Good," Gloria said. "I hope Matt and Joni let me cook when the lodge gets going. They say they will, and it's mostly going to be for breakfast, but you never know, dinner might become a regular thing."

Bethany fought to wake up. "You like working for them?"

"Sure, who wouldn't? They treat me like they do David, like we're friends."

"Did you know Matt when he came up here before? Before he knew Joni, I mean."

"Not really. I was in high school in La Plata when

he first started fixing up the lodge. I only moved to Sorrel a couple years ago. But I've always had friends here because after elementary school, Sorrel kids get bussed to La Plata."

Gloria rose and poked at the fire. "It's nice you're here. Sometimes I think Joni's bored since she lived in Santa Fe and all. A few times, she's asked me to take a hike with her. We've walked right past the ravine where those teenage guys found Krystal Decker's bones, but we never suspected she might be buried there."

"I'd be interested in seeing that spot," Bethany said.

"Who wouldn't? It's the most excitement anybody's had around here for years. I could take you." Gloria seemed her younger self again, a girl unaffected by Krystal's murder at about the same age.

****

The next morning at seven, Joni knocked on Bethany's door to say Gloria had cooked a "trial-run" breakfast. Bethany said she would be right down. She had showered already and could take a break from reading grant proposals.

Bethany praised Gloria's baked omelet and the fair-trade coffee the lodge bought in bulk. Breakfast over, Matt said Joni had convinced him to take her along to La Plata. They had to leave soon. In their absence, David would get more painting done. Bethany volunteered to help, but Matt said no, David could handle it. "Joni said you were doing your own work before breakfast. Get back at it if you need to. And take some time to relax. You're a guest. We'll see you later."

Nobody mentioned that he and Joni had to face the state police, but that fact hung in the air like a heavy fog. As Matt walked out of the kitchen ahead of Joni, Bethany whispered to her sister, "I'll see what I can find out today."

No way could she relax. She passed plates for Gloria to stack in the dishwasher and mentioned the offered hike to the crime scene. Did she have time to go right now?

"Sure," Gloria said, "I can get away for a while." She took a container out of a chest freezer. "Dinner, no problem. Let's go."

The morning sky was so blue, the air so crisp, Bethany wished the walk was for its sake alone. Gloria led her to where the lodge's driveway met the main road. They turned left, away from the town, and about a hundred yards farther, took an unmarked hiking trail. Birds called to one another, and a plane passed overhead, but only the sound of their boots disturbed a sense of remote peacefulness. Pines and other trees grew thickly.

After about fifteen minutes, a bright area of sky straight ahead made it seem as if they would walk off the edge of the world. Gloria stopped so they could rest and sip water from a canteen she had brought in her backpack. Then they continued on to where the land dropped down abruptly, forming a narrow ravine.

Following a trail at the ravine's edge gave Bethany the shivers. She stopped in her tracks. "Joni said the police believe Krystal didn't slip and fall to her death. I wonder why they're so sure."

Gloria turned around and tapped the top of her head. "The way somebody bashed in her skull, I heard. CSI stuff."

They walked in silence for a few minutes, then Gloria halted by a massive Ponderosa pine. After the discovery of Krystal's remains, no doubt, people had left flower bouquets that had since withered and a few stuffed animals—teddy bears, a blue pony, a fluffy dog. A modest, touching array.

"Look. Down there," Gloria said.

At the bottom of the ravine, yellow crime-scene tape encircled boulders and piles of displaced, smaller rocks.

"The hiker who found the bones must have slid down here," Bethany said, pointing to disturbances in the soil and its covering of dried pine needles and oak leaves. They followed the evidence of the boy's unplanned descent. The ancient Ponderosa grew so close to the drop-off, erosion had exposed the tops of its gnarled roots. Had the boy, or Krystal before him, clutched at those roots but failed to gain purchase? Someday, the old tree might topple down the ravine, she thought.

"I wonder if Krystal was killed here or down there," Gloria said.

"Here, I bet, but I suppose nobody will ever know for sure." Bethany touched the tree's bark, which felt rough even through her fleece glove. A killer could hide behind the trunk and surprise a victim, come out swinging a hefty branch or fist-sized rock and push the victim over the edge. "I don't think Joni mentioned if the police found a murder weapon."

"Not that I heard of," Gloria said.

"Do you think we could get down there safely?"

"Sure, I've done it. You'll see how the killer covered up the body with rocks."

Right, thought Bethany, the killer had hidden the body so nobody found it for almost seven years of drought. This year, flash floods had dominated the New Mexico news. Heavy rains must have eroded the ravine, preparing the scene for the hikers' discovery.

Apparently, when Krystal went missing, the police hadn't conducted a serious search of the forest. Krystal didn't take lone hikes. She had a reputation for abruptly ending relationships. It had been reasonable to assume she left town by hitching a ride, taking a bus, or going off with a mystery lover. People who had suspected Krystal was dead probably thought her body would be found along some lonely stretch of highway. Joni had said all that in several phone conversations, working up to begging Bethany to come to Sorrel.

Ridiculous to think anyone could catch the killer after seven years, Bethany fretted as Gloria led her along the trail to where the ravine became shallower, the drop-off less steep. "See," Gloria said, "We can go down here and get to the crime scene along that animal path."

The woman's agility and sure-footedness in her worn running shoes impressed Bethany. Ten minutes later, they stood where Krystal's bones had been found. They didn't step inside the sloping area encircled by tape but, from the perimeter, took a better look at what they'd seen from above. Presumably, a forensic team had tossed rocks aside to unearth the bones lodged in a deep crevice. Years ago, alone out here, the killer must have stacked rock after rock on top of the body to cover up the crime.

Suddenly, Bethany felt someone watching. She remembered the hiker standing above where she had parked at the turnout near Sorrel. Now, she glanced up at the Ponderosa pine looming over the ravine. From here, the tree's exposed roots resembled the tentacles of a creepy sea creature. The trunk divided halfway up, so the Ponderosa had a double top soaring above the other trees like a two-headed survivor of a former underwater world.

She shook off the fanciful thoughts as Gloria said, "Not much to see here."

Bethany disagreed but didn't say so. At their feet, she saw a rocky deathbed, above them a clearly defined meeting place. No other tree stood as tall or had a bifurcated trunk. Anybody familiar with this forest could find this spot if given directions. She would lay odds the killer waited at the pine for a pre-arranged meeting. No local loony had simply happened upon a victim.

Bethany's neck hurt from canting her head up at the tree, and she felt the effects of air much thinner than at home in Las Cuevas. "Do we have to retrace our steps to get back up to the trail?"

No, Gloria said. They could follow the animal path through the ravine toward the lodge. "This is the steepest part. It runs uphill a while and then levels out. I can get us back to the hiking trail. Easy peasy." She offered the canteen to Bethany, who made sure not to drink too much.

Bethany passed the canteen back. "You're quite a hiker, it sounds like."

Gloria took a sip and screwed on the lid. "Not really. I've hiked with Joni once or twice. And David and I came out here after the police left. You can see by the flowers and stuffed animals other people have done it. But you can tell they didn't know how to get down here since they left offerings for Krystal up above."

"How did you know the way down?"

"I didn't. David did. He comes out to the forest all the time. The miner's cabin he's fixing up is out here. It's pretty much a shack, so he won't live in it anytime soon. Matt has promised to help him finish it after the lodge opens. You can get to it from the main forest road, beyond the turnoff we took. And there are all sorts of animal paths to take that David knows of. He likes to run on them. He's in great shape, but he should be since he's a P.E. teacher."

And a massage therapist, a man with strong arms and hands. A man who could swing a club with ease or bash someone in the head with a rock. But David had no known motive. Glancing up at the Ponderosa pine again, Bethany tried to imagine David there but instead pictured a faceless man pitching a body into this ravine. Shaking off the image, she said, "Can you show me how to get back to the lodge?"

"Sure. It's not far. Like I said, we just follow this deer and elk path."

Soon, on flatter ground, they stopped again for sips of water. Bethany unzipped her parka; even in the cold air, she had overheated.

Gloria angled her face toward a path that intersected theirs. "I can show you something awesome if you're willing to go a little farther."

"Show me what?"

"A surprise. You game?"

Curious, Bethany followed her. They bypassed a trail Gloria said led directly to the lodge. "Don't worry. We won't get lost. This is going to be cool." After a few minutes, looking upward, she said, "Check that out."

A metal lookout tower stood high among the trees.

"Nobody's in it after fire season," Gloria said. "Let's see if we can go up."

Bethany didn't budge. "I don't think…"

Ignoring her, Gloria went straight to a stairway at the tower's base, blocked by a gate with a padlock. Gloria took the padlock in hand and opened it with a quick tug. Her laugh rang out in the forest. "Kids. They cut off the Forest Service's padlock and put on one stuffed with gum, so it looks locked. Word is a lot of them lose their virginity here. Or they come up to get high, with or without drugs, or scare themselves silly at Halloween. The Forest Service doesn't have enough rangers to stop them." She started up the stairs. "It's a tradition to climb the tower at least once. Nobody's around. Come on!"

Worried she would regret this, Bethany followed at a slower pace, catching her breath when Gloria stopped about a third of the way up at a platform that served as a switchback. They set off again, the stairs zigzagging between two more platforms before they reached the top at a small, unlocked room with windows on all four sides, an empty box except for a table and folding chair. Bethany dropped into the chair and tried to catch her breath.

The room's pine paneling bore initials scratched in the wood or written in various inks. No one had left messages as crude as in the Black Bear's restroom.

Gloria pulled a small pair of binoculars from her backpack, handed them to Bethany, and opened a window. "Look at the view!"

The forest spread out below them, enclosing Sorrel. Seeing the town from above, Bethany realized it contained more side streets than she expected. Unpaved, curving lanes branched off from the straight line of Main Street. She picked out the library, a prominent landmark, and beyond the main part of town, the school where David taught P.E. Looking almost straight down, she saw the lodge and the property surrounding it. Someone had thinned trees all around the building, giving the property more of a park-like appearance than the surrounding forest.

Gloria directed Bethany to look beyond the town to where the steep road wound its way up from the valley.

"David told me about the accident that killed the husband of the woman who runs the café and motel," Bethany said. "Lorene. I met her."

Gloria stepped away from the window. "Other people have been killed on that road. A couple teenagers died on their way back from their prom in La Plata about five years ago. I heard Matt and Joni saying maybe next spring they'll have a free post-prom party at the lodge. But they haven't figured out what to do if the Sorrel kids' dates are from La Plata. Maybe offer to let the kids stay overnight for free, girls together in some rooms and boys in others."

From the perspective of the fire tower, Bethany could literally see Sorrel as a community, not merely a street lined with businesses. If somebody died, it must affect almost everyone around here. Finding out who murdered Krystal felt as important as awarding a Foundation grant. She renewed her resolve to be of service, and to more people than Joni and Matt.

"What's that big building at the entrance to town?" Bethany pointed to it.

"The museum. A funky old place."

"Right," Bethany said, recalling the one-word sign. The building looked more prominent than from down below. A parking lot and grove of trees separated it from the mercantile and café nearer to the tower.

"What's in the museum? Joni hasn't said much about it."

"Probably because it's basically a junk heap. An old

man is paid to be the so-called curator. What the place needs more is a housekeeper, somebody to sweep the floor and dust the exhibits. Some of the stuff is from way back in the eighteen-hundreds. Mining tools, stuff from people's houses, old clothes, creepy old photos, knick-knacks. Like I said, mostly junk."

Gloria sounded so scornful that Bethany laughed. "A typical small-town collection, it sounds like. Some true antiques, I bet."

"Yeah, filthy and broken. But you know what I heard about Krystal?"

"What?"

"That she went there to look at what the ladies wore in the olden days. She made dresses and hats like those old ones for when she sang at festivals and the Black Bear. People say she sometimes dressed like a lady and other times like a dance-hall girl, and we know what kind of girls they were. A bunch of hookers. Weird that Krystal wanted to dress up like them, isn't it? But maybe Country Western singers did that in her day." Gloria made several years ago sound like ancient history.

"Who mentioned how she dressed?"

"Crush, the other night. Talk about an appropriate name for a guy. He had a big one on Krystal."

That seemed obvious. "Who says?"

Gloria shrugged. "They're whispering about it in the Bear. People who knew him back in the day. Which I didn't. Like I said, I still lived in La Plata." She frowned and looked away, then shifted gears. "Let me show you something else you can see from up here. In the other direction."

Bethany turned around to get a breathtaking view of mountain peaks, partly obscured by clouds.

"Look straight down," Gloria said. "See that skinny trail? Okay, follow it with your eyes. Can you make out a little building? It's hard to spot, but see it? That's David's cabin, the one he's fixing up."

Bethany noticed a rooftop among the trees, but the cabin would be hidden from people passing near it.

"You can see all sorts of things from here," Gloria said. "Great, isn't it?"

"A whole different perspective. Thanks for bringing me."

"I figured Joni and Matt wouldn't have time." She pulled out a pocketknife. "You need to carve your initials on one of the walls. Too bad you're not up here with a guy. Have anybody special?"

"I'm seeing someone."

"Put your initials where there's plenty of space. Maybe someday you'll bring him up here, and he can add his."

Gloria, a pragmatist and romantic rolled into one. "Did you come up here as a girl?"

"Nah, I didn't even know about this tower until David showed it to me." Gloria pointed above her head. "Here I am. GG for Gloria Geesen."

Gloria's initials looked fresher than most of the others.

"Did David carve his here, too?"

"Not that day. He'd already done it the first time he saw this place, he said. When he came out here alone."

Gloria had carved hers to the right of David's. They only lacked a plus sign to pair them in a love relationship.

"Are you fond of David?" Bethany tried not to put too much emphasis on the question as she pulled off a glove and set to work with the pocketknife.

81

"Yeah, I like him."

"A lot?"

Gloria didn't meet her gaze. "He's got twin girls not much younger than me. They're in college, and I'm only about five years older."

Bethany didn't say anything, hoping Gloria would continue.

"It's not going to happen, David and me," Gloria said, turning away to gaze out of the window with the binoculars, leaving Bethany to her carving. "You could watch people from up here, couldn't you? I guess that's why they call them spy glasses."

When Bethany finished carving BJJ for Bethany Jane Jarviss, in neat capitals, she closed the pocketknife, handed it back to Gloria, and studied other initials on the walls. She thought she recognized some of the same ones as in the ladies' room at the Black Bear. *Those girls got around!*

A musical tone sounded from inside her backpack. She answered her cell and heard her brother Don's anxious voice. "I tried to get a hold of you earlier."

"I'm at a higher point now. You know service is spotty in the mountains. My cell won't work at the lodge."

"Right," Don said. "I tried Joni's, too. No luck. David somebody at the lodge said she and Matt are in La Plata talking to the cops."

"Joni and Matt most likely had to switch off their phones in the police station."

"What's up? Do the cops have new evidence?"

"No idea. Matt has hired a defense attorney."

"That's good, but do you think our family should get one to represent Joni?"

"I don't see why. Calm down, okay, Don? Joni hadn't met Matt when Krystal went missing. The police don't want to question her. She went along to support Matt."

"As his second fiancée," Don said bitterly. "The replacement for the murdered one."

Gloria listened to Bethany's side of the conversation, not even pretending to do otherwise.

"Look, Don, I should go."

"Someone with you?"

"That's right."

"Call me as soon as you're alone."

"There's really no need, is there? Why don't you talk to Joni later, when she gets back to Sorrel? Horse's mouth and all that."

"I thought you'd fill me in."

"Go hit some balls. You said your short game needs work. Bye." She slipped her phone into her daypack. "My brother, the golfer. He's a pro on the PGA tour."

"Worried about Joni, too, right? Who wouldn't be? But you shouldn't worry about her with Matt. He's such good people. Him and Joni both. They've been so good to me I'd do anything for them."

"I can tell they appreciate that."

"They don't deserve all this trouble." She said it with a fierce passion. "Too bad he didn't meet her first, before he ever set eyes on Krystal Decker."

Bethany shared Gloria's sentiment but saw no point in dwelling on it. She took a deep breath of frigid air. "Let's go down, slowly please."

Gloria took the lead. "Heights not your thing, are they?"

"I'm not phobic, just cautious. It would be easy to

slip on these metal steps."

"I wouldn't come up here when it snows," Gloria agreed. "The stairs would be murder. Oops, I didn't say that, did I?"

Chapter 8

At the driveway to the lodge, Bethany said she wanted to walk into Sorrel.

Gloria gave her a "you must be crazy" look. "Don't you want to take a break?"

"Nope. I want to see more of the town. To keep my mind off Matt's appointment in La Plata."

"I wonder what the state cops are asking him," Gloria said.

"Me, too. I can't just sit around."

"You don't want me to make you lunch?"

Bethany thanked her but said she would get something in town.

****

Few other people walked along Main Street, but each said hello or at least nodded. She passed the library, the motel and café, and the businesses on the boardwalk. Beyond a grove of trees, she saw on her left the clapboard museum building, its narrow front faced in stone slabs fitted together like a jigsaw puzzle. The door opened to her touch.

Objects crowded a long, dim, dusty room smelling of wood smoke. Gloria was right; the place needed a housekeeper. A jumble of display cases fought for space with a barber chair, a child's school desk, a wringer washing machine. The walls were crammed with mining days photos, tools, grimy baskets, blankets, and animal pelts. From a pressed-tin ceiling hung more vintage things, notably a wicker baby carriage, a tricycle, wooden skis, a cracked saddle, a huge scythe, several rusty oil lamps, and an upside-down, tattered black umbrella.

She called hello uncertainly. At the back, a bearded man rose and peered at her through outdated, steel-rimmed glasses. The old fellow wore pants held up by suspenders over a round gut, but the rest of him looked scrawny.

"Can I help you, young lady?" He didn't come forward, so she picked her way through the maze, careful not to dislodge a shotgun here, a pickax there, a pottery urn holding walking sticks, all leaning against the display cases.

"Are you open? I didn't see any hours posted."

She had interrupted his lunch. A plate with a half-eaten sandwich rested on one of the cases. A thin flame struggled in a Franklin woodstove.

The old guy chewed and swallowed. "Open and free to the public. A whole town history within these four walls, from the spectacular but brief silver boom—eighteen-sixties that was—to the hotbed of tourism it is at present. Too bad the mines amounted to only a bunch of holes in the hillsides. No deep shafts to take visitors down, not like in some parts of the world."

He gave his unfinished lunch a longing look, but duty evidently won out over hunger. "Sid Rogers, curator. Fancy title for caretaker."

"Bethany. I'm interested in seeing your collection of ladies' clothes."

"Right over here."

He took her to the back corner past a case of molting

stuffed animals—a fox, squirrel, and beaver—which had blocked the view of glass-fronted displays of dresses on manikins in such bad shape that Bethany stifled a laugh. One manikin lacked a hand, another her wig, and a third her head. Paint peeled off faces and limbs. Surprisingly, though, the dresses had held up over time. The display included about a dozen of them—fancy gowns and everyday frocks, some on hangers due to a dearth of manikins—along with shoes and feathered hats.

"Let's have some more light." The curator flipped a switch near the cases. "Pretty, don't you think?"

"Yes, I do," Bethany agreed.

"You'd suppose women who wore the fancy getups were ladies, but most of the gowns belonged to party girls, if you know what I mean. Girls of easy virtue." He grinned. "The low-cut gowns belonged to them. This one buttoned up to the chin must've belonged to the minister's wife."

He appeared eager to launch into a lecture, but Bethany had no patience for one. "Mr. Rogers—"

"Sid, please."

"Sid, I'm not only here to see the dresses. I'm Joni Jarviss's sister. She's engaged to Matt MacGregor." She waited for the penny to drop, for him to say something, but the curator simply cocked his head. "You probably know Matt's fiancée was found dead, his first fiancée, I mean, the one who supposedly went missing seven years ago."

"Krystal." He infused the name with sadness.

She wished he would invite her to sit down somewhere, but he didn't budge. "I heard Krystal came here to see the antique clothes, that she made costumes like them for her performances."

"Pardon me, young lady, but what does that have to do with the price of rice in China?"

His sharp comment startled her, but she pressed on. "I want to learn all I can about Krystal Decker. Somebody murdered her, and Matt swears it wasn't him."

"He does, huh?"

"He thought Krystal left him."

"And you believe that? People surmise he might've done away with Krystal. But that could just be talk. Small place, big mouths."

"You can see why I need your help. Anything I can learn about Krystal might be useful. Matt is in La Plata being questioned by the state police."

"Is he? That I didn't know. Hard on him, hard for your sister. But I can't help you, what did you say your name is? Bethany. Sorry, Bethany. I don't know anything."

"You can tell me what you remember about Krystal coming in here."

"That I can do. Like you said, she looked at the pretty things in these cases. She'd sit right here and scribble and draw pictures in a little book. I'd tell her about the old days. A real nice girl, with a pretty voice. You should of heard her sing the national anthem in the park at the town festivals. Folks got teary-eyed, I can tell you."

"What else can you remember? About her coming here, I mean."

"Not much. Sometimes she brought Rusty. That's her brother. He liked the rock collection." Sid showed her a display of silver ore samples and various other rocks, identified with handwritten, yellowed labels.

"These specimens came from all over the Southwest. That big hunk of turquoise is from up near Santa Fe."

"Does Krystal's brother still come here?"

"Not once since she used to bring him."

Bethany moved toward the front door with Sid close behind her like a store associate on the alert for shoplifting. She stopped at a case holding four pottery bowls, each with a brownish animal design inside—a turtle, bird, rabbit, and buck deer. The pots were cracked, and each had a jagged hole in the bottom. Bethany knew such pots had been found at burial sites and that archeologists speculated the so-called "kill holes" were made to free the pot's spirit or that of the deceased. "These are Mimbres pots, right? From the valley not too far from here?"

"Sure are. Lot of museums have 'em."

Bethany had seen other examples. Like these, most had been found in pieces and glued back together.

An odd contraption, made mostly of copper pipe, caught her attention. At her raised eyebrows, Sid said, "It's a homemade whiskey still from Prohibition days. Mountain folks made their own hooch. My daddy told stories about drinking whiskey strong enough to grow hair on a lady's chest."

As Sid rambled on, Bethany moved toward the front of the museum. The airless, smoky room made her cough. She longed to escape, but Sid stopped her by the door to point out a photo of a bride in a fancy dress and her groom in garish, striped trousers. "That fellow died in an accident in the Sorrel family mine. Kicked by a mule the day after the wedding. Too bad he didn't take the little lady on a honeymoon."

On that bit of commentary, he let Bethany make her

exit but not before he extracted a promise to return for a "grand tour." Under a darkening sky, she flipped up her hood against the cold. What a strange place, this museum, and not only on the inside. To the back of the parking area, an RV trailer sat behind a white picket fence, a plastic one like people put around flowerbeds. Between fence and trailer, someone had placed a café table with a sun-bleached umbrella, mismatched chairs, and a barbecue grill. A holiday wreath of cloth poinsettias decorated the RV's door. *Could this be Sid's home?* But then, it was not much smaller than a typical nineteenth-century miner's cabin. She gave the RV and the museum another glance and set out for the mercantile for the chance to meet more locals.

****

The merc sold gas at twin pumps open to the sky. Faced in split pine, the building resembled a log cabin. Red, blue, and green lights strung over the entrance blinked on and off, color by color. Inside, the store was doing a reasonably good weekday business. A few customers pushed carts down the grocery aisles while others occupied tables near a deli counter in the back. At a counter like the one at The Treasure Box, the store offered sandwiches and chips as well as coffee and pastries. Shelves held *Ernie's Mercantile* T-shirts for babies through adults and boxed candy also bearing the store's name.

Bethany ordered a coffee from a girl who wore a mercantile T-shirt and looked about eighteen. The girl wrote the drink's price on a slip of paper and pushed it across the counter, saying, "Pay up front when you leave" and "Help you?" in the same breath to the next customer, a cowboy in a well-worn green coat. She made it sound as if the line were interminably long instead of only two people.

Coffee in hand, Bethany took a table and checked her watch: twelve-thirty. Several people munched on thick sandwiches. Resisting the temptation to order one, she decided to dine at the Ponderosa Café. Lorene probably knew almost everybody in town and might answer more questions. Bethany went over in her mind what she had learned so far. Krystal sang country songs. She liked to dress the part of a dance hall girl. She didn't like to hike, so why had she gone to the forest? To meet the person who killed her? Or maybe she went there to be alone. Joni thought she might have had the bad luck to encounter a lunatic killer, a stranger, who hadn't targeted a particular victim. As before, Bethany discounted that theory. Krystal must have died at the hands of someone she knew.

Bethany pried the plastic lid off the cup and sipped the fragrant, steaming brew. *Standard, decent coffee, not too strong.* She sat watching people but trying not to do it overtly. The most eye-catching one was a slim woman in a red beret. The woman dressed oddly for Sorrel, in a red-and-black plaid jacket, a short skirt, and knee-high boots. She stood talking to a husky young man clutching a broom and clearly itching to sweep around her. Beyond them, a man observed the interchange with a scowl. His fierce expression and lush, black mustache reminded Bethany of photos of the Mexican revolutionary Pancho Villa.

The woman canted her head to catch the young man's eye. Bethany heard her faint words: "I'm so sorry."

The sweeper kept his gaze on his job as the woman

reached out and touched his arm. He reacted as if she had struck him, pulling away and swinging the broom in an arc that knocked over Bethany's coffee. Instinctively, she jumped up, avoiding a splash of hot liquid. Coffee pooled on the table, chair, and floor. There were no napkins handy to wipe up the mess.

The deli girl yelled, "Rusty, put down that broom and get a towel." As he dropped the broom splat on the floor, the woman in the beret pressed crimson lips together, a look of pity on her face. Noticing Bethany, she said in a voice from somewhere back East, "He's special, you see."

Bethany understood immediately. *Krystal Decker's brother. Rusty.* He returned with a terrycloth towel and began slowly wiping up the spill.

"You have coffee on your coat sleeve," the woman said. She gestured for Bethany to move to another table and sat down across from her. "I simply said I'm sorry for his loss. He lost his sister, you might say recently, but that's not exactly accurate. I'm Jazz Marcham, by the way."

"Bethany Jarviss." She extended her hand, then realized it dripped coffee. She pulled it back, said sorry, and wiped it on her jeans.

"Jarviss. You must be related to Joni." The woman seemed flustered but struggling not to show it.

"We're sisters."

"Ah. Good to meet you, Beverly."

"Bethany."

"And everyone calls me Jazz. I have the art gallery on the boardwalk. Marcham's Fine Art."

Done cleaning the table, Rusty moved away from it, ignoring the broom on the floor until the girl behind the counter called, "Broom, Rusty. And get a mop." He picked up the broom without acknowledging the command and continued past the deli area and through a door farther back. Nobody waited to place orders, leaving the girl free to fill another cup with coffee and call to Bethany, "Here you go, ma'am."

As she started to get up, Bethany felt a hand on her shoulder. The mustached man who had been watching Jazz and Rusty said, "Let me." He fetched the coffee and a chocolate chip cookie. "Sorry about that little accident. These are on the house."

Only then did he seem to recognize the gallery owner. "Hello Jazz."

"Ernie."

For a moment no one spoke. Then Jazz said, "This is Joni Jarviss's sister Beth Ann."

"Bethany." She suppressed an urge to laugh at the woman's inability to get her name right. Or maybe because of the tension passing like a live current between the other two.

"Bethany, this is Ernesto Ruiz, owner of this establishment."

"Ernie to my friends." He leaned down, giving off a faint, pleasant wave of aftershave. For a second, Bethany expected him to kiss her hand, but he simply shook it. Large and solid, he looked comfortable in his body. "So you are the sister of Matt MacGregor's Joni. A girl with fire in her heart for her man and his great project."

Ernie's attention strayed to Rusty returning with a bucket and rag mop. Rusty ignored his employer but attended to the spilled coffee, swirling the mop with careful deliberation. When he finished the job, the overturned coffee cup still lay on the table. Seeing it,

Ernie sighed. "Rusty, the cup."

Rusty crushed it and dropped it into the bucket. He walked off, bucket and mop in the same hand, the mop leaving a wet trail behind him.

Ernie and Jazz exchanged glances. "You're good to employ him, Ernie, given his limitations."

"He does a fine job when it's routine."

"His pendants are his saving grace," Jazz said. She turned to Bethany. "I carry them in my gallery. Rusty finds stones locally and makes them into the most beautiful, wrapped pieces. It's a good outlet for him."

"For his frustrations," Ernie said.

"This is the first time I've seen him since I heard about Krystal," Jazz said. "I wanted to express my sympathies."

Ernie shook his head. "You should not have done that, Jazz. Attention upsets him."

Jazz pressed her bright lips together. "Rusty always said his sister was in a better place, something he heard somebody say once, but they probably surmised she went to L.A. The poor boy probably can't take in that she's dead. But you'd think he could accept a simple expression of sympathy!"

Ernie stepped closer to her. "For God's sake, woman! Rusty has no social graces."

She scrambled up and moved to a half-filled shopping cart. "If this weren't the only place in town to buy a loaf of bread—"

"Temper temper, my dear." A laugh rumbled in his throat.

Jazz tossed her head, an attractive, theatrical gesture that didn't dislodge the red beret.

"I'd better get going, or I'll be late opening my

gallery. Come see it. Marcham's," she said to Bethany.

"I'll ring you up when you're ready," Ernie said. He watched Jazz's trim figure as she pushed the cart between shelves of packaged foods. He stroked his mustache and made a noise like smothered thunder in his throat. "She's my ex. We're like oil and water, but she's a hell of a woman. I must tend to the register."

Bethany's mouth dropped open. *Those two married? Interested in each other, yes, but married and divorced? Really?* They shared a vibe like foreplay.

Ernie left her before she could ask more about Krystal. How well did you know the dead woman, sir, would have been good for starters if she had been with the police. But she wasn't an officer of the law or even a P.I. She should be grateful anybody would talk to her.

Chapter 9

Eating the soft cookie, drinking her coffee as other customers came and went, Bethany let her thoughts float. Then she snapped to attention as Rusty reappeared, this time without broom or mop. Barbara had said he was twenty-nine, but his reddish complexion and round face made him look younger. In contrast, the teenage girl behind the counter had an unmistakable air of authority. She said something to Rusty, who glanced nervously at Bethany and came her way. "I'm supposed to say sorry about the mess." He dropped his head so his bangs shielded his eyes.

"Accidents happen." *Poor guy to be made to apologize.* The deli girl glanced at them, but then a customer at the counter blocked her view. "I'm Bethany. You're Rusty, right?"

He didn't react to her knowing his name but reached behind his apron into a pants pocket. When he drew out his hand—a large hand with thick fingers—he concealed something in it. "Here. For you."

He held his hand closed until she extended hers. He dropped into her palm a whitish, glittering stone about the size of a quarter. "You can have it."

The stone felt warm and light. "You make these into pendants, Jazz says. I saw Barbara, at the library, wearing one."

He smiled and blushed. He didn't acknowledge the

reference to his foster mother. "I can make you one. I'll make it nicer."

He held out his hand. Reluctantly, she gave the stone back to him.

"Rusty, work!" the deli girl called.

"Oops. Got to skedaddle. That means go." He pocketed the rough stone and left without looking her in the eye.

Bethany wished he had let her keep the stone. She assumed he wouldn't remember her name or that he'd promised to make her a pendant. He appeared physically strong, emotional, and easily spooked. Jazz had set him off by simply touching his arm. Could he have pushed his sister into that ravine in the forest, then seeing her unconscious, bashed her on the head, and covered up his crime? If so, why? Because she planned to marry Matt, in a sense leaving Rusty behind?

Her coffee cup empty and only crumbs remaining of the rich cookie, Bethany looked around the store for Jazz but couldn't see her. Presumably, she had paid Ernie and gone to her fine-art shop. It would be natural to stop by there.

At the register, Ernie rang up the green-coated cowboy's purchases. The two chatted amiably. On the wall at one end of the counter, padlocked glass cases displayed shotguns and handguns, boxes of ammunition, and a wide selection of knives. The mercantile carried quite the range of merchandise. Groceries and gasoline, gourmet coffee and candy, T-shirts, and your basic weaponry. A little something for everyone.

Ernie, seeing Bethany looking, stroked his mustache. He said to the cowboy, "You come back now." As she exited behind the man, Ernie added, "You, too, miss."

****

Under a dark, cloudy sky spitting snow, Bethany walked briskly. She turned right and at the corner, crossed Main Street. *Marcham's Fine Art* fit neatly among the other shops joined by the false fronts and boardwalk. The cheek-to-jowl shops reminded her of a similar row in Cloudcroft, a southern New Mexico town that also capitalized on its Old West past. She'd visited Cloudcroft to cross-country ski the previous year with an on-again, off-again lover she no longer dated. She shook off the memory of skiing and two nights of inspired lovemaking; she had to focus on getting Jazz to talk to her some more.

The shop bell jangled as Bethany opened the door. Fortunately, Jazz was alone. She had taken off her beret and stood with her slim arms crossed and a salesperson's smile on her face.

Bethany gave Jazz a smile in return. "Hello again. I thought no time like the present to see your place."

"Good! Come in and browse. All the works are by Southwestern artists. The paintings are originals, the pottery and jewelry handmade."

Watercolors, oils, and acrylics depicted Southwestern subjects—landscapes, adobe houses, log cabins, bears, eagles, and people in traditional dress. Also for sale were painted gourds, Kachina figures, and Zuni fetishes, as well as jewelry made of silver, beads, and stones. Familiar New Mexican merchandise, of first quality, Bethany could tell.

"Could you show me Rusty Decker's pendants?"

"Certainly. They're beautiful." She went behind a case, took out two of several pendants on display, and placed them on a velvet-covered pad. Each was a single stone wrapped in silver wire with a loop at the top to slip a chain through, priced reasonably at seventy-five dollars.

One of the stones bore the partial imprint of a leaf. "It's an actual fossil," Jazz said.

The other stone resembled the one Rusty had pulled from his pocket in the mercantile. He had polished this one in some places but left it mostly in its natural state.

"He's completely untaught, but he knows what he's doing." Jazz took out another pendant. It appeared Rusty had done nothing but wrap this stone in silver wire more intricately twisted and knotted than around the other two stones.

Bethany told Jazz about Rusty's offer to make her a pendant. "He showed me a white stone like you have here. After the girl at the mercantile made him say he was sorry about knocking over my coffee."

"She would do that. Ernie has put her in charge of watching Rusty, but she takes it too seriously. You say he means to make you a present of one of his stones? That's unusual of him. He has to search all over the forest to find suitable ones. He's picky about them."

"He took it back, said he'd polish it. No, what did he say? That he'd make it 'nicer.' But I don't think he'll remember. And he doesn't even know my last name or where to find me."

Jazz shook her head. She had a thin, long-nosed face, saved from looking witchlike by unexpectedly kind eyes. "He'll probably remember to make the pendant and then agonize over how to find you. He's like that. It will bother him, poor boy. But you can make it easy for him."

"Go back to the mercantile."

99

"Which will give you a reason to check him out again, decide if he could have murdered his sister." Jazz's eyes lost their warmth. "That's why you came into my shop, isn't it? To get my take on Rusty. Wouldn't it be convenient for you if the police shifted their suspicions from Matt MacGregor to Rusty?"

"Not if Rusty's innocent. But Matt and my sister don't deserve the attention and talk they'll have to endure until the killer is identified. Sorry for sounding like somebody's outraged relative on TV."

Jazz set the pendants back in the case. "I know Matt only a little. He seems like a decent man."

"And Rusty did get pretty upset when you touched his arm."

Jazz glanced in the direction of the mercantile. "I've never touched Rusty before. He's been at his worst since his sister's bones were unearthed. Emotional and more awkward than usual. I saw a scene last week on the street. The poor fellow ran off when his foster mother asked him to tie his bootlace so he didn't trip."

"I've met Barbara Ziggerton. She appears to care about Rusty a great deal."

"Yes, despite the fact that he's difficult. Barbara encourages him to use the library, but she has to remind him not to sit on the floor and get in the way of other people, not to laugh out loud. It's embarrassing for her and disturbing for the other patrons."

"Rusty can read?"

"Some. Mostly graphic novels with cartoon drawings."

"I noticed he has big, strong hands. The stone he offered me looked so small when he held it."

"Rusty doesn't have the sensitive hands of an artist,

that's for sure." Jazz glanced at the pendants resting below her in the case. "I shouldn't say any more."

"Go on. Please."

"All right. It's probably nothing. When Rusty first came to live with Barbara, she tried to teach him not to pet her cats too hard, not to squeeze them. He never learned, and when her last cat died of old age, Barbara didn't get any others." She paused as if in reflection. "Barbara says he works out at home. Lifts weights and such." She stopped talking as if disturbed by what she'd said.

"I don't know how to ask this exactly. What makes Rusty special?"

"You mean what's wrong with him? Why isn't he normal? His birth mom did a lot of drugs when she was pregnant, more than when she was carrying Krystal. That's what the social workers told Barbara. But who knows really? Rusty seems bipolar, but Barbara says he doesn't need medication. He's rather a town project. Everybody knows Rusty and makes allowances."

"That's decent of people."

"But the way he flared up today, maybe he should be medicated." Jazz jutted out her chin. "It wasn't my fault, and Ernie shouldn't have snapped at me. Exes can be terribly quick to judge."

When Bethany didn't look surprised, Jazz said, "I take it Ernie mentioned we used to be married."

"Mm-hmm."

Jazz shook her head good-naturedly. "Briefly. He's a persuasive man, Mr. Ernesto Ruiz. Watch out for his charm."

Bethany examined the other jewelry in the case, casting around in her mind for another question for Jazz.

101

"Did it surprise you that Krystal Decker has been dead for years?"

Jazz answered at once. "Like everyone in town. We all assumed Krystal left Matt. Sorrel couldn't hold her, and neither could Matt with his plan to open the lodge. At first, she might not have believed he was serious about it. His dream didn't fit with hers of becoming some kind of star. And Rusty is a handful. Some people said she ran away from both men in her life."

"Is that what you thought at the time?"

"I didn't focus on Krystal Decker as someone special. A lot of young people escape Sorrel for bigger places."

"But you knew about it, about Krystal supposedly taking off."

"Yes, but I had my own affairs to deal with. I'd married Ernie about a year before, and we already had issues. And if you want to know the truth, Krystal Decker only made them worse. The little flirt and flatterer."

"She came on to Ernie?"

"And he loved it. I cheered when that girl cleared out of town. Not that she did. She never left, except in her fantasies." Jazz's eyes took on that kind look again. It was something she did with her eyelids. She probably studied her facial expressions in a mirror.

"Looking back, do you think there's any evidence that she would have left if she hadn't been killed?" Bethany asked. This woman couldn't know for sure, but it didn't hurt to pose the question.

"I suppose not. None directly. But there's something. Maybe I shouldn't say. I didn't tell anyone except Barbara then, and it won't do any good now."

Jazz liked to be coaxed; that was clear. "Let me be

the judge of that, okay?"

"What does it matter now? I think Krystal stole things from me. Two silver rings. Handmade and set with small diamonds. Worth several hundred dollars each."

"Why are you sure Krystal stole them?"

"I noticed them missing the day after she came into the shop and told me not to worry about her flirting with Ernie. I'd seen her all over him in the mercantile. I walked in, went to the back, and found her with her arms around his neck. The next day she came to me saying it meant nothing, that she only gave Ernie a sympathy hug. She felt so sorry about us drifting apart. I didn't believe her. She might as well have bragged about him being attracted to her."

"What about the rings? How could she have taken them while she talked to you?"

"She didn't right then. It was a busy Saturday. I saw to other customers as Krystal floated from case to case, looking at nothing special. I thought she'd wait for the shop to thin out so she could finish what she wanted to say to me. But then I didn't see her anymore. I'd taken out some rings for a man and woman to examine. When I closed the store, two rings were missing but not the ones the couple had been most interested in. I kept those in another case. Krystal could have slipped around it and slid open the back panels. People could still do that now. I've considered locking the cases, but I haven't bothered to do it. Shoplifting isn't a big problem in town."

"Were the rings ever found?"

"Not that I know of. I made the mistake of telling Barbara about the incident after Krystal supposedly left town. Barbara wanted to reimburse me for what I'd paid for the rings, but I told her to forget it, that the next time Krystal came back to Sorrel, I would talk to her about it."

"But she never came back."

"I did wonder if the rings might have been found with her bones. I didn't like to ask, though, because dredging that up would only hurt Barbara when she's mourning Krystal's death."

"Nevertheless, you should tell the police. They need a complete picture of Krystal."

"A complete picture wouldn't be flattering. Not nice of me to say, I know."

The shop bell rang again. Jazz greeted a young, parka-clad couple. Meanwhile, Bethany thought about Tom and Flora's assumption that Krystal had stolen stationery from their shop, plus their knowledge that she had gotten into trouble in high school for stealing from lockers. It sounded as if they were right about Krystal being dishonest. No need to mention to Jazz what Tom and Flora had said; best keep that to herself.

How interesting, Jazz's story about the rings. It didn't match Tom and Flora's exactly but must be the incident they had referred to. They didn't know precisely what Krystal might have stolen and disagreed about its value. They thought Barbara had reimbursed Jazz. But Jazz said she hadn't allowed Barbara to do that. *Who to believe? And did it matter which story was true? It might be more important to concentrate on Krystal's relationship with her brother.*

The gallery owner rejoined her. "Honeymooners. On a budget, no doubt! They'll look here but buy trinkets from the Whitneys." She sighed.

"Jazz, do you know if Rusty depended on Krystal? Could he have been upset about her marrying Matt?"

104

"I have no idea. Really, I don't." She watched the snow fall. "The weather is turning nasty."

"But if you had to guess? His world was about to change. Could he have been disturbed enough about the engagement to fight with his sister, maybe shove her to her death?"

Jazz raised her perfectly plucked eyebrows. "Barbara Ziggerton is a friend. I don't want to say anything that's pure speculation."

"Please, Jazz. Matt is in La Plata today being questioned by the police. They could even arrest him."

"People used to say Krystal and Rusty had a bond," Jazz said. "They'd been abused and neglected as kids. Left alone and unfed. Maybe beaten. Barbara said Krystal had been caught stealing snacks from convenience stores when their mother still had custody of them.

"I don't remember anything in particular about when Krystal went missing except wondering if she stole the rings to turn into cash," Jazz added. "But I do remember Rusty's reaction to her disappearance. Barbara couldn't console him for a long time. He thought Krystal had abandoned him."

Jazz stopped talking as the shop bell signaled the entrance of two women bundled in heavy coats and scarves. One said, "Just browsing."

Bethany stepped in front of Jazz to stop her from moving toward them. She dropped her voice. "Rusty's extreme reaction might have been from the act of murder—from killing his sister because she dared consider deserting him, or because she planned to marry Matt, another way of leaving."

"I think you're wrong." Jazz looked alarmed.

"Barbara said the first week without his sister, Rusty kept asking, 'Where is Krystal? Where is Krystal?' After weeks of telling him she'd gone off to be a star, Rusty came to some sort of acceptance. As Ernie remembered today, Rusty started saying Krystal had gone to a better place."

"Heaven. That's what people mean. I wonder who put that phrase into his head."

"One of the old-timers probably." Jazz watched her customers, saw they didn't need help, and fixed her gaze on the boardwalk. Snow fell steadily on it and the angled, parked cars. "I wouldn't want to be in your place. You're not going to make any friends raking all of this up. You should leave it to the police."

Bethany knew she had worn out her welcome. But she said, "I can't leave it to them. They probably don't have the resources to investigate such a cold case. Matt might be charged simply because he's the convenient suspect. I'm scared the police won't find the real killer."

Jazz gave her that kind-eyed look, this time tinged with pity. "And you think you will. I doubt that very much. What experience have you had?"

Bethany didn't hesitate. "I discovered who murdered another young woman. In Albuquerque. Not too long ago."

Chapter 10

Bethany stepped onto the boardwalk, not waiting for Jazz's reaction. The thought came unbidden: Did Jazz kill Krystal for coming on to Ernie? No woman whose marriage is in trouble wants a younger, beautiful woman giving the husband a "sympathy hug." But if Jazz had committed murder, would she have mentioned what could be construed as a motive?

Exhaustion hit Bethany in waves, that and a queasy feeling in her stomach, making her regret succumbing to the free cookie at the mercantile. And why the parting shot at Jazz Marcham? Now it would be all over town that Bethany Jarviss had been involved in a previous murder. For how could Jazz not spread such a titillating fact about Joni Jarviss's sister? The woman relished telling stories.

After the intense conversation, Bethany badly needed a break. The Ponderosa café beckoned as a place to rest and think. Snow struck her face as she scooted across the street. Shivering, she took a booth in the Ponderosa's front porch to avoid a table full of laughing customers in the inner dining room. From the booth, she couldn't see the others and wouldn't be disturbed.

Minutes passed with no sign of a waitress. Someone should have heard the bell, which sounded exactly like the one at Jazz's gallery. Bethany took a pen and notebook from her daypack as the same waitress who had served her before arrived with a menu and a smile.

"Good to see you again, miss." The waitress—Trudy—spoke in the soft local accent, likely influenced by regular contact with Texas tourists. Today, she wore a sweater with a red-nosed reindeer on the front.

Without checking the menu, Bethany ordered the soup of the day.

Trudy frowned. "You've had the beef barley. That's our best one. Lorene made chicken noodle. It's kind of plain but good."

"Sounds perfect." Left to herself, she held the pen still as she mused about what she had learned about Krystal. Her foster mother, Barbara, and other locals knew Krystal wanted to be a star and that she hoped a man would be the ticket to a new life. David said his ex-wife in Santa Fe had viewed Krystal as a young woman on the make. If life with Matt in Sorrel had been shaping up to be unbearably constricting, what would Krystal have done?

Seven years ago, most people believed she had left Matt. If she had intended to do that, had she planned to go alone or with a man, the person who murdered her? But why would that man kill her? It made no sense unless she changed her mind at the last minute and decided to stay with Matt. It could have driven a man madly in love with Krystal to violence.

Most people described her as exceptionally beautiful. The studio portrait in Barbara's office had proven that. But Tom at The Treasure Box said Krystal was pretty but not special. Maybe he took that attitude because she had shown no interest in him. Maybe that's why he gladly pegged her as a thief. Could he have murdered her? Probably not. But his information merited consideration. While the school thefts and theft of stationery were petty offenses, Krystal also had stolen valuable rings. Unless she stole for kicks or suffered from kleptomania, it could be assumed she took the rings to convert into cash after she left town.

Crush, however, didn't think Krystal planned to leave, or to be more accurate, said she hadn't told him of any plans. But then she wouldn't, would she, if she didn't mean to include him in them? Or perhaps he had lied in denying any knowledge of what Krystal was up to. Gloria said Crush had been in love with Krystal. His bar customers still gossiped about his passion for her. But while Crush gave Krystal a job and platform for her performances, like Matt, he couldn't help her realize her dreams of stardom. Did Krystal feel sorry for Crush even as she played up to him? If she then turned a cold shoulder to him, let him know she would soon be gone, how might he have reacted?

Bethany wished she could give credence to Joni's suggestion that "some pervert" killed Krystal, some "oddball" living in a miner's cabin in the forest. But Joni was grasping at straws. No one else had mentioned her theory or any reclusive, potential killers by name. Possible, but a long shot.

Bethany wrote it all down. Next, she turned the page, wrote *Matt,* and set down the pen. Unable to put on paper the negative things people said about him, she went over them in her mind. Crush and Sid at the museum both believed Matt killed Krystal. In Crush's view, Matt had been holding her back from "her destiny." And Sid sounded concerned Joni might be in danger from Matt. *Please goddesses, no*.

Bethany stared at the journal's almost-blank page

until the waitress brought a steaming bowl of soup and a plate of homemade rolls.

"Careful, the soup's real hot," Trudy cautioned and went on her way.

Bethany lifted her spoon and sipped the wholesome broth. Her stomach ached, but she made herself eat. It wouldn't do to get sick from anxiety; Joni depended on her.

She noticed the snow turning to sleet. The melted stuff covered the street. What must the mountain road be like? Scary in clear weather, treacherous today. Officials might close it. Would Joni and Matt make it home?

Bethany pushed her bowl aside, having only managed half the soup and one of the rolls. When Trudy returned to clear the table, Bethany snapped out of her troublesome reverie and ordered coffee. "No, make that tea." She asked for chamomile, remembering David drank it. Maybe it would soothe her stomach, calm her fears.

****

"How's it going, hon?"

Lorene, the café owner, set down a cup of hot water and a teabag. "Saw you sitting here, all alone, and thought you might need cheering up. May I?" She slid her stocky body into the opposite side of the booth. "I heard through the grapevine about Matt and Joni going to La Plata today. Darn police. Won't leave him alone, will they?"

Bethany said no, but naturally, they wanted to interview him again. Maybe he could remember something helpful.

"They think he might of done it, don't they?" Lorene's blue eyes, under heavily mascaraed lashes, expressed concern as well as curiosity.

Bethany made the tea and took a sip. It tasted truly awful. She put sugar in it, but that did nothing to improve the insipid taste. Tired of talking, she wished the woman would leave her in peace.

The spiral notebook lay between them. Bethany slipped it and her pen into her daypack. Watching her, Lorene said, "Find out anything to get Matt out of the mess he's in?"

"Maybe. I don't know. Like you told me, Krystal supposedly wanted to leave town. But if she was seeing another man, somebody she might have planned to go away with, there's no evidence of it. Nobody remembers hearing anything concrete about him."

Lorene brushed invisible crumbs off the table. "A man staying at my motel might of got her britches off at least once. I just remembered. That's what I came to tell you."

"What? You saw her with a man other than Matt?"

"Not me, no. One of my waitresses. When the motel office is closed, folks come to the restaurant to get a room key. I recall the waitress telling my cook about a local girl, Krystal, I'm pretty sure, going into a fella's room."

"You say you didn't see him?"

"Sorry, no."

"You're not sure your waitress saw Krystal?"

"I only caught the edge of a conversation. Heard the word 'engaged.' I can't think of any other engaged girl that would of fit the bill." Lorene propped her chin on a plump hand. "Maybe I shouldn't of said anything."

Bethany took a deep breath and tried not to get too excited. "Who checked him in? Not Trudy. She would have been a kid back then."

Lorene made a throaty "ha" sound. "She's still a kid to me. I can't remember everybody who worked here once upon a time. They come and go, high school kids and older ones. None of them stays long, but that's not a big problem. There's always a new one needing a job."

Bethany put a hand on Lorene's arm. "This could be really important. Do you keep records? Ones that would show who worked for you? Maybe the waitress could describe the man, remember his name even, and say for sure if the girl was Krystal."

"I keep old pay stubs with my tax records, but that far back, it's all buried deep."

"What about a guest book? Don't motel guests have to sign in?"

Lorene shook her brassy head. "Only in the movies."

"Well then, could you look for those pay stubs? If you could find out that waitress's name, I'd like to contact her."

Lorene looked sorry she had mentioned a mystery man.

"I know I'm grasping at straws, but anything might help," Bethany said. "Please look through your records."

"Sure, okay. You know, I did always wonder why Krystal would cheat on Matt. What's the point of an engagement if you cheat? I can see it with unhappy married folks. I really can. People feel trapped, and then they meet somebody they can't resist. Next thing, they're divorced and remarried. And usually no better off. Once was enough for me."

What Jazz Marcham had said about Ernie and Krystal came to mind. Had Ernie been the mystery man in Krystal's life? No, that was absurd. Everyone knew him; he wouldn't have rented a motel room on Main Street for a tryst. But Jazz had suspected something more had been going on between him and Krystal than the so-called "sympathy hug."

"Weather's getting worse," Lorene said. "Not a lot of snow, but what there is looks nasty, don't it? Road outside of town is going to be a mess."

The woman must always worry about driving conditions. "I'm so sorry about your husband's death," Bethany said.

"You heard about that. It didn't happen on a day like this, though. We had perfect weather and a clear road. Then some idiot in an RV takes his half out of the middle on a blind curve outside of town. Flint was a trucker, but he wasn't driving his big rig that day. We went over the edge, smack into a pine tree, or we would of tumbled down the mountain. The idiot didn't even stop. Probably didn't realize we ran off the road. I thought *this is it for me,* but I never lost consciousness and only got cuts and bruises. Flint wasn't so lucky. Killed instantly." She blinked but kept her composure.

Bethany said she was sorry for having brought it up, but Lorene said that was okay; it was a long time ago.

"You must miss him."

"I do. We had a hard marriage, though, with him on the road so much. I always thought he'd retire some day and be around more to help with this place. I don't think he would of believed I could of kept from going under without him. You're not married, are you, hon?"

"I'm seeing someone."

"Well that's nice. Serious?"

"No, we're still having fun."

Lorene hooted with laughter. "That a girl."

As they talked, the café had completely cleared out, the group in the main room exiting through the porch in a noisy rush to the bell's jangle. Moments later, the bell signaled the arrival of three women who called friendly hellos.

"Regulars," Lorene said. "Bridge players. A few more will show up pretty soon. Trudy can take their orders, but they like me to stop by and say how-de-do. Known 'em all for years. Want something else to drink? Black tea?"

Bethany glanced at her nearly full cup of chamomile. "No, but next time that's what I'll order, or coffee."

"David's about the only one who asks for chamomile. A healthy drink, but it tastes like green grass, don't it?"

Firmly back in the present, Lorene left to chat up the regulars. She probably would forget about looking up the pay stubs. And even if Lorene unearthed the name of the waitress, could that former employee be found or remember anything helpful about the mystery man? Bethany doubted it.

The café's porch served as a repository for other Sorrel information. While the windows displayed see-through, handwritten *Merry Christmas* and *Happy New Year* messages, the inner wall remained as it likely looked all year—plastered with local photos and news clippings. Bethany got up to take a closer look from an empty booth. Several articles, mounted in black-edged document frames, were from the *Mining Monthly*, a newspaper she hadn't seen for sale in town.

Thumbtacked to the wall unprotected, too large for

ordinary-sized frames, were a yellowed front page and double-page spread from the same newspaper's May edition a decade back. The articles promoted a Memorial Day weekend festival, *Old Timers Days*. The front page listed the events and showed kids in a pie-eating contest from the previous year. The two-page spread included articles about a parade, food booths, and contests, as well as a feature about the museum. The writer, avoiding calling the place a disorganized mess, mentioned *a wealth of collected items*. The closely cropped photos didn't show the state of disarray but concentrated on the whiskey still, the baby carriage, several Mimbres pots, and Krystal, modeling a low-cut, antique gown.

She wore white lace gloves and held a fragile-looking parasol. With her hair piled high under a feathered hat, she appeared older than in the senior photo in Barbara's office. A caption identified her as *Krystal Decker, 21*, and reported that she would sing at the festival's outdoor stage in the park.

In another picture, Sid Rogers, identified as the museum curator, sat proudly by the woodstove. The reporter had gleaned information from Sid about the owner: *Gerald Sorrel, 80, a resident of Desert Breeze Care Center in La Plata*. Sorrel had lived in the house most of his life, amassed the collection, and then opened his home as a museum. He was pictured as a boy with his father and mother. The man would be eighty-nine or ninety now if still living, Bethany calculated.

Another separately framed article from seven years ago reported winners in various festival categories. Lorene Callender had taken third place for the Ponderosa Café float. That had to have been after her husband's death. She must have made a valiant effort to keep the business going and participate in the community.

As Bethany studied the wall displays, more women entered the café. She glanced into the main dining room, where the bridge players sat with decks at the ready, chatting while the newcomers placed their orders with Trudy. Like the waitress, they all wore gaudy Christmas sweaters. Grinning, Bethany returned to her booth, left enough cash to include a tip, and stepped into the darkening afternoon.

Too bad she hadn't driven here. She set off on foot, almost at a trot. On the forest road, her cell phone vibrated. Low battery; the phone probably had been searching fruitlessly for service.

****

No one greeted Bethany at the lodge. In her room, she plugged the phone into its charger and tried to call Joni's cell. Still no service. From the third-floor phone, she reached Joni's voice mail and left a message. "Just checking in. I hope everything's going okay." She tried to reach her mother but heard only the familiar, soothing recording. At the beep, she hesitated, then said, "Hi, Mom. Things are fine here. Joni and Matt went down to La Plata, so I've been checking out Sorrel. Talk to you later." No sense in saying Matt had been summoned by the police. That would only make the folks worry.

Without undressing, Bethany lay down on the bed, pulled the quilt up to her chin, and tried to nap. For at least an hour, images and thoughts of Krystal bounced around in her brain. The woman had been bad news for Matt, no doubt about it. But had he been bad news for Krystal? Was Joni safe with him? *Yes, of course she's safe. Sure she is.*

Bethany awoke in the dark. She fumbled to switch

on the bedside lamp and read 6:10 on her watch. She freshened up in the shared bathroom and headed down the two floors to a deserted lobby. She turned on the chandeliers, found where to plug in the icicle lights to brighten the exterior, and flipped on the floor lamps she had helped Joni assemble in the enclosed porch. There, someone had set a fragrant pine tree in a metal stand and left next to it dusty boxes of decorations. Gloria, she assumed, or David. Poking through the boxes, Bethany found ball ornaments, strings of glass beads, and silver tinsel—familiar, vintage decorations.

The lobby felt chilly, so Bethany set about building a fire. As she struggled to get it going, David came down the stairs with another box.

"Found the lights." He said it with satisfaction. "That attic is a jungle, but the great explorer has triumphed."

From the opening between the lobby and porch, she watched him climb onto a stepladder and start at the top to string the lights around the tree. "I had to dig deep up there to find these beauties. Matt said his uncle always stayed here over the holidays and never failed to put up a Christmas tree."

David sounded determinedly cheerful, but Bethany, frustrated by her lack of fire-building skills, didn't play along. "Have you heard from Joni and Matt?" she asked.

He kept stringing lights. "Not a peep, but they should be back soon, wouldn't you think?"

"No idea. First, my cell phone almost died from trying all day to get service. Then when I got back, I left Joni a message, but I haven't heard from her."

He stepped down from the ladder and picked up the bellows. Instead of taking over with the fire, he handed the tool to her. "Try this. Pump it gently."

She did as he said, and soon the fire caught hold. "Thanks. Sorry, I'm not in the best of moods."

David went to the kitchen and came back with glasses of white wine. "We need a drink. Then let's get this monster tree decorated."

"Yes, let's."

They clinked glasses. She felt grateful to have something practical to do.

****

Half an hour later, the decorating done, they sat sipping the last of the wine.

"David, do you know many of the locals?"

"Some. Why?"

"Because it's likely that somebody in town murdered Krystal Decker."

When he didn't respond, she asked, "What do you know about Jazz Marcham, for instance?"

His glass jiggled in his hand. "She can't be your prime suspect!"

"No, more of a source of information. It's interesting that she and Ernie at the mercantile were married for a while. I met him, too."

"Yeah, he caught her on the rebound when she first came to town, after a nasty divorce in Minnesota by all accounts. Nice woman. Adds a touch of class to Sorrel. But Ernie's a scoundrel in his way."

"In his way?"

"You must have seen. Women seem to go for his type. Mr. Macho."

As he spoke, headlight beams flared against the windows. Joni and Matt were back.

"We saw the tree lit up in the porch," Joni said. "It

looks great!"

"A team project," David told them.

"Thanks, you guys," Joni said. "That's the perfect place for it. Are those Matt's uncle's ornaments? The glass balls are exquisite. How did you find them in all that attic clutter?"

David brushed off Joni's praise. "It wasn't too hard with the boxes labeled *Christmas*. So how was your day?"

Matt gave a bitter laugh. "The last half hour on the road required nerves of steel. What a slippery mess. But not as bad as being grilled by the state cops. They're going to have to come and arrest me if they want to talk again."

He unzipped his coat, pulled off his knit cap, and dropped onto a love seat. "Four hours of questions and more questions while Joni sat cooling her heels in the waiting room. They don't know squat about what happened to Krystal, and they don't seem convinced I can't help them."

"They had to ask," Joni said.

Her reasonable tone infuriated him.

"Ask! They *asked* me when a couple of them came to Sorrel right after the discovery of Krystal's bones. The first time they were polite. Today they were rude SOBs, insinuating they have something on me. They don't. But they'd like to pin the murder on me and go back to texting their girlfriends or whatever they do to waste time."

Joni sat down beside him and tried to take his hand, but he pushed hers away. "They asked him the same questions over and over, about the days before Krystal disappeared," she said. "Did they fight? Did he expect her to leave him? Those kinds of things."

"I can tell it," Matt insisted. "You weren't in the room."

Joni met his gaze, acting as if his harsh words didn't hurt. She unbuttoned her tailored, black wool coat—a conscious choice, Bethany assumed. In Joni's theater work, she had learned about appealing to an audience from rubbing elbows with actors. Today, she had smoothed her usually spiked hair. She wore so little makeup her face looked colorless. *Has she eaten anything since breakfast?*

"What did you say to the police?" David asked.

Matt rubbed his forehead. "No to everything. No, Krystal wasn't going to leave me. No, we didn't fight. No, I didn't kill her. No, I don't know how she ended up buried under a pile of rocks. That La Plata lawyer let those damn state cops badger me. Tomorrow, I'm calling the defense attorney in Santa Fe my lawyer there recommended. The man supposedly is a genius at criminal law. It'll be expensive but worth it to be protected from those bastard cops."

Chapter 11

Gloria returned in time to hear Matt's rant. She hesitated at the edge of the group and when no one said hello, went into the kitchen. Through the open doorway, Bethany watched her spoon stew into a pot on the stove. She unwound her long scarf, glancing toward the lobby, straight into Bethany's line of sight. No doubt Matt's comments had upset Gloria. Despite the blazing fire, Bethany felt chilled to the bone by his vehemence.

When Matt wound down, Joni said, "The kitchen cabinet! It's in the SUV. I didn't wait in the station the whole time. I went to the store and picked up another cabinet. Remember, we were one short."

"Right," Matt said, regaining his composure. "I'll go get it."

But David insisted he do it. Joni went with him to the lodge's entrance and beeped the SUV open with her remote. She came back and frowned at Matt, who didn't budge. "I'll go help Gloria," she said.

Alone with Matt, Bethany said, "I found out some interesting things. By talking to people in town."

"Who also think I'm a killer, right?"

"Some do. But that's natural, isn't it? For people to suspect you."

"Crush Dobbs, for one."

"Uh-huh."

"Who else?"

"The museum's curator mentioned people are gossiping. But he didn't say he thinks you're guilty."

"That old coot? He lives in an RV. That so-called museum is a junk heap. I'm surprised you bothered with it."

Bethany shrugged. "It's one of the town's main attractions."

"I guess so, since the Sorrels used to live there. The last one, Gerald, is in a nursing home in La Plata."

"He's still alive? His name and a family picture appeared in a news story I saw on a wall in the café."

"Yeah, he's still breathing, but he's not in good shape. Alzheimer's. He wouldn't know anything useful, and I bet Sid Rogers doesn't either."

"It's hard to say. Sid said Krystal liked to look at the antique gowns there, for inspiration for her performances. That she sometimes dressed like a woman would've in the Old West."

"Yeah, come to think of it, she did, for Old Timers Days. She got a kick out of it."

Bethany's wine glass wasn't quite empty. As she drained it, Matt asked if she'd spoken to anyone else.

"Quite a few people, actually, at the café, the library, and two of the shops. Most people are on your side, Matt. Lorene at the café has heard talk about you, but she doesn't believe you harmed Krystal. Nor do the Whitneys and Barbara Ziggerton."

"The Whitneys are good folks. And Barbara's great. She thought the world of Krystal."

"She said you are a 'genuinely good man.' "

Matt's expression brightened. "She was in favor of the engagement and really devastated when we thought Krystal left us."

Bethany took a chance. She didn't want to get Matt more upset, but she had to be truthful.

"Barbara wasn't all that complimentary about Krystal. Even though she described her as beautiful and talented—and clearly loved her—she said some critical things, too."

"Yeah, I expect so. We talked a lot after Krystal disappeared. Barbara suffered as much as I did. Krystal had gone off before, but Barbara never thought she'd do that to me. She's probably still in shock now we know Krystal never had the chance. I went to Barbara's house when the cops told me about finding the body, but they'd already informed her. We broke down and cried. I've called her since then to see how she's doing, but it's awkward."

David pushed a packing box through the doorway, interrupting them. He must have dragged it across the ground; wet grit soiled the bottom. Matt helped him carry the box into the kitchen where Joni said something too low for Bethany to make out.

Matt returned immediately and dropped onto the loveseat as if drained of energy. "David's going to unpack the cabinet. A better right-hand man you couldn't ask for."

Right-hand man, a secondary person. She wondered if David saw himself that way.

Matt ran a hand over his mouth and jaw and rotated his head. If he had a headache, he didn't admit it. "What else did Barbara say about Krystal?"

Bethany pulled her thoughts back to the foster mother. "That Krystal always thought somebody else would determine her fate, that she didn't work hard enough, at anything, it sounded like. And she said

Krystal stole things. That seemed to trouble Barbara the most. I heard about the stealing from the Whitneys and Jazz Marcham, too. Apparently, it escalated over time. Krystal first took things from other kids' lockers in high school, then she shoplifted a box of writing paper from the Whitneys, and then she probably stole two silver rings that went missing from Jazz's gallery."

"Silver rings from Jazz? I never heard about that. Barbara told you Krystal stole from Jazz?"

"No, she didn't. Jazz did. And the Whitneys alluded to it but didn't know specifically what Krystal might have stolen. Jazz and the Whitneys told me two stories about that. The Whitneys think Barbara paid Jazz for whatever Krystal may have stolen from the gallery, but Jazz said she wouldn't let Barbara reimburse her for the rings. Jazz was sure, though, that Krystal took them."

Matt leaned farther forward, elbows on his legs, hands covering his chin and mouth, the picture of puzzled worry.

"Did you know about Krystal's thefts?" Bethany tried to ask gently.

"Only about what she did as a kid. She told me she shoplifted little stuff—snacks, candy, nothing valuable—from convenience stores when her foster parents wouldn't give her treats, before she came to Barbara. She said the locker incident happened right after Barbara became her and Rusty's foster mother. After that, she never stole at school, she said. She owed it to Barbara to behave for taking such good care of them. If they needed anything, they got it. I can't believe Krystal would have stolen anything from anyone in Sorrel. What did you say she took from The Treasure Box?"

"A box of stationery. Before she met you. I don't know how old she would have been, but I got the impression she'd finished high school. The Whitneys didn't say they had proof except she wrote to a boyfriend using the same kind of stationery that went missing and sent the letter from their shop when it also served as a post office."

"It must have been a coincidence she used the same type of stationery. Maybe Barbara gave her some as a present."

"Maybe. But then what about the rings? I think they are much more significant because Jazz said Krystal stole them shortly before she went missing. It makes me think she took them to pawn, to finance getting out of town."

Matt slapped a hand against the wooden arm of the chair. "That's not true! I don't believe she stole any damn rings. I'm going to go talk to Jazz about it, tell her to stop spreading rumors!"

Even in the subdued lobby lighting, Bethany could see the blood rush to his handsome, freckled face.

"Please don't do that," she said. "People have been talking freely to me. If you complain about it, there's a chance everyone will clam up."

"Fine, but don't believe trash talk about Krystal. She was a beautiful person, and I loved her."

He raised an anguished face to Joni as she came toward him from the kitchen.

Joni's expression mimicked his. "What about now, Matt? Do you still love her? Do you love a dead woman?"

He jumped up and hugged Joni to him. "No! That's in the past. You're my world now, sweetheart. You have

125

to know that."

Bethany weighed telling them the worst, about the rumor of Krystal sleeping with someone else, that Lorene remembered her going into a man's motel room. But she'd wait for a better time.

With a twist of her slight shoulders, Joni freed herself from Matt's embrace. "Gloria has to be at the Black Bear soon. Let's have some of her stew before she goes."

He glanced over her head at Bethany. "Good idea. And some of that wine Bethany and David have been drinking."

"David poured me a glass," Bethany said. "The last of what I brought, I think."

"Then we'll open a bottle of ours." His determinedly upbeat voice sounded false, but at least he was shaking off his bout of anger and self-pity.

Over dinner, Joni made a fuss about the Christmas tree. She had David tell in detail how he'd found the pine near his cabin and hauled it back behind the lodge's three-wheeler. Bethany could see how much the attention surprised and pleased him, especially when Matt added his less effusive but genuine-sounding thanks. Only she seemed to note that Joni ate very little.

After the meal, Matt and Joni went upstairs, Gloria left for her shift at the Black Bear, and David stoked the fire in the lobby. Then, Bethany and David decided to add the last touches to the tree, thin silver icicles they draped over the limbs.

He stood back to examine the overall effect. "You can't beat a real tree."

Bethany agreed. "It smells so—I don't know—so spicy. Way better than air freshener."

"Did you notice the cones?" Eagerly, he broke off a light-brown one. "This tree's a Douglas fir. You can tell by the cones. See these little projections? They look like the tail and back legs of a squirrel. The school kids learn the squirrel's name is Douglas and he's furry."

She took the cone from him and examined it, then set it on a branch among the ornaments.

David sounded genuinely caught up in the holiday spirit. "I'm going to cut boughs for over the doorways, but not until right before the party on Friday. Geesh, only three days from now. But let's not think about that tonight. We've got to believe everything will fall into place."

His sensitive face, narrow like the rest of his slim body, seemed alight with emotion. He looked more poet than P.E. teacher, a good fit with young kids. He wasn't the muscular type who got off on being called "coach" by high school athletes.

He asked if she would like more wine or the coffee Gloria had made before she left. Bethany opted for the coffee. David said to stay put and admire the tree; he'd get them two cups.

"Sure you wouldn't prefer chamomile tea?" Bethany asked. "Lorene seems to think it's your favorite beverage."

"Lorene! She prides herself on knowing what her customers prefer. I needed to cut down on caffeine after the school year started. I'd gotten the shakes from too many bad cups of coffee in the teachers' lounge. So I asked for chamomile. Lorene didn't have it, but by the next time I went to the café, she'd made a point of getting some, just for me, she said. Since then, I don't dare order anything else. Actually, that's okay with me. I'm going easy on the caffeine. Gloria made decaf. Cream? Sugar?"

Black would be fine, Bethany said. While he went to get the coffee, she replaced the unused ornaments in the boxes, closed the lids, and pushed the boxes off to the side. Maybe David could find a place to stow them down here rather than all the way up in the attic until the tree came down in January. A quietly competent person, he might think of that. While he was out of sight, she admired the lodge's main floor, once again taking in the wagon-wheel lights, the wood-framed chairs upholstered in fresh, colorful fabric, and the newly enclosed porch. She'd never asked Joni how much all the improvements cost.

When David brought their coffee, Bethany decided to see what he knew about Matt's financial situation. "Matt must be fairly well off to be able to finance all the work on the lodge."

David turned the mug around in his smooth hands. "He's in demand as a financial adviser. He landed some big accounts in La Plata and the valley, a good thing since there's not a lot of money in Sorrel. But don't think he expects to make a bundle on this place. It's a labor of love. He's always assumed the lodge will be a tax loss for a few years until some guest cabins are built."

"He mentioned guest cabins. And the plans to build a cabin for him and Joni to live in. David, do you know if Krystal had life insurance?"

"If you're thinking Matt did away with her for the insurance payout to put it into the lodge, you're wrong about that. He's been open about inheriting money from his uncle along with the lodge itself. He did say Krystal had a policy, paid for by Barbara Ziggerton, with Rusty as the beneficiary. She never tried to have Krystal declared dead, so Rusty didn't collect on the policy, but now I suppose Barbara will make sure that happens. She told Matt when Krystal's remains are released, she'll pay for the cremation. She made sure he knew she would pay for it personally, not from any insurance money Rusty gets. She said the insurance money will help take care of him. Matt said she's also setting aside money of her own to help support Rusty after she's gone. She's an extraordinary foster parent. Matt thinks the world of her."

How much did the policy amount to? Bethany wondered. What would that seemingly decent woman do to provide for her special-needs foster son? Kill her troubled foster daughter, expecting the body to be found soon, but the murder to go unsolved? Krystal stole things, possibly cheated on her fiancé, and may have intended to leave Barbara and Rusty behind as she pursued her singing or acting career. Maybe Barbara decided she'd had enough of Krystal, that this time the girl wasn't going anywhere. Bethany said as much to David.

He looked at her as if she were crazy. "That's completely farfetched. You suspect everybody, don't you?"

"It's the way my mind works. I can't help it."

"Matt told me you figured out who killed that college student. My girls live on campus at UNM. I was relieved it didn't happen in a dorm. How come the police didn't discover the truth?"

Bethany's jaw ached from talking to people all day. She wanted nothing but to go to her room, lie down, and get away from the task Joni had assigned her. But she said, "The police wrote it up as an accident, not a push down the stairs."

David shook his head. "The poor girl. But I bet her mother got some comfort from learning what really happened."

"Not really. She took it hard when she found out her daughter had been deliberately killed."

They each took a sip of coffee. In the silence that followed, Bethany decided to confide in him. "Today, I went to the café again, and Lorene told me something troubling. She said when Krystal was engaged to Matt, she spent the night at the motel at least once with another man. Lorene never saw the man, but she said one of the waitresses checked him in."

David reared back in surprise. "I don't believe it. Krystal and another man? Is Lorene sure?"

Patiently, Bethany repeated Lorene's information. "If she can figure out who the waitress was, I'm going to try to contact her. What I wonder is if Matt knew Krystal cheated on him."

A pained expression crossed David's face. "I'm sure he didn't."

"David, I can't help thinking about something you said in the café. That after Krystal disappeared, Matt told you she'd realized he wasn't going to be the rich husband she expected. It makes me think she might have been considering breaking off her engagement to him, especially if she had another prospect."

He picked up his mug, found it empty, and set it down. "It's true Matt didn't do as well back then as he does now. He'd just launched his career, and it takes time to build a client base. I don't want to even think about what you're saying. If the police found out Krystal slept with somebody else, they'd immediately conclude Matt

130

saw red and killed her." His right hand tapped the top of his thigh. He didn't seem to notice.

Another idea occurred to Bethany. "Or maybe the police would explore the possibility that the mystery man murdered her. Somebody who wanted her to leave Matt. Maybe she met this guy in the forest, said sleeping with him had been a mistake, but he wouldn't accept that."

"Maybe, maybe. It's all as thin and slippery as today's snowfall, the kind that melts by morning. I don't think you should mention any mystery man to the police. It could look bad for Matt. And I shouldn't have told you he thought the size of his bank account disappointed Krystal." He leaned so close she caught a whiff of coffee-scented breath. "Usually I don't repeat what people tell me. It's pretty much a requirement for a massage therapist."

Bethany didn't respond. She couldn't promise David not to tell others what she found out.

He tended to the fire, which always seemed to need more wood. When he turned around, she could feel his eyes sweep over her like a doctor sizing up a patient. "You look all in. How about one of my fifteen-minute massages? I've got a chair in that closet." He gestured to a door under the stairs. "We can do it right here. You'll feel a lot better."

He didn't give her time to refuse but set up the massage chair. "Sit down and put your face in the so-called donut hole. Here, let me adjust the pillow."

Once before, Bethany had experienced a chair massage in the Las Cuevas mall. She had felt exposed and had worried someone might snatch her daypack off the floor while she kept her eyes closed. But this time, with no one else near, she relaxed.

David worked skillfully on her shoulders. "What did you do today besides grill the natives? No, don't answer. Breathe."

While he attended to her tight back, he talked about his twin daughters at the university in Albuquerque, technically young women but really still girls who hadn't totally gotten over the divorce. He was excited but nervous about their upcoming visit in January. He wouldn't be able to make his cabin livable by then, so they'd stay at the lodge. The cabin had only two rooms, so eventually, they would get the bedroom, and he would sleep on the couch. Maybe later he could add a third room with twin beds for them. But what if they wanted to bring boyfriends?

As he talked more to himself than to her, Bethany's consciousness floated off to a serene place. What a relief to let go of her worries.

Sooner than expected she felt the movement of air from head to toe as David swept his hands a few inches above her body. "All done," he said. He took her hand and helped her up.

"That was wonderful. What do I owe you?"

He gave her a mock stern look. "Nada for friends. Ever." He brought her a glass of water from the kitchen while she sat by the fire. Putting the massage chair away, he moved smoothly and efficiently. What an appealing, middle-aged guy despite the gray at his temples! Why had his marriage failed? David seemed like a man who needed a woman and would be good to her, not someone destined to be single.

He rejoined her by the fire. "Drink your water. You need to hydrate."

She checked her watch. He'd worked on her for half

an hour, not fifteen minutes.

"Bethany, can I ask you something?"

"Sure," she said, surprised.

"Do you like Matt?"

She wanted to say yes, she did, but she stopped to truly consider the question. "I don't know him well. Neither do my parents. We only met him a couple times before Joni got engaged to him."

"That's an answer, isn't it? He's not usually so focused on himself. Normally, he doesn't complain about people like he did about the lawyer. Obviously, he needs one more experienced in criminal law."

"Why are you telling me this, David? I understand Matt's under tremendous stress."

"I'm just saying. He has a lot to process. He's a decent man. He'll be a good husband to Joni."

"Of course."

"It would help if you believe in your heart Matt is innocent. Stop treating him like a suspect. He needs us on his side. To stand by him."

Chapter 12

David didn't wait for Bethany to respond but headed up to his room. She wanted to stop him and protest that she stood on the side of truth, whatever it turned out to be. Instead, she sat alone staring into the fire, listening to its crackle and sizzle, smelling its pungent smoke. When it turned to orange embers, she went into the porch and unplugged the Christmas tree lights. The porch felt chilly. No one had turned on the electric baseboard heaters, and no curtains covered the windows. Looking into the blackness outside, she shivered.

In contrast, her room felt overly warm with the space heater blasting. On the bed, Joni lay curled up in her robe and slippers. She slept, clutching a fistful of wet tissues. She probably had cried herself to sleep like when, as a child, she took refuge in her room after throwing a tantrum. She'd been a willful kid, but she didn't often go in for crying jags these days. *What had happened?*

Bethany turned off the heater and touched Joni's shoulder. "Wake up, Little Bird."

Joni rubbed her eyelids. "What time is it?"

"After ten. What are you doing on my bed?"

Joni slid against the headboard, fiddled with the pillows behind her back, and blew her nose. Her white-blonde hair, so carefully smoothed down for the police station visit, stood up all over.

Bethany sat on the edge of the bed. The massage and her stint by the fire had made her want to do nothing but get some rest without seeing anyone else tonight. She sighed. "Tell me."

"Matt's not over her. He won't deny it."

Oh-oh. "What happened, Joni?"

"I came back from the bathroom and found him with a newspaper clipping he's had in his wallet for years. He tried to put it back, but I grabbed it and looked for myself. He kept the story and picture about his engagement to Krystal. God, that woman had big hair!"

Bethany smiled, remembering Krystal's high school photo in her foster mother's office in the library. "What did Matt say about still having the clipping?"

"That he'd never thought to take it out of his wallet. Supposedly, that's what I caught him doing, throwing it away. But I don't believe him. He's in love with a dead woman."

"Do you really think that's true?"

"He didn't say he isn't. He told me to grow up and get real."

"Then you came in here to have a good cry."

Joni squeezed the wad of wet tissues. "I thought I could stand by Matt no matter what, but Bethany, if he still loves Krystal, how can I marry him?"

Fresh tears trickled down her face. Bethany reached into her pocket for a clean tissue. She handed it over and watched her sister dab her eyes and blow her nose. Devoid of makeup, Joni could have passed for twelve.

A knock sounded on the door as Matt called, "Bethany, are you in there? Joni?"

Joni slid closer to the headboard. "What do we do?"

Bethany opened the door a crack. "Joni's a bit upset

with you."

Matt whispered, "She's overwrought because of the awful day we had. Not thinking straight."

"Matt?" Joni's voice resembled a mouse's squeak.

Bethany stepped away as Matt went to Joni and enveloped her in his arms. Bethany left them alone, going straight for the sofa outside her room. She lay down, pulled a Mexican blanket up to her shoulders, and tried to blot out Matt's voice reassuring Joni that he loved her and only her. She dropped into sleep, hoping he meant what he said.

****

Sometime later, Joni shook her none too gently. "Go back to your room. Matt and I are okay now. Really. He tore up that clipping right in front of me. I overreacted. The thing is, he has to get over his anger at Krystal for leaving him now he knows she didn't. It's not that he still loves her, but he feels guilty for misjudging her. I can understand that. Besides, now he realizes he was only infatuated with her. He didn't understand real love until he fell in love with me."

Was that so? Bethany barely had the energy to go back to her room and undress. She straightened the bed covers. The sheets felt warm to the touch, evidence that the lovers had gotten between them. Bethany fell into bed, astounded and amused at the audacity of Matt and her sister. Maybe their relationship would be fine. Maybe Matt realized he would gain nothing from holding onto his feelings for his first fiancée.

****

Bethany awoke thinking about the announcement of Matt's first engagement. If that had been in the press, what else could she learn at the library about Krystal?

She would go there this morning to find out if it had a newspaper database. She might also ask Barbara Ziggerton about David's information about Krystal's life insurance policy. Did Rusty, not Matt, stand to benefit from it?

At breakfast, Matt and Joni acted as if they'd never argued. David and Gloria both looked less rested than the engaged couple. Gloria, her ponytail bobbing despite her obvious weariness, produced crisp bacon, scrambled eggs, salsa, and warm flour tortillas. Everyone made their own burritos.

"You're a fantastic cook," Bethany said after her first mouthful. "Perfect breakfast on a cold day."

As they ate, Matt talked about the party for locals and the open house. "We should have a good turnout for both events. People know the lodge will benefit the town. The motel and a few private cabins for rent never have met the demand for lodging. Those places will still be full, but with guests staying here, Lorene will have more people eating at the café, and every other business—the mercantile, the Black Bear, the shops—will have more customers."

"Who's invited to your events?" Bethany asked.

"On Friday, businesspeople, the top school officials, Sid from the museum, Barbara, a few others," Matt said. "On Sunday, anybody who lives in the Sorrel area, La Plata, and beyond could come by. The open house is being heralded through social media, on bulletin boards all over town, and in the La Plata newspaper.

"Too bad Sorrel doesn't have a paper anymore," Matt said. "The *Mining Monthly* went out of business a few years back, but people read the *La Plata Citizen* and a free shopper. We have no idea how many people will come Sunday. Road conditions will have a lot to do with it."

Bethany thought, but didn't say, that people with an interest in Krystal's death, along with newspaper and TV reporters, might show up in droves. "If you're swamped with people, will you be able to handle it?"

"Sure," Matt said, a little testily. "We want people to see the lodge, don't we? We've even hired fiddlers for the party for the locals."

Gloria described a mouth-watering Friday buffet: sliced ham and barbecued beef that she planned to make and deli salads catered by the mercantile. Pies supplied by Lorene's café. Plus wine, beer, and sodas. "The plans for Sunday are pretty simple." She moved around the table, offering refills of coffee. "Sodas, cookies, popcorn—stuff like that."

Joni listed the door prizes: poinsettia plants, boxes of chocolates, and baskets of fruit she would need help assembling.

"Have we got enough temporary hired help?" Matt asked.

"No problem," Gloria said. "Two girls for the open house. I asked around and got the most reliable ones."

"I bought Santa hats for the girls to wear," Joni said. "They'll look cute in them. And Santa's elves, little kids David teaches, will hand out candy canes."

"Right," David said. "And for both events, I'm giving five-minute chair massages. Upstairs in the massage room but with the door open so people can look in and see how it's set up."

"Be ready to book people for whole body massages," Joni said. "But leave some slots open for all of us after Sunday. We're going to need the full treatment from you."

"But who will work on David?" Gloria asked. "There's nobody else in Sorrel."

"True," he said. "I'll have to go for a long run and soak in the tub upstairs. And then folks, I'm going to get serious about fixing up that cabin of mine so the twins can stay there with me next summer."

"We'll help you," Joni promised. "Won't we, Matt?"

Matt patted David on the shoulder. "Yes, indeed, buddy. It'll be our next project."

Did he sound sincere? Bethany wondered if Matt would come through for his friend. He put his needs first and expected those around him to fall in line with what he wanted to accomplish. But would he pay people back for their efforts, or would he busy himself with new personal goals—building cabins behind the lodge, for instance?

As the group broke up, Bethany noticed Joni had only eaten part of a burrito. *Say something or not?* The opportunity passed as Gloria cleared the table. Joni said somebody needed to paint two bedrooms on the second floor before she could hang the dreamcatcher mobiles she'd bought.

Bethany helped paint until Joni said to take a break, that she could handle the rest. Now, if ever, was the time to bring up the subject of anorexia without naming it. Steadying her breath, Bethany agreed they'd made progress. "Joni…I wonder if you might want to give Mom and Dad a call. Check in."

"I can't call them yet. Not with a cloud hanging over Matt's head." Joni crossed her arms in an automatic, defensive pose.

"Then how about calling your counselor? You've said you can tell her anything, that she's a good listener. About relationships as well as health issues."

"Relationships. Issues. You sound like a counselor yourself. Why would I call her when I have you? Besides, I haven't seen her for months. No need."

"Half a burrito isn't breakfast."

"It was for me. I made mine too full." Joni's chin jutted out like when she was a kid, and almost every discussion had turned into a battle.

No use pushing any further. "I love you, Little Bird. You know that."

"I love you too, Big Turkey." Joni grinned.

"That's an old one. Gobble gobble." Bethany flapped her arms and checked her watch. "The library must be open by now. I want to look up old articles on Sorrel. And whatever I can find on Krystal."

"You have a hunch."

"Not really. Nothing to get excited about. Just research."

Joni brought her thumb to her mouth and nibbled on the nail. She had stripped off the polish for the trip to the police station.

"Better do your nails again." Bethany said it gently.

Joni stared at her right hand as if she had no idea how it had gotten to her mouth. "Filthy habit."

Bethany touched her sister's cheek. "You need to take care of yourself."

"I know," Joni said. "Don't worry about me. Find out who killed that woman."

****

Bethany tried not to disturb the library's peaceful atmosphere. She practically tiptoed by the elderly man she had seen before. This time he dozed in an armchair, an open book on his stomach. A woman who had been among the reading-club group staffed the front desk. Her badge read *Carmen Montoya, Volunteer*.

Bethany asked if the library kept copies of the *Mining Monthly*. The volunteer said sorry, the newspaper went out of business five years ago.

"I'm actually looking for old issues, maybe in an online database?"

The woman huffed, but softly. "Database! We wish. It's on microfilm. You probably don't remember what that is, do you?"

They shared a laugh, and Bethany said she had used microfilm once or twice. "A lot bigger rolls than for old thirty-five-millimeter film cameras, right?"

"Yes indeed. Come with me."

The volunteer opened a file cabinet filled with boxes of film. A gray metal viewer sat nearby. "How far back do you need?"

Deliberately vague, Bethany said, "Maybe a decade or ago? I'm not sure."

"Let me know if you have problems using the machine. You can print from it, a quarter a printout."

The system seemed terribly cumbersome. "Are back issues of the newspaper anywhere online?"

No, the volunteer assured her, only on microfilm. "But we should have issues from Krystal Decker's time, if that's what you're looking for."

Bethany inwardly cringed. "How did you know?"

The woman had eyes so dark the irises and pupils seemed to merge. She glanced over a shoulder. Apparently concerned someone might hear her, she moved closer. "Barbara was upset after you talked to her.

I don't think she even tasted my biscochitos at our book club's get-together. She mentioned you're Joni Jarviss's sister."

"Bethany Jarviss."

The woman's face softened. "Barbara has suffered for years, and now your sister must be suffering, too, what with all the talk."

"What are people saying?"

"Anybody who knows your sister has sympathy for her. She's in my prayers."

Bethany stepped back to regain a measure of personal space and bumped the microfilm machine. "People are gossiping about Matt, I suppose?"

"They would, wouldn't they? Some think the worst of him, but most believe he's a good man and hope he had nothing to do with what happened to Krystal. They're sorry for his situation. People say he can hardly marry your sister until it's known for sure who did that awful thing to his first fiancée. The truth must come out. It must. Good luck looking at the old papers." She pointed out the boxes labeled *Mining Monthly*, arranged by year.

"Ms. Montoya?"

"Yes?"

"Did you know Krystal?"

"No, I moved here afterward, from El Paso. My husband and I have a small house in town we used as a weekend place before he retired. You know, I hadn't seen that graduation picture of Krystal on Barbara's desk until after you came here the first time. She said she took it out to show you. Now it seems she can't put it away again. That dead girl is on her mind all the time. Well, I'll leave you to your research."

Bethany set out to find the pages from the *Mining Monthly's* decade-old issue she had seen in the café, to look again at the photo of Krystal modeling a dress in the museum. With fumbling fingers and little patience, she opened a small box, extracted a wide roll of black-and-white film, and spooled the film onto the viewer. It seemed to take forever, but finally, the screen displayed the issue's front page. She skimmed over the promotion of *Old Timers Days*, then cranked the machine's handle until she came to the inside page articles about the event, including the article encouraging people to visit the museum during the festival.

Seeing the photo of Krystal a second time didn't reveal anything new. Krystal liked to play dress-up and sing. Nevertheless, Bethany got out a few quarters and printed the page, which showed Sid Rogers by the museum's woodstove.

Which other *Mining Monthly* issues should she examine? Bethany did a quick calculation. *Krystal disappeared seven years ago. Might as well start with January*. She returned the first roll of film to its box and found another roll. *What a cumbersome process!* The January front page showed kids sledding outside of town, announced a Forest Service tree-thinning project, and recapped a choral performance at the grade school. Bethany gave the film reader's crank another turn.

On page two, she hit the jackpot, presumably the article Joni had caught Matt looking at—the engagement announcement and photo. The brief story portrayed him as a Santa Fe financial adviser whose "hobby" *(how would he have reacted to the pejorative word?)* was restoring his family's hunting lodge with plans to open it as a bed-and-breakfast inn. The writer described Krystal as a talented Sorrel singer and La Plata High School graduate and made no mention of her foster-child status, simply stating, *The couple's parents are John and Patricia MacGregor of Santa Fe and Barbara Ziggerton of Sorrel.*

In the engagement photo, Krystal had teased her hair to maximum volume. In a ruffled blouse, she showed plenty of cleavage as she leaned against a younger version of Matt. He appeared proud and self-conscious in the clichéd pose.

How thoughtless of him to have kept the clipping in his wallet after he became engaged to Joni. Had he been about to throw away that scrap of paper, as he told her? Bethany would bet money he wouldn't have destroyed it if Joni hadn't seen it. Bethany fed another quarter into the machine and made a print. She wasn't sure why she wanted one, mindful that Joni would disapprove.

Raising her arms over her head, she leaned back and stretched.

At her side, a young voice demanded, "Whatcha doing?" A little girl about four years old—a serious child in blue-framed glasses—peered at the machine's screen.

"Looking up old newspaper stories," Bethany said.

The girl raised her chin and wrinkled her nose. "In that box? That's not a computer."

A harried woman hustled up and took the girl's hand. "I lost track of her. Sorry if she's bothering you."

"Not a problem," Bethany said, turning the machine's crank. "She's curious about the microfilm reader."

The girl, on tiptoe, watched newspaper pages move along the screen.

The woman shook her head. "Wow, that's an

antique! It should be in our museum." She drew the curious child away. "Well, I hope you find what you're looking for."

Under her breath, Bethany said, "Whatever that is." Turning the crank with increasing speed, she scanned the rest of the issue but saw nothing of interest. She viewed successive issues from the same year. The March issue's front page contained the article, *Town Mourns Loss of Flint Callender.* The truck accident that killed Lorene's husband in February merited only a brief recap to a readership already in the know. A fund had been set up in aid of Lorene Callender. An obituary appeared on page two and, beside it, a photo of flowers, stuffed animals, and candles near the café's entrance. Bethany skimmed the pages and moved on. She felt sorry for Lorene but needed to stay focused on Krystal.

Nothing else caught her attention until a July article headed, *Sorrel Woman Still Missing.* The county sheriff's department and state police were *seeking help in locating Krystal Decker, 24, of Sorrel, missing since late April.* The story described her much the same as in the engagement announcement—as a well-known local performer and graduate of La Plata High School. It emphasized that neither her foster mother, Barbara Ziggerton, nor her fiancé, Matthew MacGregor, had heard from her since April 28. MacGregor would pay *a $50,000 reward for information leading to Krystal's whereabouts and safe return.*

The *$50,000 reward* surprised Bethany. Matt hadn't mentioned offering one. Did Joni know he'd done that? Did she know about this article in the *Mining Monthly*? If Matt killed Krystal, offering the reward had been a clever way to divert suspicion from him.

Trying to be patient, Bethany viewed the microfilm rolls for the rest of the year. Only once more, in the September issue, did she find a mention of Krystal still missing and the reward still on offer.

What had the *La Plata Citizen* published about Krystal's disappearance? Bethany hoped the library had a database of the daily's back issues. She found the volunteer, Carmen, shelving books and with her help, soon signed onto the lone, public computer near the microfilm machine. "Computer printouts cost a quarter, too," Carmen said. "You pay up front."

An hour's database search yielded a few *Citizen* articles from when Krystal went missing and several published since the discovery of her bones. Bethany realized she hadn't seen a newspaper at the lodge or looked for a newspaper rack at the mercantile. Had Joni and Matt read these reports?

The *Citizen* reported, on an inside page, Matt's offer of the $50,000 reward. Apparently, the police had dutifully questioned him, Barbara, Rusty, and several other Sorrel residents after Matt insisted Krystal wouldn't simply leave him. The articles implied the police believed she did leave; they found no evidence to the contrary. A few follow-up reports rehashed the basics. The last story from seven years back included a quote from an exasperated police detective, who said the case remained open, but adults had no obligation to inform anyone about their *whereabouts*. That old-fashioned word again.

News reports over the last three weeks took a different tone. They characterized Matt as a murder suspect now engaged to Joni Jarviss of the *wealthy and socially prominent northern New Mexico family*. The articles mentioned the family's oil business and the Jarviss Foundation. They portrayed Matt as well off in his own right and inaccurately labeled him a *financier* rather than a financial adviser.

Bethany hit the computer's print key several times. The printouts were in black ink, so the newspaper's color photos came out looking almost as ancient as the photos in the museum.

Short on coins, Bethany took a twenty from her wallet and went to pay but couldn't find Carmen. No old man snoozed up front. She glanced at the most recent *Citizen* and saw nothing about Krystal in it, then checked the stacks for the helpful volunteer. The woman must have gone to the restroom or Barbara's office. Hearing Barbara in there talking, Bethany went cash in hand to interrupt the women.

But Barbara was alone and on the phone. A groove between her eyebrows deepened at the sight of Bethany in the doorway. After a few moments, she said, "That should work well. Yes, fine. I'll be ready for you."

She replaced the handset and noticed the twenty-dollar bill Bethany held out.

"I made some computer printouts," Bethany said. "Carmen Montoya helped me get set up, but I couldn't find her to pay."

Barbara started to rise. "How many pages did you print? Certainly not twenty dollars' worth. We'll have to go up front to get your change."

Bethany put the twenty on Barbara's desk. "I don't need change. Can I talk to you for a minute? I found out about Matt's $50,000 reward." She watched Barbara's face but couldn't read her expression. "Apparently, he's still offering it."

Barbara settled back into her chair. "I suppose so. As I told you, he's a genuinely good man. He wanted to find out what happened to Krystal seven years ago, and now he will want to know who did away with her."

"Did away with her" sounded stilted to Bethany but better than saying "murdered" in reference to one's foster daughter.

"I'm having doubts about Matt." Bethany blurted it out. "About whether he's innocent. I'm worried about my sister."

Today, Barbara wore her pageboy tucked behind her ears, silver button-shaped earrings, and the pendant crafted by Rusty. "I can only repeat what I told you before. Matt would never have harmed Krystal."

Bethany's heartbeat quickened. "I heard some things about Krystal from other people in town that make me think she might have been a liability as a fiancée for Matt."

"Some things? Such as?"

"How Krystal stole from kids' lockers and might have stolen a box of stationery from The Treasure Box, and how she took two silver rings from Jazz Marcham's shop that you may or may not have reimbursed Jazz for. The Whitneys think you did, but Jazz says she wouldn't let you pay her."

Barbara smoothed her hair behind her left ear. "Jazz is a good friend. I offered, but she said no. But I don't see how this relates to Matt."

"May I sit down?" Bethany asked.

The librarian gestured to the extra chair, her reluctance obvious. Bethany settled in without apology.

"A fiancée known to be a thief must have been quite a liability for a professional money manager," Bethany

148

said. "I've been thinking how angry it would have made Matt to realize he'd gotten engaged to a dishonest young woman, or to say it more kindly, someone with a problem like those troubled actresses in the news years ago."

"Yes, it's possible Krystal suffered from kleptomania. And I knew my girl could be a fantasist, firmly believing she would be 'discovered' by someone who would whisk her away from Sorrel."

"But Matt didn't intend to take her away. You said he wanted her to work hard on the lodge the way my sister is doing now. But Krystal didn't share his commitment to the project. I've been thinking how frustrating it must have been for Matt, if he realized how much of a dreamer she was, how immature."

Barbara fiddled with her pendant. It went beautifully with a heather sweater. The woman knew how to create a dignified look. *Perhaps as a shield against pain.* But Bethany could not worry about hurting Krystal's foster mother. "I heard something else from Lorene Callender."

Barbara's eyes flicked toward the doorway but quickly came back to meet Bethany's gaze. She sat up straight, like a schoolchild facing an oral exam.

In response, Bethany straightened her own spine. "Lorene said Krystal stayed at the Ponderosa Motel with a man. Someone other than Matt, she meant. A waitress doing double duty checked him in and mentioned it. But all these years later, Lorene can't remember the waitress's name. And Lorene never knew the man's identity."

Barbara raised eyebrows as neatly groomed as Jazz's but said nothing.

"I've been thinking if that's true, Matt has another

motive for killing Krystal. If she cheated on him."

"Or this unidentified man could have killed her," Barbara said. "Did Lorene tell the police?"

"No. Maybe she thought Krystal had run off with some guy. She wouldn't have said anything that would have hurt Matt, would she?"

"Or Lorene wouldn't have wanted to get involved. Why tell you now?"

Bethany shifted in her seat. She had left her parka on in the chilly outer room, but in the warmer office, she started to sweat. "Lorene knows I'm looking into Krystal's murder. She cares about Matt and Joni. Like you, she doesn't think Matt did anything wrong, no matter what people are saying."

Barbara touched her hair again, seemed to realize she was fidgeting, and folded her hands on the desk. "Townspeople who frequent the Ponderosa Café are saying a great deal. You can be sure of that. Lorene must be hearing all sorts of talk about Krystal's death."

"Do you go to her café?"

"I do," Barbara said. "It's convenient and affordable. And Lorene makes marvelous soups and desserts."

As the librarian spoke, Carmen Montoya stuck her head into the office and said she was back from lunch. Barbara told her the preschool director had phoned. The children would arrive in a matter of minutes for the holiday story time.

"Get them settled, will you?" Barbara asked. "I'll be along to read to them. And Carmen, here is Bethany's cash for some computer printouts. She doesn't need change."

With the volunteer out of earshot, Barbara said, "Is

there anything else? If not…"

From beyond the office, a male voice called, "Hi Carmen! How's it going?"

"My foster son." Barbara said it as if in warning.

Rusty barreled into the office. "Hi Barbara! I'm going home. Ernie doesn't need me anymore today." He saw Bethany. "Hi you! I know you! Hi!"

He wore a red knit cap pulled down to his roving eyes. He breathed as if on speed as he grasped Bethany's hand and shook it too hard and too long.

"Hello, Rusty. We met at the mercantile yesterday," Bethany said.

"That's right, Barbara. I gave her a stone, but I took it back. I'm going to put wire around it so she can wear it around her neck. On a chain. Like yours, Barbara."

He switched his focus to Bethany. "What's your name?"

"Bethany Jarviss."

"Want to come to tea, Beth Annie?" He blushed. "If you want to, I mean. Can she, Barbara? Come to tea? We have sandwiches with our tea. Sometimes we have cake, don't we, Barbara? Can she come? Today, I mean. For tea?"

Bethany could hear children outside the office and over them, Carmen's voice and that of another woman. Organized, cheerful chaos.

Barbara stood up. "Of course, now that you've extended an invitation, Bethany can come to tea if she wishes."

A coolness to the words signaled Bethany to decline, but she couldn't pass up the chance to see where these two lived and the possibility of finding out more about Krystal. "I'd love to come. Thank you, Rusty."

"Well, then," Barbara said, "I'll draw you a map." She did it quickly on a notepad with Rusty breathing down her neck. She wrote an address below the simple sketch and handed over the paper. "We live quite close to here. Tea is a ritual for us after the library closes at four. Now Rusty, why don't you go home for a while? Did you have lunch?"

"At the merc. But tea will be nice later. You come, Beth Annie. See you." He pushed up his knit cap and left them.

Chapter 13

Equally ready to get away from the warm office and Barbara's chilly demeanor, Bethany said, "I won't keep you. Sounds like you've got a full house of kids for story time."

"All under five. Easy to please."

"Is Rusty?"

"Sometimes, not always. If you get to know him, you'll see. He hasn't invited anyone to tea in years. He must think you're very special." She smiled but not with her eyes.

****

At the lodge, Joni was making lunchmeat sandwiches. "I'm going to take some food to Matt. He's upstairs painting and won't take a break. We might get it all done."

Bethany announced she had a tea date at Barbara's house. "Rusty invited me. On impulse at the library."

"Ooh la la, the boy fancies you."

"No, he doesn't, and he's not a boy."

"He acts like one. Matt's glad he's not going to be his brother-in-law. Oh, don't give me that holier-than-thou look. I know it's not PC, but Rusty can be a project." She cut the sandwiches into halves.

"Rusty may be loud and ungainly," Bethany said, "but he makes those beautiful pendants. And I thought maybe when I go to the house, I can learn more about

Krystal's life."

"You might. Sandwich?"

Bethany took a half and said thanks.

"Did you find out anything at the library?"

"Background about Krystal. Joni, I haven't seen any newspapers around the lodge and wondered why."

"Matt won't have them here anymore. We both got sick of the headlines like *Murder in the Mountains. Who Killed Krystal? Fiancé Questioned in Singer's Murder.* Matt won't let us watch the TV news either. He says we need to focus on the lodge, and he's right."

"What do you want help with before tea?"

"Matt and I can get the painting done. You could iron some new curtains."

Bethany groaned. Joni knew how much she hated ironing. "Thanks. And by the way, you have paint on your nose."

Joni rolled her eyes. "Bet I don't, but now I'll have to look, won't I?" She picked up the tray of sandwiches and held it out.

Bethany took another half. "This should do me until teatime. Be sure to eat one yourself."

She'd aimed for a light tone but wished she could take the last few words back as Joni pressed her lips together and gave a curt nod.

Alone in the kitchen, Bethany recalled the days after Joni's divorce. Joni had the diamond removed from her engagement ring and made into an earring stud. She threw herself into new relationships with vigor. Until they fizzled. Once, she came close to being hospitalized, but with counseling and the family's support, she had regained her health. *Matt had better not let Joni down.* She could bounce back from despair only so many times.

****

At twenty to four, Bethany set off, on foot again, to find Barbara's house in the fading daylight. In town, Christmas lights provided cheer.

Having memorized Barbara's map, Bethany turned right toward the grade school and soon found the two-story house—a white clapboard with a modest-sized front porch. Pine trees dotted a tidy yard. The house sat between a similar one and, beyond a stone wall, an overgrown, vacant lot.

Rusty opened the door almost as soon as Bethany knocked. He didn't offer to take her coat or let her remove her gloves; he grabbed her by the hand and led her into the kitchen. The teatime fare included elegant sandwiches, peanut butter cookies, and chocolate sandwich creams. Three china plates and matching cups and saucers had been set out.

"No cake today." Rusty pushed out his bottom lip. "Barbara didn't have time to make one."

Bethany slipped out of her parka and pulled off her hat and gloves. What could she and Rusty talk about? But then Barbara appeared in a checked flannel shirt and jeans. Bethany was surprised; she supposed she expected Barbara to dress at home much as she did for work. But the flannel shirt suited her, made her seem friendlier than her library persona. Bethany relaxed, determined to enjoy being a guest.

Rusty poured the tea, not spilling a drop. The sandwiches were exquisite. Thin slices of rye bread were filled with a cheese spread. Barbara admitted modestly that she had baked the oat bread spread with butter and raspberry jam.

"Homemade jam?" Bethany asked after the first

delicious bite.

"Yes," Barbara said. "By a neighbor, not by me."

Tea, she said, had been a tradition in her house since she started taking in foster children. The kids could count on coming home from school to a ritual snack and then, after a break, do their homework or household chores.

Rusty interrupted her. "No crusts on our sandwiches today. Barbara let me eat them before you came."

Barbara's shoulders twitched. "I must admit I don't usually cut off the crusts, not for Rusty and me. But when I fostered little girls, they liked to help make tiny, crustless sandwiches."

"Finger sandwiches for Halloween," Rusty said.

"We put 'fingernails' on them with cream cheese," Barbara explained.

Bethany asked how many children she had fostered over the years.

"Thirty-six. Some for very short periods of time, some for years."

"I'm the last," Rusty said. He frowned. "And Krystal. She was the last, too."

Barbara raised the plate of cookies. "Rusty made the peanut butter ones all by himself."

"I didn't make the other ones. They're from the merc," Rusty said. "Have one of each, Beth Annie. Or two of each. I'm having two of each."

"I will, thank you."

Barbara seemed far off in her thoughts as Bethany compared sandwich cookie eating techniques with Rusty. She removed the top of hers, ate it first, and then consumed the white filling with the bottom. Rusty popped an entire cookie into his mouth and chewed vigorously, mouth closed, smothering his laughter.

That earned him a disapproving glance from Barbara, but then she shrugged and turned to Bethany. "Krystal and Rusty were enough family for me when they came here, so no more other fosters. And after Krystal left…" She glanced at Rusty. He seemed unaffected by her words as he eyed another cookie. "I couldn't," Barbara said. "I just couldn't. No more, you see."

"Show her the picture, Barbara," Rusty said. "The one Jazz made."

"More tea?" Barbara asked.

When Bethany said yes, Rusty said he'd pour. "Show her the picture."

"All right, Rusty. I'll go get it from the living room."

Rusty held the teapot in his big hand above Bethany's cup. "Say when."

Barbara returned with a poster-sized collage of children's school portraits mixed with casual, family shots. A younger Barbara appeared in several of the snapshots. There were photos from birthday parties, Christmas gatherings, bike rides, camping trips, softball games, trick-or-treating—all cheerful scenes.

"Here's me and my sister," Rusty said. In a Christmas candid, they wrapped their arms around each other. Younger than in her graduation photo by a couple of years, Krystal directed a Hollywood smile at the camera. Rusty, a cute, chubby boy, gazed open-mouthed at his sister with love.

"Jazz had me give her all the pictures I never put into photo albums and made this as a remembrance," Barbara said.

"Do you hear from many of these kids?"

"More than you might expect."

"Show her what's under the tree," Rusty said.

"After she's finished."

"I am," Bethany said, taking a last sip of tea.

"Show her now."

The living room contained an artificial Christmas tree and, on the mantel, a lineup of holiday cards. Barbara replaced the collage on the wall nearby. "I hear from many of the children, grownups now, at this time of year," she said. "It's very gratifying. By the twenty-fifth, the mantel will be filled with cards."

"The presents," Rusty said. "Show her."

Below the tree rested a modest number of wrapped gifts. "They're from my most thoughtful fosters," Barbara said. "They send presents for Rusty and me every year. Socks and candles and candies and games."

"We open them Christmas morning," Rusty said. "We love it, don't we, Barbara? Hey, Barbara, can I show Beth Annie my room? I made the bed."

Barbara smiled indulgently. "Surely. If Bethany is interested."

"Of course I am."

Rusty clomped up the steps. When Bethany started to follow, Barbara stopped her. "Foster children run the gamut, like all kids, from the precious darlings to ones you can't do much for. Some of them have called me about Krystal, expressing their condolences. When the police release the remains, I expect some of the ones within driving distance will attend the funeral."

She sat down on the sofa, took a tissue from her pocket, and dabbed her nose. A wave of emotion passed from her to Bethany, who put on a happy face and went upstairs to the sound of Rusty calling, "Beth Annie, hurry up!"

The uncarpeted stairs, stained a dark brown, dipped in the middle. At the end of a narrow hall, Bethany found Rusty in his room smoothing a quilt on a lower bunk bed. "I didn't do a very good job when I got up. But now I did."

The room might have belonged to a boy who loved horses rather than a man almost thirty years old. The quilt squares depicted horses in their many roles: running free across a plain, pulling Conestoga wagons, and supporting cowboys, Indians, and English riders. The curtains featured jockeys and their mounts. Framed photos of fine-looking horses hung on every wall.

"You must love horses very much," Bethany said, stepping into the room.

"I guess."

"You have them all over the place."

"This is a boys' room," Rusty said. "It's got horses. The girls' rooms don't."

Oh, so Barbara decorated this room for any foster child, not Rusty in particular. "Rusty, how old were you when you came to live with Barbara?"

He squinted with the effort of thinking. "I don't know."

"About eleven or twelve?"

"Yeah, I guess."

"Did other boys stay in here, too?"

"Yeah, I said they did."

He hadn't said, but Bethany let it slide.

"It's a nice room, Rusty. I see you've got hand weights and a computer."

A laptop sat closed and unplugged on a child's desk. At one time, this room must have had two small desks on opposite sides, but now an adult's desk provided a larger surface for Rusty's craftwork. The desktop held an assortment of rough stones, squares of sandpaper, and small implements lined up like a surgeon's tools.

"And here's where you work with the stones."

He picked up one of them. "This is your stone, Beth Annie. I'm making it nicer for you."

He flipped on a desk lamp and held the stone under the light. He had started to polish one side of it. She hoped he would leave it mostly unaltered.

The desk had a shallow center drawer and three deeper ones to either side. Rusty opened the top right-hand drawer and took out a roll of fine silver wire. "I'll fix it so you can wear your stone around your neck. When you wear it, it's called a 'pin dent.' "

"A pendant." Something gentle passed between them. She looked forward to getting a beautiful gift from this special man. She could feel only friendship coming from him. With relief, she realized he didn't view her as a potential girlfriend, even though they were much the same age.

"I made a pin dent for Krystal. Want to see it?"

From the lowest right-hand drawer, Rusty pulled out a book—*no, a personal journal*—with a glossy purple cover. A leather cord, attached to a flat, brown stone with creamy swirls in the center, encircled the journal. Leather strips almost as thin as thread encased the stone.

Bethany's heart beat in her throat as Rusty unwrapped the cord. "You can hold it," he said, handing the pendant to her.

The beautiful piece of jewelry captured her interest, but she longed to see inside this journal of Krystal's, if indeed that's what it was. But she ignored the book as Rusty set it on his desk. "You wrapped the stone in leather, Rusty, not the usual silver wire. Nice job." She handed the pendant back.

"Hide," Rusty said. For a second, Bethany thought he wanted her to conceal herself, then she realized he meant the tanned animal skin. "I cut it myself," he said.

He picked up a pair of scissors. "With this. Like skinny shoelaces."

"You did a good job, Rusty. The stone is lovely, and the wrapping is too." She gestured toward the purple book. "Is this Krystal's journal?"

"Krystal kept it shut with this." He swung the pendant back and forth on the leather strip. "Smart, huh?"

"Did she give you the journal?"

"I can have it. It's okay for me to have it."

Trying to keep the excitement out of her voice, Bethany asked, "Have you read it?"

He shrugged. "It's just girl stuff."

"Rusty, would you let me borrow it?"

He looked puzzled and nervous. "I keep it in my desk. With the pin dent."

She took a deep breath. "You know about Krystal, right, that somebody hurt her all those years ago?"

"Krystal's in a better place." He said it solemnly. "I know that means she's dead." He sank to the floor, folding his legs in an awkward imitation of a yoga pose. He buried the pendant in his hand with the leather strip hanging out like an animal's tail. "I thought Krystal ran away, Beth Annie. But she didn't."

"No."

"She didn't mean to leave us." Rusty sniffled, then cleared his throat. "Barbara told me she didn't. Somebody stopped Krystal."

As Rusty rocked back and forth, Bethany picked up the journal and fanned its pages. The pages pulsed with cramped, cursive writing in blue, purple, and orange ink as well as drawings of flowers, butterflies, and here and there a unicorn, a dragon.

"May I read Krystal's journal? To see if it provides any clues?"

He looked confused. "Clues?"

"Clues to what might have happened to her. Who hurt her."

"Clues like in the Hardy Boys?"

"Yes, exactly."

"Like in Nancy Drew?"

"You've read Nancy Drew books?"

"No, they're for girls. Barbara put the Hardy Boys in the attic when I grew up." He stared with distaste at the laptop on the boy's desk. "She got me a computer. I don't like it."

His expression brightened. "I read books. They're called graphic novels."

Barbara, in the open doorway, interrupted them. "What's going on? Rusty?"

He scrambled to his feet and held out the pendant. "I showed Beth Annie the stone I made nicer for Krystal."

Bethany held up the journal. "The leather cord with the pendant held this journal of Krystal's closed. I asked Rusty if I could borrow the journal to see if she wrote anything that might be useful."

"She's looking for clues. Like the Hardy Boys." He said it seriously. "Like Nancy Drew."

Barbara hesitated but said, "You won't find anything in that journal, Bethany. I've read it, and believe me, there's nothing. It's from Krystal's high school days, her senior year, if I remember correctly. But if Rusty is willing to lend it, go ahead."

"You can read it, Beth Annie." Rusty held out the pendant on its thong.

"Oh no, you keep that. Let me just borrow the journal."

"Okay, Beth Annie."

He put the pendant back in the drawer, and the three of them stepped into the hall.

"Want to see Krystal's room?" Rusty asked. "It's a girls' room right here."

When Barbara didn't object, Rusty opened the door and flipped a switch. Bethany blinked at deep purple walls, empty of decoration, marred by nail holes and remnants of clear tape.

Like Rusty's room, this one held a set of bunk beds. Here the desks, each with a straight-backed chair, matched. Two chests of drawers had mirrors above them. The bedspreads and curtains, in a pink-and-yellow rose design, clashed with the purple walls. The room held no personal possessions.

"Krystal painted the walls purple?" Bethany asked.

Barbara fingered a button on her flannel shirt. "Yes, I allowed her to do that after the last of the other foster girls moved on. When she turned eighteen. Purple was a popular color back then."

"But she didn't change the bedspreads or curtains?"

"I said I'd gladly pay, but she never got around to it. Typical of Krystal, to start a project but not quite finish it."

"What's missing from the walls?" Bethany asked.

"Pictures," Rusty said. "Lots."

Barbara leaned across an empty desk and pulled a scrap of clear tape off a wall. "Krystal cut pictures from magazines. Famous singers and movie stars, some of the more prominent models in ads for perfume or what have you. I left the room as it was for a year. One day, I took all the pictures down and threw them away. I thought I'd paint the room afresh for new girls after I heard from Krystal, if she informed me that she didn't intend to come back. But time passed, and as I said, I didn't take in other foster children."

"Did Krystal live here after she and Matt became engaged?"

"Yes, officially. The lodge was no place for a couple to live. Matt basically camped out in one room. Sometimes Krystal stayed with him there, or in Santa Fe, but I believe she still considered her room here a sort of refuge."

Downstairs, Barbara sent Rusty to retrieve Bethany's parka and daypack. "I appreciate that you're trying to find out what happened to Krystal, but please don't upset Rusty. He still misses her so much."

A wave of dismay coursed through Bethany's nerves. She asked, "Are you sure it's okay for me to borrow the journal?"

"It's fine, but it won't help you." She sounded hopeless.

Rusty followed Bethany to the porch and watched her go down the steps. As she turned onto the gloomy street, he called out as if on the job at the mercantile, "Thanks for coming! Have a nice day!"

****

In her bedroom, Bethany read the journal with compassion for the teenager who had poured out her heart in alternating colors of ink. Krystal wrote mostly about boys in school, using only their initials. She devoted pages to who looked at her in class, who brushed an arm against her chest as they passed in the hall, who she was *working on* to take her to Homecoming. Beside an entry in purple ink, she had sketched in blue a rough picture of a boy, ST, with a broad face and small ears.

She wrote extensively about the dance, a new dress Barbara let her buy, the corsage from ST, how great he played football, but how that left her sitting in the stands with other *team widows* during the game. She mentioned that the Homecoming queen and her court lived in La Plata *of course* and that no Sorrel girl had a chance because the La Plata kids always voted for their own.

After Homecoming, Krystal wrote passionately about various boys for brief periods, sometimes only a week or so. Girls came up in the journal as competition for the boys, never as friends. Krystal had drawn a witch with a wart on her long nose and under it, the initials *CM* after the girl started dating a boy Krystal wanted *for my own*.

Krystal mentioned performing a solo at a holiday concert. *The audience clapped and clapped!!!* she wrote, with three exclamation points. She didn't mention teachers or schoolwork. She only wrote about Barbara when her foster mother granted or denied a request.

For the senior prom, when Barbara suggested looking at a consignment shop in La Plata for a formal gown, Krystal called her a *mean cheapskate* but later wrote that Barbara changed her mind and would let her buy a new dress. Krystal got the dress but did not go to the prom with a boy she had her eye on. But her nobody-special date fawned all over her, the most glamorous girl at the prom. Since another girl wanted him, it was *good for my image* to be seen in public with him, like movie stars paired for publicity. She described her strapless, off-white dress—*almost like a wedding gown*—a jeweled evening purse, and *an adorable faux fur* white jacket. It appeared Barbara had shelled out plenty for Krystal's prom wardrobe.

A light rap on the bedroom door pulled Bethany back to the present. "Come in!"

Joni entered and spied the journal. "Oops, I'm interrupting. Doing some writing?"

"No, this is a journal of Krystal's that Rusty had. He and Barbara let me borrow it. It's from Krystal's high school days."

Dropping onto the bed, Joni said, "So no help to us."

"I suppose not. But what she wrote about her prom shows that Barbara catered to her. She bought her a special jacket for that one night. For my senior prom, I borrowed mom's satin stole."

"Sounds like you. I wouldn't have worn that old thing!" She drew a square in the air.

"No. You wore your denim jacket. And a dress that barely covered your butt!"

"Mom didn't approve of it or that I didn't have a date, but she didn't say so."

"She wanted you to have a good time."

"I guess. She and Dad and some other parents did spring for a stretch limo. A bunch of us singles piled in, screaming our heads off. Prom wasn't a momentous, formal event like back in your day."

"Krystal saw prom as huge. She wrote about it with such feeling."

"Poor girl." Joni got off the bed. "Don't let her get

to you."

Bethany barely heard the door close as she read on. Krystal wrote that for the prom, Rusty made her a special pendant, a *sweet* thing to do but *totally inappropriate* wrapped in leather. Bethany realized the pendant had to be the one on the leather strip encircling the journal. After Krystal put it on at the house to please Rusty, she stuck it in her purse as soon as she drove off with her date. She hadn't hurt Rusty's feelings by telling him the pendant didn't go with her prom dress. In a small way, her sensitivity countered the self-centered picture she painted of herself. Krystal ran out of pages in the journal before she wrote about the prom dance. She must have had another journal in which she described the important night.

Chapter 14

Bethany went out to the third-floor lounge to use the phone. She looked up Barbara's number in the skinny La Plata phone book that included entries for Sorrel and a few small towns in the valley. Barbara answered on the third ring and said she didn't have any other journals of Krystal's. "I think she only kept a journal for a short time. I'm sorry I can't help you. Did you find anything important in the one you borrowed?"

"No," Bethany admitted. "She started to write about her senior prom night but stopped when her date picked her up. She wrote a lot about boys. I thought if she kept a journal toward the end of her life, the person who harmed her might be mentioned. I know it's a long shot, but…"

"You're trying to help. I realize that. But I don't know what to say. I gave Krystal that blank book for her birthday. She probably didn't bother to get another journal after she filled up that one."

Replacing the phone on its base, Bethany doubted old journals would help her anyway. In her room, she went through the newspaper clippings again, pausing to study the engagement photo. Had Krystal ever loved Matt, or had he simply been a desirable partner for a budding star?

Bethany heard no one other than herself on the third floor. Where were Joni and Matt? No matter; she needed a break from thinking about them. She deserved a soak in the claw-footed tub in the community bathroom. She undressed in her room, slipped on her skimpy travel bathrobe, and clipped her hair above her head. At home, she took showers most of the time but once in a while indulged in a long bath. Now she turned the white enamel-coated taps, poured in fragrant bath salts left conveniently at hand, and sank into the wet warmth. Hoping the hot water wouldn't run out, she watched with satisfaction as the level rose in the deep tub.

Immersed to her chin, she felt a keen, unexpected longing for Nathan. Would her sporadic relationship with that cowboy get serious if they saw each other more? He might enjoy staying at this lodge as a break from the trailer, supplied by the ranch owner, that he basically bunked in when he wasn't on horseback or an ATV. He never had been married, which at first surprised her, but then neither had she. Mentally, she listed his good points: considerate lover, good dancer, moderate drinker. He had cleaned up nicely when he accompanied her to a charity dinner a few weeks ago. They talked about seeing each other over Christmas, maybe at the ranch, maybe in Las Cuevas. Then she left for Sorrel and, until now, gave little thought to those vague plans with Krystal's murder demanding her attention.

But her work demanded attention, too. Her laptop contained more than a dozen applications from communities for grants. She had skimmed them but needed to read them in detail. The day after Christmas, her father expected to hear her recommendations, an annual tradition, before making his decision. At this point in the process, she always felt the pressure. She had traveled to each of the communities that put in applications, had seen their needs first hand, and would be the liaison between the Foundation and the winners. She would also help the applicants not awarded grants to apply to other funding sources. The most promising also-rans would be encouraged to reapply to the Jarviss Foundation with stronger applications next year.

Reluctantly, Bethany pulled out the tub's rubber stopper. The bath had relaxed her muscles but not her brain. Better put in time on the proposals before dinner.

Dressed, she took her laptop to the lounge and worked for an hour until Matt came up the stairs and announced he had hired a lawyer from Santa Fe.

"The guy's got his own plane and can fly down to the La Plata airstrip if I need him. A friend of mine who's also a client made the initial contact."

Bethany took a deep breath. "That's good. Do you have a minute? I want to talk to you about a few things."

He selected a sagging armchair and crossed his feet at the ankles. "What things?"

"For one, something David said. But he didn't want me to mention it, so I hope you can keep this between us. I didn't promise him, but I won't go on if there's a chance what I say will get back to him."

Matt uncrossed his legs. "Sure, sure. Whatever it is, it can't be anything incriminating."

She repeated David's mention at the café that soon after Krystal went missing, Matt said she might have realized he wasn't going to be a rich husband.

"I may have said that, but so what?"

"David said you sounded bitter."

"Yeah, because I thought Krystal left me. David's a good listener. I probably said a lot of things to him."

He looked at Bethany as if trying to work out a puzzle. "Oh, I see. You think Krystal was about to dump me, so I went into a rage and murdered her. But I didn't. That never happened. Bethany, I've said all this before, more or less, haven't I?"

She ignored his question. "There's something else. Something intriguing and potentially serious. Lorene said one of her waitresses checked a man into the Ponderosa Motel and that Krystal stayed in his room. Did you know she was unfaithful to you? Maybe planning to leave you for another man?"

"No way. What waitress? Somebody with bad eyesight and too much of an imagination."

"Lorene said she can't remember. She plans to look through her old records."

"For God's sake, Bethany, you don't consider this to be more than gossip? Lorene probably made it up."

"Why would she do that?"

"Okay, no, Lorene's a good woman. She wouldn't lie, but some teenage worker must have. Did Lorene ever tell this story to the cops?"

"No, she likes you. All those years ago, she kept it to herself to protect you, and as far as I can tell, she hasn't told anyone but me now."

"Lorene thinks what, that I knew about the guy and killed Krystal because of him? By the way, why did she tell you? She barely knows you."

"She's a good judge of character." Bethany waited until he smiled at the joke. "People do tend to talk to me. But I actually think Lorene told me because she's on your side. Maybe Krystal did plan to leave you for some other man you didn't know about, who, for some reason, killed her. And another thing, you offered a reward,

171

$50,000, something it seems a guilty man wouldn't do." Bethany heard herself tossing him a lifeline.

"How did you hear about the reward?"

"I went through back issues of the *Mining Monthly* and *La Plata Citizen* at the library."

"Enterprising of you. You're seriously checking up on me." He said it lightly but couldn't quite cover up his surprise and anger. "I offered the reward in a rash moment. Back then, I couldn't have paid that kind of money to anybody."

He rubbed his forehead and blinked a few times. "And now it's coming back to haunt me. I got a call from a lawyer for the family of one of the boys who found Krystal's remains. He thinks his client and the other boy are entitled to equal shares of the reward. He said I advertised it for anyone who had information about her whereabouts. Well, they certainly discovered her whereabouts, didn't they?"

Bethany winced at the bitter, self-pitying rant. She tried to remember the self-confident, appealing optimist Joni had introduced her to not so many months ago. If she were Joni, she might be ready to bail on this new and not improved version of her fiancé.

"I don't think you should worry too much about the reward, Matt. According to the *Mining Monthly*, you offered it for information leading to her whereabouts and safe return."

"Did I really? I can't remember. Do you have the article? I never kept what the papers printed about Krystal's disappearance."

"I do. Wait a second."

She got the article from her room and handed it to him.

Relief showed on Matt's face. "I'm going to call that lawyer and fax him this. You might have saved me $50,000."

"Matt, one more thing. I've been wondering: Is Joni eating enough?"

"Yes, she is. When we first met, she told me about the problem she used to have. But she's over that now. She swears she is. And you know she doesn't like anyone monitoring her."

"I know, but I can tell she's lost weight. You've seen her every day for months, so it's not obvious to you. She needs looking after."

"I do look after her. Don't worry about that."

Bethany bit her lip. It seemed disloyal to mention Joni's skills at pretending to eat or to drink milk, at deflecting attention from herself, at concealing sunken cheekbones with makeup. *Matt has no idea.* With a nod, she let him go down to the office. He could never know the hungry, neglected, nearly silent five-year-old new little sister whom Bethany, at ten, couldn't bring herself to resent.

She shook off that memory and went back to her room, where Krystal's journal and the other newspaper stories lay on the pine desk that resembled the boy's desk in Rusty's room. Again, she studied the photo of Krystal in the museum. The sleeves of the nineteenth-century dress were a trifle short for her, details not immediately noticeable because of poor lighting. Krystal's figure merged with the display case behind her. A better photographer would have posed a person against a less-cluttered background. Bethany picked up the stack of microfilm and computer printouts. She flipped through them one by one. She ought to return to the museum as

173

soon as possible to talk to Sid again. He wouldn't have told her everything that might be useful, not in only one interview.

****

That evening, after a dinner that Joni only picked at, Bethany knew she would go stir crazy if she didn't get out of the lodge where everyone seemed on edge. Matt and David put up the last kitchen cabin, saw that it hung at a slight angle, and did the job again. Joni, her voice tense, recited a list of other projects she wanted done before Friday. As Gloria loaded the dishwasher, David, his eyes on the wall clock, got in her way. He had scheduled a client—Jazz Marcham, who suffered from chronic back problems. "I dropped off a few flyers that she's going to put in her shop and asked her to come take a look at my setup and get a free massage."

When the kitchen buzzer alerted them to someone at the front door, David said, "I'll go. It's probably Jazz."

Bethany could hear him greet her. Her voice rose as she praised the holiday decorations, then their voices mingled with their footsteps as they went upstairs.

Gloria said she was off to the Black Bear. "Crush could probably do without me when business is slow. It's decent of him to give me weeknight hours. Anybody want to come liven the place up?"

Matt and Joni said no thanks, but on impulse, Bethany said she'd come for a while and then walk home. Joni protested that she would freeze; call when she needed a ride back.

It would be no problem to go get her, Matt added.

"If you're still there at closing, I'll bring you back," Gloria said.

While Gloria waited for her, Bethany dashed up to

the third floor to get her parka. A hand-lettered *Body Work in Progress* sign hung on David's massage room door. Soothing music came from within, but no conversation. Remembering David's professional touch when he'd given her the chair massage, Bethany envied Jazz on his table getting the full treatment.

****

The bar felt as dead as Gloria had predicted, with only four other customers in the place—three pool players in the back and a silent old man in a corner. Gloria wiped tables while Bethany took a barstool and ordered a white wine. The overhead TV showed a high-stakes poker game in progress—in Las Vegas, Crush said.

"Las Vegas, Nevada, or Las Vegas, New Mexico?" Bethany asked as he set her drink in front of her.

"Ha-ha. Nevada. Not a lot of high rollers in New Mexico's Vegas. Just a bunch of college kids. Cowboys and cowgirls."

"And students from all over the world," Bethany said.

"Well, here's to them." Crush raised a half-empty beer glass from behind the counter.

They clinked glasses companionably. She took a sip and set her glass down. One of the pool players in back let out a whoop of glee. Crush grinned lazily in their direction. How many drinks did he put away in a day of bartending? Seeing her looking at his beer, he said, "I can nurse one of these babies for hours, waiting for somebody to buy me a real drink."

Bethany shrugged off her parka and put it and her daypack on an empty stool. "And what would a real drink be?"

"Not wine." Crush grinned. "A whiskey would do it."

"Let me buy you one."

He poured himself a shot and downed half of it. "First one all day. Thank you. How goes the gumshoe job? I've heard you've been all over town talking to people the last couple days."

"Says who?"

"Everybody and nobody. I can't name names. That would be talking out of school."

A middle-aged couple came through the front door and ordered drinks and a pizza from Gloria. She got two beers from Crush, took them to the couple, and then went to the end of the bar and through a swinging half-door to the kitchen.

Bethany took her first sip of wine and made a face. "What is this anyway? I didn't notice."

Crush got the bottle for her inspection. "Extra dry," she said.

"What's wrong with that?"

"Nothing, but this one tastes like vinegar. A wine may be inexpensive…"

"Cheap." He repressed a smile.

"But it shouldn't taste this tart. Not when first opened."

"I don't get a lot of call for wine, not during the week. I can't throw away a whole bottle after I serve one drink out of it."

She sniffed her drink. "It smells like vinegar, too. When did you open it?"

"Last week? Can't exactly remember."

They both laughed.

"Dump it out, okay?" Bethany dug in her daypack

and pulled out some cash. "Will this cover a bottle you've yet to uncork?"

He took some of the bills and pushed the rest back. "That'll cover the whiskey and a glass or two of wine. You don't need to buy the bottle."

He moved to a refrigerator at the end of the bar. Beyond him, over the swinging door, Gloria stood in profile, apparently waiting for the pizza to cook. She yawned and tilted her head from side to side. Bethany didn't envy her balancing two jobs.

Crush made a production of opening a new bottle and pouring a thimble's worth into a clean glass. "Taste that, milady."

She swirled the wine, sniffed, tasted, nodded. She watched him fill her glass. "I actually don't know much about wine."

"But you know what you like." He drank the rest of his whiskey. "What have people been saying to you?"

She glanced around the bar, not wanting anyone to overhear. Gloria was still in the kitchen. The old guy dozed in the corner, and the couple gazed at the TV.

Bethany became serious. "I've learned a lot about Krystal."

"Like what?" he demanded.

She toyed with the wineglass stem, turning the glass around and around on the counter, then stopped the nervous motion and thrust her hands in her lap.

"Not everyone was as enamored with Krystal as you, Crush. I've heard she stole things, starting with items from kids' lockers in high school."

"I don't believe it."

"Barbara Ziggerton says it's true. And as an adult, Krystal stole from shops in Sorrel."

"No way. Not Krystal. What shops?"

"I don't want to say. The owners can mention it to the police if they want to. They didn't back when it happened. And there's something else, something that might relate to Krystal's death. When Krystal was Matt's fiancée, a Ponderosa Motel employee saw her go into one of the rooms with some man, and she didn't mean Matt. Do you think Krystal would have cheated on him? He doesn't believe it, but if it's true, that man could have killed her."

"Whoa, girl. Wait a minute. Krystal sleeping with some guy in the motel? That would have been plain stupid. She wouldn't have done anything so public. Unless…"

"Unless what?"

He poured himself another whiskey. "You don't have to buy me this one. It's my bar. I can drink up the whole supply if I want."

Bethany took another sip of wine. "Okay, fine. Please finish what you wanted to say."

"She wouldn't have cheated on Matt in a way that would be sure to get back to him unless he cheated on her first. Yeah, she might've slept with some guy to teach Matt a lesson."

"But Matt wasn't unfaithful to Krystal."

"No? You didn't know about that, obviously. And why would you? He wouldn't tell Joni, would he? His brand new love of his life. He'd keep his past hidden. But he did cheat on Krystal."

"How do you know?" Surely, Crush was making it up. "Can you prove it?"

"I heard it through the grapevine." He looked away from her to the TV poker players.

She felt sorry for this guy who had loved Krystal. He needed to face the fact that she hadn't been the innocent lovely he'd imagined.

"You're going to have to do better than that, Crush. It's a serious accusation against Matt. Slander."

"I'll tell him to his face if he comes in here." Crush leaned over the bar and said in a low voice, "Okay, here's the deal. You tell me who Krystal supposedly stole from, and I'll tell you who said Matt cheated on her."

He took off his rimless glasses and polished the lenses with a bar rag, giving her time to think. Already, she'd probably shared too many things people had told her. Lucky she wasn't a professional investigator; she'd never develop any confidential sources. But if she wanted to call Crush's bluff, she had to mention people by name.

"The Whitneys at The Treasure Box," she said quietly. "Krystal almost certainly stole a box of stationery from them." At his scornful look, she added, "Yes, I know. An incidental item. But that's not all. Jazz Marcham says Krystal stole two valuable rings from her shop. Barbara knew about it. It happened right before Krystal went missing, so it's possible Krystal did it with plans to pawn the rings to get some cash."

"Jazz is sure the thief was Krystal?"

"She noticed the rings had disappeared right after Krystal visited the shop."

Crush put his glasses back on. His face took on a solemn expression. "If Krystal wanted to leave Matt after he cheated on her, she might've lifted a couple rings from Jazz for traveling money. And like I said the first time you came in, Matt is the most likely person to have killed her. If he knew she slept with somebody in the motel, he wouldn't have stood for it, even though he cheated first."

"Your turn. Crush, how do you come to think Matt cheated on Krystal?"

While they talked, the smell of cooking pizza filled the air. Gloria delivered the pie to the middle-aged pair and moved to the end of the room to check on the pool players. "Ask her," he said, nodding in Gloria's direction.

"Gloria? No. She couldn't have been more than a teenager when Krystal went missing."

"Yeah. Ask her."

"That's not good enough, Crush."

"Look, Bethany, it's sticky, okay?"

"As sticky as this countertop?"

"Touché." He took up a rag and made small, slow circles on the worn wood. "It's better if it comes from Gloria. She just told me yesterday, and I think she wants you to know, too. But she's afraid it might get Matt in trouble. Unlike me, she thinks he's innocent. She works for him, so she thinks she knows him. Likes him and your sister, too. But Gloria likes everybody."

"I don't see how she can know anything from so far back when she was, what, in high school?"

"Ask about her senior year. Ask her. That's all I'm going to say. Now, how about another glass of wine?"

"No thanks. I'm going to walk back to the lodge. Tell Gloria, will you? She drove me here and offered me a ride back later."

"I can tell her that her shift's over. You can talk to her now."

"No, don't cut her hours short on account of me. I'll see her later."

"You do that, Bethany. Listen to what she's got to say and then judge if Matt MacGregor should be in handcuffs."

****

Setting out on foot, she realized how much the temperature had dipped since sunset. She stopped near the library to flip her hood up over her knit hat. Maybe she should have called Matt from the Black Bear for a ride, but that was ridiculous. She'd be back at the lodge in ten minutes. Walking along a nearly deserted Main Street, she wondered if the lodge could truly succeed with so little nightlife in Sorrel. The Ponderosa Café had closed at nine o'clock, and the shops had shut their doors hours earlier.

How good it would feel to be home in Las Cuevas, a small city sure, but one with an all-night diner, a couple of decent coffee shops, and her favorite hangout since high school—a twenty-four-hour family restaurant. Someone she knew would be at every one of those places at this time of night. Friends would take a break from reading or working on their laptops to talk. Compared to her city, this town felt like a black hole. No wonder Krystal had wanted to get out of it.

Lost in thought, she jumped when someone honked at her. Gloria pulled up and rolled down a window. "Crush insisted I go home. He's paying me for a whole shift. Get in. You must be freezing."

Bethany welcomed the heater's blast. Gloria surprised her by pulling to the side and parking. "Crush said I have to mention something I've been thinking about since they found Krystal's remains," Gloria said. "I told him after you and I took that walk. I had to tell somebody, and now he insists you hear it."

181

Gloria's voice quivered, and her ponytail shook. "I hope I'm doing the right thing. I really, really like Matt and don't want to get him in trouble. I'm not talking to the cops, okay? I'm telling you because that's what Crush thinks is best."

"What is it?" Bethany demanded. "Sorry. That came out way too loud." She placed a hand on Gloria's shoulder to comfort her. "Take your time, but keep the engine running, okay?"

Gloria gave a little laugh and spoke in a rush. She had been a senior in high school in La Plata the spring Krystal went missing, one of four girls who skipped school on a Friday after lunch and drove up to Sorrel, scaring themselves on the turns. Their parents wouldn't be any wiser, and the principal didn't care where last-semester seniors spent their time so close to graduation.

The story was taking too long. "What happened? Did you get into some sort of trouble?" Bethany asked.

"No, nothing like that. The school and our folks never found out."

"What did you do?"

"Not us. And it didn't mean anything at the time. We parked on Main Street by the Hike N Bike, the outdoor store that's not open this time of year, and we saw them."

"Who?"

"Matt and Krystal, as it turns out, not that I knew that. They were having a whopper of a fight right on the street. She cried and called him names, a bastard and what all. She didn't say what he'd done, but I could guess: He'd been cheating on her. He yelled at her to calm down, but she wouldn't. She planted her feet and shook her head, and I remember how her hair flew all around her shoulders. You should have seen her!

"The guy—Matt—went after her and grabbed her arm, but she shook him off and started walking toward us. We turned our heads and pretended to look at the shop window. I remember a mountain bike with about twenty gears. It looked awful expensive. Then I heard an SUV door slam and saw Matt drive off past Krystal, not stopping for her to get in. Later, when I saw her picture in the paper and read about him offering a reward, I recognized them. But I didn't tell anybody."

"Because you'd skipped school?"

"No, like I said, our parents and teachers wouldn't have cared. The adults almost expected it of us seniors at the end. But see, one of the girls had a key to her brother's car and borrowed the car without him knowing. He was a junior, stuck in school all day. He even stayed over lunch for math tutoring before Finals. She filled up the car with gas afterward. He never noticed the change in the mileage."

When Gloria finished her story, Bethany considered its implications. "You're sure you saw Matt and Krystal?"

"Positive. About a week before she went missing. I never read a word in the papers about any argument. Matt sounded clueless about why Krystal would leave him. I thought of telling somebody when Krystal's body was discovered that she'd called him a bunch of names. I took that to mean he cheated on her because a boy did that to me senior year. But I probably read too much into their fight. I like Matt so much."

"And he employs you part-time and gives you a place to live." Bethany said it softly. "But you think he should have told the police everything that went on between him and Krystal, don't you?"

"Yeah, I sure do." She pulled onto the road. "Crush thought I'd feel better when I told you, but I don't. I feel sick inside."

Chapter 15

The lodge's white lights at the entrance twinkled as if in anticipation of good times to come. But could anyone truly celebrate the opening with Krystal's murder unsolved?

"Thanks for the lift, Gloria," Bethany said. "Do you think Crush will tell anybody else what you told us?"

Gloria said no; he would keep the story to himself. "But he really thinks Matt's the killer. He's worried about Joni and about you and me, too, all of us girls at the lodge."

"Most likely, that argument had nothing to do with Krystal's death. Maybe you should ask Matt to explain. He might tell you it was about something different than you assume. He might have a good reason for not saying anything about it to the police, then or now."

"You don't sound all that convinced." Gloria turned off the engine. "I'm starting to feel creeped out at the lodge, and I used to love it here."

"You're not going to quit? That would devastate Joni."

"I guess not. Crush can't hire me full-time, so if I quit the lodge, I couldn't afford to get an apartment, and I don't want to go back to La Plata and live with my folks. My mom keeps bugging me to come home. She's been reading the newspaper and worries Matt did it—not that she knows him—and she never met Krystal. If she knew I heard that argument, she'd be up the mountain in a flash to drag me home by my hair." She adjusted the stretchy band on her ponytail and stared through the windshield.

"I appreciate that you told me, Gloria. I'm going to keep talking to people about Krystal."

"The police asked all sorts of questions when her bones turned up, but as far as anybody knows, they didn't find out much. Have you?"

"Nothing that I can see helps." Bethany got out of the car to avoid more questions. She had learned quite a bit, but did any of it relate to Krystal's death?

At the front door, Gloria stopped. "If I tell Matt what I overheard, he'll probably fire me. Then he'll turn out to be innocent. You've got to find out who's really guilty. That's the only way out of this nightmare for all of us."

She ran into the building and up the stairs without waiting for Bethany to reply.

****

Alone in her room, Bethany vowed if she didn't learn anything useful soon, she would beg Gloria to risk Matt's ire and tell him about the argument she'd overheard. Matt wouldn't fire Gloria, would he? Joni wouldn't let him. Right before the two opening events, he wouldn't be able to find a replacement. Bethany bet the overheard argument had nothing to do with Krystal's disappearance and death. Joni simply could not have gotten engaged to a murderer.

Bethany felt her body tremble. The lodge's heating system left something to be desired. She turned on the space heater and sat at the desk, staring at the engagement photo of Matt and Krystal. *What did they argue about? Had he been unfaithful?*

Once again, Bethany examined the museum photo, studying Krystal's pose. She looked so coy, wearing lace gloves, holding a parasol, and exhibiting what would have been an indecent amount of cleavage for a nice girl in the nineteenth century.

Maybe she should show this photo to Sid Rogers along with the one of him in the newspaper's center spread. That might jog his memory. Maybe he knew more than he had recalled or been willing to say during their first meeting.

****

Determined to find out something, anything more about Krystal, Bethany drove in the morning to the museum as snowflakes pelted her windshield. She took along open-house flyers and the newspaper story with its accompanying photos of Krystal and Sid.

At breakfast, Gloria had given no sign of having confided in Bethany the previous evening. She served whole-wheat pancakes studded with chopped pecans that got rave reviews from David, who then went off to teach at the grade school, saying he'd be back to help in the afternoon. To Bethany, his cheerfulness seemed overdone but well meant. Matt and Joni barely took time for breakfast; they talked about nothing but what they needed to do for Friday's party.

Bethany parked near Sid's truck and RV trailer, noting another vehicle in the lot, an SUV like her own. Sid huddled by the potbellied stove with a woman it took Bethany a moment to recognize: Flora Whitney from The Treasure Box. The two stopped talking as Bethany approached. Flora smiled in recognition but didn't rise with Sid.

"Hello, young lady," he said. "You stopped by the other day."

"I did," Bethany said.

Sid looked from Bethany to Flora. "Flora is here to twist my arm to be Santa Claus for the school kids again. I resisted as usual, but she's a strong lady when it comes to arm twisting."

"I am." Flora gazed up at him. "I organize Santa's visit every year. Tom and I donate treats and little gifts, and so does Ernie at the merc." She got to her feet with effort, and Bethany remembered the bad hip. "Sid, you come in the back door as always."

"I know, I know. You'll have the Santa getup, and I can change in the toilet by the teachers' lounge. Put that itchy white beard over my gray one. As per usual."

Flora gave him a fond smile. "You enjoy it, you old rascal. Making children happy."

"I do at that."

"Remember, it's the last day before the holiday break."

"Yep, but I bet you'll remind me again." Sid grinned at Flora.

"That reminds me," Bethany said, pulling out the flyers. "Joni asked me to spread the word about the lodge's party. And here are some open-house flyers if you'd be so kind as to display them here and at The Treasure Box."

"All right, dear," Flora said. "I'll add them to the ones David dropped off."

Bethany felt a rush of embarrassment. "Are we getting a little pushy?"

Flora rocked her body to the side as she pocketed the flyers. "No, of course not. It's good to see the lodge coming to life. Tom and I plan to be there for sure. How about you, Sid?"

"After I close up here." He looked uncomfortable, no doubt remembering how he hadn't held back his view of Matt earlier.

As soon as Flora left, Bethany showed him the printout from the *Mining Monthly*.

"I'd forgotten about this story," he said. "Thought I kept a copy but never did. I told you Krystal liked the old dresses. Forgot I let her put one on for Old Timers Days. It was the newspaper gal's idea. Young girl did the write-up and took the photos, too. Where did you get this? It's not a press cutting."

"No, a microfilm copy from the library." When she held out her hand for Sid to pass the page back, he did so with reluctance. "I should have made an extra copy for the museum, but I didn't think of that," she said. "I can give this to you when I'm through with it."

"That would be nice." He stood between her and the way to the dresses.

Bethany said, "Excuse me," and squeezed between him and the hodge-podge of museum items. He stayed nearby as she looked from the photo to the display cases until she identified the gown Krystal had modeled, now worn by a manikin missing a hand. A folded parasol rested at the manikin's feet. But this wasn't where Krystal had stood for the photo. Consulting the printout, Bethany moved to where a glass case held four Mimbres pots. Krystal had posed before this case, which had held *five* pots.

Bethany could feel the hairs on the back of her neck rise. "Sid, where's the fifth pot?"

"Say what?"

"In the photo, there are five pots with geometric designs. See for yourself. But now there are four. Mimbres pots are valuable, aren't they, especially if they're fairly intact? Where's the missing one?"

She whipped around and looked Sid straight in the eye.

The old fellow's gaze dropped, but he said nothing.

"Where did it go, Sid?"

"No idea. None at all."

"I don't believe you," Bethany said. "I've been learning a lot about Krystal, and one of the things I've found out is that she was a thief. I wish Flora hadn't left. She would back me up. She and Tom told me Krystal probably took something from The Treasure Box, something small, true. But they also said she stole from kids' lockers in high school, and before she went missing, she stole jewelry from Jazz Marcham's shop. I think she also stole a pot from this museum, didn't she?"

The old man's body sagged. Gone was the jolly gentleman with the paunch who would delight children as Santa Claus.

"Let's sit down, Sid. You can tell me all about it."

She led him back to the stove's warmth and sat holding the printout in her lap. He opened the glass-paned door and added a log. Bethany waited for him to speak. When he did, she could barely hear him.

"I don't know when it happened or what she did with it," Sid said. He cleared his throat. "That pot just vanished, and I never got a chance to ask her about it. She vanished, too."

Bethany felt sorry for the man. What a failure as a curator. "Was the pot very valuable?"

"Oh, yes indeed. Those pots can bring thousands of

dollars. I didn't even miss that one, not at first. Krystal came here a bunch of times. She looked at the gowns, drew them, played dress-up for that newspaper story, and brought her brother to see all the rocks. I let her have the run of the place."

"When did you realize she stole a pot?"

Behind the steel-rimmed glasses, his eyes avoided hers.

"Not when she disappeared, not at first. But then one day, the same young newspaper gal, the one who did that story on Old Timers Days for the *Mining Monthly*, came back to talk to me. The second time she came, she'd been hired by the La Plata paper.

"She remembered how pretty Krystal looked in that dress but how it was too tight, so she couldn't button it up the back, something you couldn't see in the picture. Since she'd snapped that photo of Krystal, the *Citizen* let her come up to Sorrel to do a write-up on Krystal as a missing person.

"Well, anyway, while she talked, I happened to look at that showcase and realized one of the pots wasn't there anymore. Krystal must have rearranged the four of them so I didn't see a gap in the row. I never noticed until that day the reporter gal came again."

"Are the other four pots valuable?"

He scoffed. "Reproductions. I had a university professor, who came in one time, take a look. He said, 'Sorry, they're not the real thing.' I never told him we used to have a genuine one."

"Do you know for sure?"

"No, but if it wasn't real, why did Krystal steal it? I figured she did her research. She looked over the whole collection. That pot might've been the only valuable thing we had. 'Course I could be wrong. Maybe the pot wasn't worth a plug nickel. But anyway, I never told a soul, not Mr. Sorrel in the nursing home. Not nobody. And nobody's ever asked until now."

"Sid, do you think Krystal died because of that pot? Maybe after she stole it, someone found out and took it from her."

"Could be. I've thought about it a bunch. I don't know, young lady. Heck, maybe Matt did her in for it. I heard he wasn't exactly flush, that he was sinking a fortune—borrowed money—into that old hunting lodge."

"But after Krystal vanished, he didn't finish renovating the place. It wasn't as if he had extra money for the project."

He shrugged. "Maybe he offed Krystal and hung onto the pot until he thought it'd be safe to sell it. But what do I know? Except that I failed in my duty to the museum and Mr. Sorrel."

Bethany commiserated with the old guy slumped in the chair. "You should tell him and the police. It's only right, and it may be an important clue to Krystal's death."

"I've been thinking about that myself."

"Well, do it then, okay? Why don't you go down to La Plata? Talk to the police, tell Mr. Sorrel. Is he able to have visitors?"

"The old gentleman's got his good days and his bad days. He lives mostly in the past, but sure, I can get in to see him."

"It's the holidays, Sid. Before you play Santa, do the right thing. Does he have any relatives?"

"Great-great-nieces and -nephews, none of 'em close by, enough of 'em so they're not expecting to inherit a fortune. He never married and doesn't have kids of his own."

"Does the museum have insurance? Maybe you could report the pot missing, and Mr. Sorrel could collect."

"Insurance? He can't afford it. I'm paid peanuts. Insurance? That's a laugh."

****

She slid behind the SUV's steering wheel and sat considering Sid's assumption that Krystal stole the Mimbres pot. At last, she was onto something significant, more so than the argument between Matt and Krystal. But suppose the theft of the pot was what they argued about, not about Krystal cheating on Matt or him on her? He would have been shocked that his fiancée would steal. Or, if not shocked, did he kill her, take the pot, and sell it so he could continue restoring the lodge? Unlikely, but still possible if he were running out of money and obsessed with the project. *No, no, no. Matt wouldn't have murdered his fiancée so he could open a B&B*.

She started the engine and heater. *How dark the sky looks today! An omen of other bad things to come?* Ideas whirled around in her head like the snowflakes in the air. Something Sid had said nudged at her consciousness, something more about Krystal. Closing her eyes and tilting her head back, she breathed deeply to calm herself and tease out the memory. *Got it!* Sid had mentioned Krystal sketching the dresses when she visited the museum. What did she do her drawings in? A sketchbook or journal, probably. Maybe she wrote about stealing the pot. Barbara didn't know of any journals of Krystal's except the one from Rusty's desk. Where had

Krystal kept her possessions at the time she disappeared? Had she kept some at the house and others at the lodge? Barbara said Matt camped out in one room. Krystal stayed with him, although the house remained her home base. What had happened to Krystal's things at both places? She needed to find out.

On impulse, she stopped at the mercantile, hoping to see Rusty. If he knew what had happened to any belongings in Krystal's room, he would say so. He was a guileless person.

She was in luck; she found him stacking a grocery shelf with canned goods.

"Hi Beth Annie. I have to do this right. See, green beans. The big letters have to go in the front." He straightened the can carefully.

She admired his work. "You're doing a good job, Rusty. May I talk to you for a minute?"

He looked up and down the aisle. "It's not my break. I can't stop until Ernie tells me it's my break."

"You can keep at it. I'll be quick," Bethany assured him. "I've been reading Krystal's book, her journal, the one you let me borrow. Sid at the museum said she drew pictures, too, pictures of the dresses there. I thought maybe she drew her pictures in blank books, like the one you loaned me with the purple cover. Do you know if there are more of her books like that around somewhere?"

Done shelving green beans, Rusty moved down the line, away from Bethany, and reached into an open carton of canned peas. "I helped Barbara put Krystal's things away. To save for when she came home." He concentrated on the cardboard box between them. "Barbara had me use duck tape."

194

"Think, Rusty. Did you box up any books Krystal wrote or sketched in?"

He lined up a can of peas and reached down for another one.

"Please think hard, Rusty. It's important."

He straightened up, a can in each hand. "Krystal had some books in her room. On a shelf. A bunch of them. Storybooks for girls. Nancy Drews. But not the books she wrote in. She kept them in her secret place."

"Books she wrote in? A secret place? Where? Can you tell me, Rusty?"

"I am telling you! Behind her storybooks."

"She hid her journals behind a row of books?"

"I put all her books in the box. I put other stuff on top. I used way too much duck tape, Barbara said. She called it a waste."

He turned away to shelve the two cans. Bethany moved around the cardboard box to get closer to him. "What stuff? What did you put on top of the books?"

"I don't know. Just stuff. From her room. Girl stuff."

"You mean things from her dresser, like her brush and comb, perfume bottles, makeup, those kinds of things?"

"Yeah, I guess. I don't know. I got to do the peas, okay, Beth Annie? It's not time for my break."

"Right you are, Rusty. Thanks for talking to me. One more thing, how many boxes did you put duct tape on?"

"Just one. I used too much tape. Barbara made me stop."

****

Walking over to the library, Bethany tried to conceal her excitement. She had to talk to Barbara again. Carmen

Montoya, staffing the front desk, said Barbara was in the stacks. Bethany said thanks and moved on, sensing Carmen's shrewd, black eyes tracking her.

"Patrons try to be helpful, but they really shouldn't reshelve books," Barbara said. "We have signs telling them not to. Three mysteries are upside down, and one's facing the wrong way. Certainly people know we put the spines to the front."

Bethany waited as Barbara righted the mysteries. "I just saw Rusty doing a job like yours, only with canned vegetables."

The librarian looked pleased. "Rusty helped out here before Ernie hired him. It's nice to know his volunteer tasks taught him something useful. But why were you talking to him? Not about any fuss he's caused, I hope."

Bethany said Rusty wasn't in trouble. Leaving out any mention of the missing pot, she told Barbara about Sid's story of Krystal sketching and Rusty's memory of what might have been journals hidden behind other books. "He said he boxed them up together, put some of Krystal's other belongings on top, and sealed the box with too much duct tape. I wondered…"

"I do know the box you mean. While I was packing away Krystal's things, Rusty came into the room to say someone was on the phone. I told him to help. When I got back, he had taped a box shut. The boy used so much tape I called him on it. Duct tape is expensive."

"It's possible that box contains journals or sketchbooks you didn't know about. Where is it?"

"Still in the attic with the rest of Krystal's possessions, I suppose. There weren't many boxes, not even with what Matt brought back from the lodge. Krystal stayed with him there, as I told you, but she kept her bedroom at home, too, since I didn't have any other foster girls.

"Not long after she went missing, I got so angry at her for leaving yet again without a word to either Matt or me that I started to clear her room out. I wasn't aware Krystal journaled past her senior year. But she liked being dramatic, so keeping a stash of journals nobody else knew about must have excited her."

"Didn't the police search her room or ask to look through the boxes?"

"They looked in her dresser drawers, her closet, and under the bed. They didn't disturb her books, that I recall. She kept a lot of knick-knacks in front of them, miniature decorative boxes, stones she and Rusty collected, a set of Russian nesting dolls I gave her one Christmas—those kinds of things.

"I don't think the police moved them. They did look closely at the clothes and other personal items she left at the lodge, Matt said. When they didn't find anything helpful, he brought those things to me. The police focused on her missing backpack and what Matt remembered her wearing when he saw her last. I'm sure the police assumed she had left Matt. I got the impression at the time they didn't believe for a moment anything bad had happened to her. She always kept a toothbrush and makeup in a small daypack—like yours."

She indicated the pack slung over Bethany's shoulder. "When she left those kinds of things behind at the lodge and at home, it didn't mean she hadn't left us. She'd run off before with only what her backpack contained. It was found with her bones, much degraded."

Chapter 16

Seeing Barbara's distress, Bethany waited a beat before pressing on. "Will you look through the box Rusty taped up? See if there are journals or sketchbooks? I'd like to examine anything you find."

Barbara hesitated. She patted her hair, held back today with two silver combs. "I have a meeting tonight. About the senior center holiday gathering."

"I think it's important to move on this as fast as possible."

"All right, when I go home at lunchtime, I'll look and get back to you. The box in question shouldn't be hard to find. But it's going to take a sharp knife to cut through all the duct tape, which I'm sure Rusty termed duck tape, am I right?"

"Lots of people call it duck tape."

"That they do." The librarian turned her attention back to the mysteries. "These aren't even in alphabetical order."

****

Leaving the SUV sit where she'd parked it by the mercantile, Bethany stopped at the Ponderosa Café to think and make some notes. At midday, diners filled half of the tables in the main room, but no one occupied the porch. She chose a booth in the back corner next to the wall rather than by a cold window.

She jotted down her hope that Barbara would find

the duct-taped box. How ironic to be journaling about a fellow journaler. She hoped Krystal had written in detail about the weeks and days before her murder. However, she doubted that Krystal would have mentioned stealing the pot. But wouldn't it be a piece of luck if she did just that, naming a potential buyer who turned out to be the killer? *Please, powers that be. Let this be the solution. Let the killer not be Matt.* She sent the plea to Joni's goddesses.

Almost ten minutes passed before Trudy, the same waitress as before, brought a menu. She seemed harried. "I didn't see you. The mirrors don't show who's this far back. People usually stick their heads in the main room first if they're going to sit out here."

"Sorry, I didn't know. There's no rush." She ordered coffee, then added a tuna sandwich so Trudy would view her as a legitimate lunch customer, not simply taking up space.

Left to herself, Bethany went over the notes she had written since arriving in Sorrel. When no fresh revelations dawned, she closed the notebook and looked at the framed news clips above her booth.

The waitress returned and poured coffee. Steam wafted up to Bethany's nose as she took a sip.

"Your sandwich will be right up." Trudy spoke in a friendlier voice this time. "I see you looking at that picture of Lorene's husband. You know he passed, right?"

Bethany had been studying a newspaper photo above the booth. In it, Flint Callender held a trophy cup topped by a horseshoe. A caption identified him as the winner of the town festival's horseshoe pitching contest. "Lorene told me he died several years ago."

Trudy set the glass coffee pot on the table and glanced over her shoulder. "He was a hard man, people say, with a name that fit him perfectly. 'Hard as flint,' you know. Everybody says he could be a right bastard to Lorene."

"How so?" Bethany took another sip of coffee and looked closer at the photo. Flint, a big man, appeared cheerful and harmless.

"He was a trucker. Like now, Lorene pretty much ran the café and motel. When he wasn't on the road, he didn't help much around here. Yelled about any little thing he didn't like. Knocked her around. And you know about truckers, a girl in every town. At least, that's what I've heard for as long as I can remember. Lorene's real sweet, so she didn't deserve all that. She's a good boss."

"She does seem like a nice person."

"The best. I'll see if she's got your order ready. Here, let me top off your cup."

Bethany wrapped her hands around the warm coffee cup. *You never know about couples.* Nathan, a man of few words in public, could be quite the talker in private. He could say the most romantic things about her eyes, skin, and hair when they made love. He had met Joni and Matt only once, at a casual Jarviss family barbecue. The two guys behaved civilly but didn't hit it off. Bethany suspected Matt's job as a financial adviser intimidated her cowboy. On the way back to her house, she offered a leading comment about Joni and Matt, something like, "They make a good pair, don't they?" Nathan responded with a nod and hmph sound. Had he said anything at all? She couldn't remember.

****

Someone had left a pile of fresh pine boughs in the

lodge for more decorating, Bethany assumed. She didn't find anyone on the main floor. Upstairs undisturbed, she used the landline to call Nathan's cell. Expecting to leave a message, she contained her surprise at his familiar, easy-going "hello."

"It's Bethany. Am I disturbing you?"

"Never, darlin'."

The "darlin'" came across as a jokey, old-timey term of endearment. She wished she could see the smile that accompanied it.

"Didn't recognize the number," he continued in a normal voice. "I can take a break. I'm only painting a fence."

"A fence? I would've thought the ranch had wire ones."

"It's the picket around the Carters' house. Warm day for December, so the missus has me slapping on a coat of white."

She commiserated with him. His job often involved more domestic chores than ranch work for his nearly retired employers. But he never liked to dwell on that. Quickly, he turned the focus to her. "Are you still in Sorrel with Joni?"

When she said yes, he asked if the cops had caught that killer. No, she said, and as far as she could tell, no one was about to be arrested. "Joni firmly believes Matt is innocent." She waited a bit for his response but heard only silence. "Nathan, are you there?"

"Yep, still here."

"I've been wondering. When you met Matt at my folks' place, you didn't say much about him or about Joni and him as a couple."

"What's going on, Bethany? You're worried about

her. You think he did it, don't you?"

"No! I don't know. He's got a quick temper, though. And I heard about an argument he and Krystal had on the street years ago."

"You ask him about it?"

"Not yet, but I should. The young woman who overheard it works at the lodge. She thinks Matt cheated on Krystal, but she's only guessing. I wonder if Krystal did something to make Matt angry. She shoplifted small items and might have stolen things of real value. Maybe Matt found out and confronted her."

"Whoo-ee. A thieving girlfriend. Not good for a guy managing other people's money."

"She was his fiancée."

"Even worse."

"Nathan, what do you remember about Matt?"

"I didn't pay him much mind at that party. We had a fine time back at your place after it, I do recall."

Bethany's skin warmed at the recollection. "I recall it, too. But seriously, what do you think about Matt? You talked to him for a little while."

"Okay, let's see. What did we talk about? That lodge of his. Hunting and fishing out of it with his uncle. Fixing it up for the public."

"Did he say anything about his job as a financial adviser?"

"Nope."

"He's able to keep doing that from Sorrel. While he's running the lodge with Joni's help. She says she's as much into Matt's dream as he is."

"That's good, right?"

"I guess. Joni's decorating the place like a theater set. It's like the eighteen-hundreds with Wi-Fi but without decent central heating. If Matt and Joni can't make a go of this place, she'll be devastated. As it is, she's exhausted with all the work and worry."

"Maybe you should go back home and take Joni with you. Get her to spend Christmas with the family."

"She wouldn't even consider that. She and Matt are opening the lodge for the holidays." She gave him the details. "Maybe you could come to the open house. It's a long drive, I know, but I'd love for you to be here."

He said he'd check with the Carters. As they said their goodbyes, he added, "Look out for your sister, Bethany. I used to be as crazy about bull riding as this Matt guy is about his lodge. Ladies would tag along behind me like puppy dogs on the rodeo circuit. That's great for a man's ego. If I hadn't hurt my hand real bad, I might still be breaking girls' hearts and not thinking a thing about it."

Nathan had said more about Joni and Matt than he'd ever said about anyone else, Bethany realized. Good thing she hadn't told him about her full-out effort to investigate Krystal's death. She didn't want him worrying about her safety. Would he come to the open house? She hoped so. She was growing quite fond of this cowboy with the damaged hand.

In her guest room, she turned on her laptop and read proposals for community grants. All too soon, she would have to meet with her father to give him her recommendations. When she'd done enough, she went out to her room's small balcony. The weather had turned blue-sky perfect, but that could change quickly. The forest beckoned. Time for a walk to clear her head and get some exercise.

Passing David's massage-therapy room, she heard a

woman's moaning coming from behind the closed door. The moaning definitely sounded sexual. What kind of massages did David do?

Downstairs, as she went by the office, the phone rang. She snatched it up and heard Barbara leaving a message: she had located the duct-taped box.

"Did you find any journals?"

"None you'd be interested in. There are five of them, all from Krystal's high school years. She wrote dates in them, so I can tell they're from long before she met Matt. There's one from the rest of her senior year."

"The one right after the journal Rusty loaned me. Thanks for looking anyway." Bethany willed her voice to be gracious to hide her disappointment.

"I did wish for something more," Barbara said. "Pardon me. Just a moment."

Bethany heard Barbara blow her nose and then, "I'm on the phone, Rusty."

Seconds passed in silence until Barbara returned and apologized for keeping Bethany waiting. "Rusty's home from the mercantile, and I must get back to the library. I do wish that box had yielded better results."

Bethany thanked Barbara for trying. As she set down the phone, David and Jazz passed by the open office door. They walked close together, David with his hand on the small of her back. So Jazz was the woman who'd enjoyed more than a standard massage from David. Both were single, so why not? Nevertheless, Bethany felt uncomfortable at having heard Jazz's cries of pleasure.

She stuck a note for Joni on the kitchen doorjamb, took a pair of binoculars from a lobby table, and set off on the snowy road through the forest. Thoughts of Jazz and David, herself and Nathan, Joni and Matt, and Lorene and her abusive husband Flint swirled in her mind, mixed with the disappointment of Barbara not finding any useful journals of Krystal's.

She hadn't been paying attention to the beautiful landscape. Deliberately she focused on it, immediately hearing bird sounds mingle with the winter breeze in the treetops. She breathed in the forest scents as she followed the way Gloria had shown her.

The fire lookout tower loomed up ahead before long. On a whim, she opened the jimmied padlock and climbed up, her boots slipping on a light layer of snow covering the metal steps. At the first turn, she stopped, nervous about trespassing, but who would see or care?

Up top, she held onto the railing, caught her breath, and took in the view through the binoculars. Today, Sorrel looked almost deserted, except in front of the mercantile, where a truck was parked at one of the unsheltered gas pumps. As she watched, Sid from the museum replaced the pump nozzle, moved his truck to a space by the store, and went inside. Bethany hoped he had filled up to make the drive to La Plata to report the long-ago theft of the Mimbres pot to the police and Mr. Sorrel.

Sid seemed a decent man, one who would do the right thing. If Krystal had stolen a pot several years ago, the police needed to know. They could investigate who might have killed her for it. But what a long shot! If the pot had been acquired by a private buyer, which was likely the case, there would be no trace of the transaction. The public might never see that pot again.

"Beth Annie! Hi Beth Annie!" The unmistakable voice of Rusty boomed up at her from the tower's base.

She had been so intent on observing Sid, she hadn't seen Rusty approach. The gate stood open; nothing stopped him from clambering up the stairs. "I'm coming up, Beth Annie," he called, stating the obvious with gusto.

A frisson of alarm passed through Bethany's body. Rusty was so strong, so loud, so apt to get worked up. She had never been alone with him, not like this. She tried to hide her dismay as he reached her, talking a mile a minute. "Joni told me you went for a walk. I walked here, too. I know the forest real well. Krystal used to say, 'Rusty knows the forest like the back of his hand. He can go by himself.' "

An expression of self-satisfaction crossed his face. He came so close she smelled his frosty breath, sweet like that of a child eating peppermints. But this big guy was no child.

She willed herself to sound calm. "Why did you come all this way, Rusty?"

"To find you, Beth Annie." He held out a plastic mercantile bag. "For you. What you wanted."

She took the bag from him. "Rusty, could you step back some? That's good, thanks." The bag contained three journals. "Are these Krystal's? Let's go into the lookout room. It's a little bit warmer in there."

He watched her take the journals out of the bag and line them up on the table. "Rusty, where did you get these? On the phone, Barbara said the duct-taped box didn't have any from just before Krystal disappeared."

Rusty stared at his boots.

Bethany waited, but Rusty didn't speak or meet her gaze.

"Rusty, come on, you can tell me. You brought me these, walked all the way to find me. Where did you get these journals?"

He mumbled something so quietly she had to ask him to repeat it. "Didn't put them in the box. The other book either."

"You kept these journals back as well as the other one you loaned me?" The question bounced off the walls on which dozens of people had carved their initials.

He bobbed his head but still didn't look at her. His breath came faster.

"Why did you keep them? Rusty, look at me. Why?"

"They're pretty." He ran a gloved hand over them.

One had a green cloth cover with five-pointed stars drawn in black marker. Bethany opened the journal to see entries from May to October over ten years ago in Krystal's small cursive, plus doodles of flowers, spirals, and the like. There were also pencil sketches of objects in the museum. Bookmarking where the journaling left off before the remaining blank pages was a blue tail feather from a Stellar's Jay.

The other two journals had handmade, brown-paper covers. Colored-pencil sketches of flowers and butterflies decorated one of them. A quick look inside told Bethany it was a more recent journal than the clothbound one. The third journal's paper cover bore hand-drawn stars, hearts, arrows, whorls, and geometric rickrack designs in black and red ink. This journal was wrapped in a cord tied to a white arrowhead about an inch long. Bethany couldn't tell if the arrowhead was a relic or a modern copy.

"Did you make this arrowhead nicer for Krystal? Attach it to this black cord?"

He shook his head, a firm no.

"Do you know where Krystal got it?"

Another headshake.

Bethany unwound the cord. The journal began the Christmas before Krystal's death and ended April 27, the day before she went missing. It was filled with cramped writing and drawings of hearts, flowers, stars, swirls, and other symbols in blue and black inks. Trying to contain her excitement, Bethany thanked Rusty for bringing her the journals. "I'm looking forward to reading them."

"I'm going to get in trouble. Barbara's going to kill me." Rusty shifted his feet and kicked the table leg.

Alarmed at his agitation, Bethany assured him that would not happen. "She'll understand why you didn't put these journals in the box. You wanted to keep something of Krystal's, right? Something personal."

"I put them in my underwear drawer, under my socks. Barbara never, never looks there. I put all of Krystal's other stuff in the box. Barbara said I used too much duck tape." He sounded like a worried little boy.

She wondered how much he had gleaned from the journals. "Did you read these?"

"No." He looked at his boots again. "But I can read. Books with pictures. You know that, Beth Annie."

She slipped the journals back into the mercantile bag. "I remember. Graphic novels. But you didn't read these journals? Any of what Krystal wrote?"

"Nah. I can't read Krystal's writing. It's too small and curly."

"Right," Bethany said. "It would be hard for anybody to read, but I'm going to do my best to decipher it."

"Dee-sigh-what?"

"Decipher. That means to figure out what Krystal wrote." She longed to begin reading but would hold off until she could do so in private.

"Beth Annie, will you talk to Barbara? So I don't get in trouble? She'll be mad I didn't put all of Krystal's stuff in the box."

Bethany moved outside to the railing with Rusty behind her. "Tell you what, Rusty. I'll call Barbara and explain that you kept these journals."

She tried her cell phone but failed to get service. "I'll phone her from the lodge. She won't be mad at you."

"You sure?"

She pasted a bright smile on her face. "Yes, I am."

"Okay, I'll come clean. That's what Ernie says. 'You screw up, Rusty, you come clean and tell me. Then clean up your mess.' "

Bethany remembered the spilled coffee incident. Rusty might be an artist with stones and silver wire, but he was a clumsy guy otherwise. He probably made a lot of messes.

"Rusty, did you ever come up here before today?"

"A few times." He said it reluctantly as if she might disapprove.

"That's okay, Rusty. I can see by all the initials a lot of people climb the tower. Are your initials here somewhere?"

"Yeah, I guess." He didn't look too sure.

"Can you remember where?"

It took him a while, but eventually, he found a simple RD and above it, a tiny, cursive KD.

"Your and Krystal's initials," Bethany said. "Are Matt's somewhere?"

His head bobbed and weaved as he scanned the mass of letters. Finally, he pointed out a dark MM. "Maybe here, when Matt was a kid? Kids do this stuff."

"Kids' stuff. Right you are." She found no evidence of Krystal and Matt as lovers. Krystal probably had tried to impress her older fiancé with her maturity. She wouldn't have suggested they come up here. He might have done that as a boy but not with her.

Bethany started down the stairs, Rusty one step behind. At the landing where the stairs turned, he bumped into her. "Rusty, can you stay a couple steps back, please?"

"Sure, no problem, Beth Annie."

No longer did she consider him a threat. This developmentally challenged man did his best to relate to other people. He followed exactly two steps back the rest of the way. At the tower's base, Bethany adjusted the lock to appear secure. They set out side by side in the fast-dimming daylight.

By the time they reached the lodge, it was after four o'clock, late enough for Barbara to be home. Bethany took Rusty into the office. Joni, at the computer, said sure they could use the phone. Joni raised her eyebrows when Bethany reached Barbara and said Rusty had brought three more of Krystal's journals that he'd had all along. Bethany plopped the bag on the desk.

At the sight of the journals, her sister's blue eyes widened. "Oh, goddess."

"I'd like to read them as soon as possible," Bethany said to Barbara. "Rusty is right here and is going to explain about them. Yes, he's fine. He went all the way to the fire tower in the forest to find me while I was out walking."

Rusty shot her a look of gratitude as he took the phone and told Barbara he had followed Bethany's footsteps in the snow. He said he didn't put the journals into the "duck" taped box but kept them in his room in his underwear drawer. His face, scrunched up in anxiety when he began to tell Barbara, relaxed at her reaction. He said, "Yes, ma'am," and hung up. "She asked can you give me a ride home, and I said yes. Is that okay? Or she'll come get me if I'm a bother."

"You're no bother at all. You're a big help," Bethany said.

"Definitely no bother," Joni added. "What's the arrowhead all about?"

He shook his head. "Dunno."

She touched the Stellar's Jay feather. "And the feather?"

"I found it. In the forest. Krystal liked it, so I said she could have it."

"When was that?" Bethany asked.

He shrugged. "One time. Krystal and I went walking. She hated walking, but she liked finding stones for me to make nicer."

"Why don't we let Bethany go upstairs to read the journals while I get you something to eat?" Joni said. "We've got some banana nut bread."

Rusty went with her happily.

"Thanks for the journals, Rusty," Bethany called to his back.

He turned, enveloping her in a tight hug. Through his heavy coat, she could feel the firmness of his muscles. Without a word, he spun around and followed an amused Joni into the kitchen.

Bethany hoped Joni would have some banana bread, too, that the anorexia was at bay for now. She felt heartened by knowing that she and Joni had a new friend in Rusty, one more person for whom to discover the identity of Krystal's killer. Maybe now, with the additional journals, she had a fighting chance of doing that.

****

She sat on her bed with the journals on her lap. If she believed spirits could make contact with the living, she might think Krystal had engineered the finding of these books. She didn't believe that but hoped reading them would be worthwhile.

She opened the one with hand-drawn stars on its green cloth cover. Krystal wrote about dropping out of college in Albuquerque and bumming around northern New Mexico and Colorado with a guy. *I love him but he can't afford to support me and I don't have much money of my own so I'm back with Barbara.*

Bethany skimmed entries made over several months in which Krystal mentioned sending long letters to the guy, identified only as ZD, to his parents' address. Krystal assumed he got them; the post office didn't return them. Bethany wondered if Krystal wrote on the stationery she stole from The Treasure Box. No way to tell, and what did it matter?

Krystal's last sentence mentioning the guy read, *I'm in true despair over ZD.* She made an occasional reference to college. The last read, *I couldn't stick it. Booorrring!*

A full year after beginning the journal, Krystal quit writing and instead filled it with sketches of flowers, stars, and swirls in colored pen. After those, she made detailed pencil drawings of the museum's 1800s apparel: dresses, hats, gloves, shoes, and a parasol. After those, she drew other museum objects: an antique tricycle, a row of dusty soda bottles on a windowsill, a broom, a pickax and other mining tools, a wooden ironing board and old-fashioned iron, piles of books, and Mimbres pots. Krystal drew competently but without particular artistic skill, as far as Bethany could tell. Why had she visited the museum so often to sketch? To make plans to steal a pot?

Or perhaps not at this point. After the sketches came more of Krystal's small, cramped writing focusing on an upcoming gig to sing on stage during Old Timers Days over Memorial Day weekend and how she had posed for a photo for the newspaper. *The dress was too small. It wouldn't close in the back. But nobody will be able to tell in the picture.* Then she pondered what to wear on stage: *A long skirt and blouse and my boots I guess. Nothing as fancy as in the museum. Where would I get something like that? There's not enough time to make a costume so I'll improvise.*

Krystal wrote about performing *the old numbers mostly, but some new ones too*, and that people clapped and whistled. She left off journaling until September 15, when she wrote about listening to a band at the Black Bear. She talked music with the lead singer, BT, who one night, on the spur of the moment, asked her to perform with him. *He dragged me up to the mike. He only sings his own stuff but I picked it up fast.*

Krystal wrote breathlessly in her tiny cursive that BT asked her to travel with the group. *BT is the lead but he's gonna write new material for the both of us.*

The last entry, on October 16, merely read, *My new life with BT! Bring it on!* The Stellar's Jay feather lay between that page and the remaining blank ones.

Chapter 17

Bethany wiggled her jaw and yawned. She should have started with the latest journal. She unwrapped the black cord and dangled the arrowhead in front of her face. Too bad Rusty didn't know anything about the arrowhead. Had someone given it to Krystal, maybe the person who killed her? Had her killer, or Krystal, attached it to the cord? Had Krystal worn the arrowhead as a necklace or only used the cord to secure the journal?

Bethany studied the stars, hearts, arrows, loops, and rickrack designs on the homemade cover's front and back. The designs resembled those on the Mimbres pots in the museum. But while the ancients' embellishments formed pleasing patterns, Krystal appeared to have randomly doodled.

The journal began: *Today M asked me to MARRY him! MERRY Christmas!* A string of stars and hearts followed, then *His gift? A diamond ring with little rubies. His dead gramma's. The ring is pretty even if the diamond is no rock. M was so proud of himself, giving it to me this morning with toast and coffee on a tray. Breakfast in bed like in the movies. I said yes yes yes!*

Krystal wrote about Christmas dinner at B's house and how M gave *nice presents to B and R.* She finished with *M's special and I love him love him love him!* and a line of intertwined hearts.

After an entry about cross-country skiing with Matt

some days later in fresh snow, Krystal had tucked into the journal their engagement announcement from the January *Mining Monthly*. Bethany again examined the studio shot of Krystal leaning against Matt and read the flattering descriptions of Krystal as a talented singer, Matt a Santa Fe financial adviser who aimed to turn the hunting lodge into a B&B.

What did these two have in common except an apparent sexual attraction? Perhaps that both dreamed of better lives. Years later, Matt still clung to the same dream, renovating the lodge with the help of a new fiancée. Would any woman do? A chill rippled through Bethany's body. She turned on the space heater and resumed looking through the journal.

On January 5 of the last year of her life, Krystal mentioned R—Rusty obviously—who could be made happy by the littlest things. She wrote about a walk she and her brother took in the forest after the snow melted, collecting stones. *Rusty begged me to go.* No mention of arrowheads.

On January 14, Krystal wrote that the lodge was freezing. M had learned the price of putting in a new heating system would be sky high. It was so cold in M's bedroom at the lodge Krystal slept in her old room at B's house. M had refused an offer by B to stay there. *M is being a STUBBORN JERK,* Krystal wrote.

Next, nearly a month after the engagement, Krystal complained, *M is a big bore. All he wants to do is work work work on the lodge. It's too much & too hard. Why can't we live in Santa Fe? It's like I'm buried alive. M's got to see that. He knows I have to get out of this stupid nowhere town!*

On February 15, Krystal wrote that M had gone to

La Plata and come back with a dozen red roses on Valentine's Day. *M made a fire in the lodge and I stayed overnight. He zipped two sleeping bags together so we sure weren't cold!* She had drawn a smiley face next to the sentence.

Krystal had been writing in blue ink up to February 17, when she switched to black. *Everybody's talking about FC's accident yesterday. The whole town's in complete shock! I am thinking so many things about F's death it's hard to put it in words.*

The journal contained a sketch of a skull and crossbones. Below it, Krystal had written, *Some people are blaming F for his own death, saying he drove too fast, but that's not right, is it? God, the people in this town. Shooting off their mouths about something they know nothing about!*

The sentences stood out as uncharacteristic of Krystal; they didn't relate directly to her. Bethany gave this entry particular thought. What had Lorene said about the accident that killed Flint but barely injured her? Flint swerved to avoid an oncoming vehicle in their path on the mountain road's blind curve. Flint wasn't at fault, but maybe that hadn't been public knowledge when Krystal wrote in her journal. Krystal must have known Flint for years. His sudden death had yanked her out of her normal self-absorption. How ironic that a few months later, Krystal met her own death.

After the February 17 entry, Krystal picked up writing, in blue ink again, about wanting to leave Sorrel, but *M kisses me and says when the lodge is up and running I'll love it. He says I can sing for the guests. But that's someday. NOT SOON ENOUGH.*

On March 3, she wrote, *I have to show the world I'm*

216

SERIOUS about my entertainment career. Carpe deeum! (sp?) Seize the day like they taught us in school. gogogogoforit!

On March 30, Krystal penned one line: *All according to plan but I can't tell a living soul.* Had Krystal stolen a pot and sold it? If so, she didn't mention it. Below the sentence, she had drawn a rough shape, an outline. Bethany set the arrowhead on top of it. It fit perfectly. Why had Krystal traced around the arrowhead? The object hadn't meant anything to Rusty, or so he said. He seemed sincere enough, but maybe he could tell lies and maintain that innocent expression.

Bethany had grown stiff with tension and tiredness. She did a few stretches, raising her arms overhead and touching her toes. She had to keep reading.

Krystal hadn't written again until nearly a month later. On April 25, three days before Matt claimed he last saw her, she made a final journal entry: *M will be mad at me but it's for the best. I do love him. But we don't want the same things. I thought he would support my dreams, but I guess he expected me to forget them once we got engaged. He is SO WRONG about that. My dreams are who I am. I will do whatever to make them come true. B sides with M but there's another side to the story.* Below the last few words, she had drawn a heart divided in two by a jagged line. The left side of the heart was labeled *M,* and the right side *K.*

The naïve drawing disturbed Bethany. She felt sorry for the girl but even worse for Matt. Krystal would have jilted him. Had she announced she planned to leave him? Is that what the fight Gloria witnessed had been about? And if so, had Matt killed Krystal? Or if he was innocent of murder, what else had happened in Krystal's life after she wrote the last passages? Too bad she hadn't written more in her final days.

Bethany closed the journal and took a few deep breaths. The room felt warmer now, thanks to the space heater. She yawned. It would feel good to take a nap. But she couldn't go to sleep, not now.

She opened the previous journal—from before Krystal had even met Matt—and immediately was mesmerized. Krystal must not have kept a journal for a long while because she started this one by recapping several months away from Sorrel, when she had gone to California hoping to start her music career. *I've missed putting my heart on paper,* she wrote. Below the statement, she had sketched a heart filled with rows of teardrops. What a contrast to the flowers and butterflies in colored pencil decorating the brown paper cover. She must have wanted to begin a fresh journal on a positive note but couldn't help writing about what troubled her.

The new guy in her life and his friends planned to form a band with her as the lead singer, or so they said. When they came into the Black Bear one night, she saw them as her ticket to fame. But they were more into alcohol and drugs than music. In San Diego, the new guy, BT, made it clear he didn't care if she slept with the other guys; he even expected it. She refused and parted company with them fast. *They spent most of my savings. I had to get along the best I could. My light fingers got me food and some clothes. Thank God I bartended before so I got a job and made friends with some girls that had a place.*

Krystal described her efforts to land a singing gig. She told about performing at a Holiday Inn lounge for *a bunch of grayheads who call me dear.* That job didn't last long. Krystal considered trying to find her birth mother but didn't know where to start. Reading between the lines, Bethany imagined how dejected and lonely Krystal must have been in California. She wrote: *I'm taking the bus home. Barbara's agreed to pick me up in La Plata. She always understands and takes me back.*

Next came half a dozen pages covered with sketches of the antique dresses. Krystal made several drawings of particular elements such as lace collars, buttons, and a pair of gloves. One sketch might have been a photograph; it showed the dresses in their case and behind them a line of four pots, just like now. Maybe she drew the scene after she stole a pot. It wouldn't have been hard to simply take one out of a case when Sid wasn't looking, slip it into a tote bag or under a jacket, and walk out with it.

Then Bethany read an entry that made her catch her breath: *I've seen something I bet nobody else has. The proof is in my journals and right before everybody's eyes in the P C. Do I dare make something of it? Four not five.* Below it was a sketch of the same four pots in a line, a more rudimentary drawing than on a previous journal page. Under the pots, like a long caption, ran a string of letters: *sdiditsdiditsdiditsididit.* What did it mean? The nonsense word began with the letter *S* and the word *did* jumped out. Bethany put her finger on the letters after the *S* and drew it to the right. *Sdidit.* Did *S* stand for Sid? Did Krystal mean to say *Sid did it* over and over? Sid did what? Yes, of course. Sid stole the pot, not Krystal!

Bethany put the open journal face down and picked up the oldest of the trio. She stared at Krystal's drawing of five, not four, Mimbres pots decorated with various geometric designs. Krystal had seen and sketched five pots before she left town—in the time before she met Matt—but only four when she returned. But what did she mean by the proof being visible in the *P C*? What did *P C* stand for? Personal computer? No, it had to be the Ponderosa Café. The proof was in the newspaper articles on the café's wall.

Hurriedly, Bethany sorted through the printouts she'd made at the library and found the ones promoting the Old Timers Festival. She had seen the same pages in the café. One of the photos depicted a line of five Mimbres pots in their case before one went missing, something Krystal noted because she inadvertently had made before-and-after sketches of the pots. Who had seen the photo? A pot collector, probably. Someone who offered Sid a great deal of money to remove the pot from the case. Then he moved the four pots closer together. In the cluttered museum, Sid hadn't thought anyone would notice.

Bethany saw what a fool she had been, going to Sid with the suspicion of Krystal being the thief. True, Krystal stole small things, including a couple of rings from Jazz's shop. But she hadn't stolen an antique worth thousands of dollars.

Bethany picked up the journal again and read the next entry: *I can keep a secret. I'm a reasonable girl. Needy but not greedy. I told that to S and he said okay. Simple as that. Finally, good fortune! The flip side of my usual bad luck.*

It sure looked as if Krystal had blackmailed Sid. She almost said as much in her journal but didn't spell it out.

Then she wrote on an entirely different subject: *I met a guy—MM—yesterday at the 4th of July celebration at the park. He's good looking and super nice compared to*

*those loser band guys. Mmmmm! Older but not too old.
Our teeny tiny town can't afford fireworks but SPARKS
FLEW between the two of us.*

Reading several more references to *MM*—clearly
Matt—Bethany learned he took Krystal to the Black
Bear and on four-wheeling jaunts. He impressed her with
his lodge plans.

Struggling to read the tiny writing, Bethany stopped
and rubbed her eyes. She hated to intrude on an account
of Matt's personal life. At least as Krystal began using
Matt's name, she made only oblique mentions of their
physical relationship: *Matt knows how to make a girl
happy in and out of bed. Matt's a great lover. Matt's
really into me. Matt thinks I'm sweet.*

The journal contained no entries in August and only
one in September, on the twenty-third. Krystal headed
the September entry *A DECISION* in large capital letters.
*I need to stop meeting S. Tell him it's all right. I don't
need it anymore. Not with M in my life.* A casual reader
would think Krystal wrote about a lover, but if *S* stood
for Sid, she must have intended to stop blackmailing
him. She had found a golden goose in Matt and couldn't
risk him discovering she was anything other than a
sweet, young thing.

Bethany closed the journal. Nothing in it pointed to
Matt as the killer. But Sid, sure. He probably sold the pot
to a private buyer and made payments to Krystal to keep
her mouth shut. Maybe he killed her before knowing she
planned to stop making him pay once she'd gotten
serious about Matt.

Had Sid used the money from the Mimbres pot for
two big-ticket items in plain sight all along: his truck and
trailer? Bethany had seen him gassing up the truck.

Would he go to La Plata to tell the police and Mr. Sorrel that Krystal had stolen a pot? Maybe, if he thought Bethany didn't know the truth. *Or he might make a run for it. Yes, that was more likely.* He'd probably filled up at the mercantile for his getaway, not a mere drive to La Plata. But he might still be at the museum.

She crammed her arms into her parka and rushed down the stairs. In the kitchen, Rusty and Joni sat with mugs of tea and a nearly empty plate of banana bread. "Come on, Rusty, I'll drop you at your house on the way to the museum. I've got to talk to Sid again."

"Why Sid?" Joni mouthed over Rusty's head.

"I just figured something out. Something I need to check," Bethany whispered.

Joni said she could drive Rusty home, no problem.

"Okay, see you both later."

"Come back and tell me all about it," Joni said as Rusty reached for the last slice of bread.

Bethany crossed the lobby at a trot, nearly losing her balance on one of the Southwestern rugs covering the polished wood floor. She drove less than cautiously on the slippery road into town. As a dusting of snow hit the windshield, she slowed down at the *35 MPH* sign on Main Street. As she turned into the museum parking lot, she saw that not only was Sid's truck gone, but so was his trailer. The plastic picket fence lay flattened on the ground, marked by vehicle tracks. Sid had left in a hurry.

A red sports sedan was driving out of the lot. Bethany powered down her window and asked a woman in the passenger seat, "Did you by any chance see a truck and trailer pull out of here?"

"Yes, we did. The man at the wheel said the museum is closed for the holidays."

"Did he go that way?" Bethany pointed toward La Plata.

The woman nodded. "My husband told him to be careful on the road. We just came up for a day's shopping and had no idea how steep or winding the road would be. We probably shouldn't have taken the time to see the museum anyway but should get back to our motel in La Plata before the roads get bad."

The woman kept talking. Bethany cut her off with a thanks, and before the husband could move the car, backed up and whipped around it. She headed out of Sorrel and down the mountain to see if she could catch a glimpse of Sid's truck and trailer. Driving as fast but as carefully as she could, she negotiated the blind curves and hairpin turns with her heart in her throat, finally spotting Sid up ahead where the road straightened out some. His truck lights and the trailer's backlights gleamed. Knowing they still faced more curves and a steep, downhill slope, she kept a safe distance behind him.

What now? What should she do? When she got to the valley floor, she could try to get cell service, call 911. But what could she say? That she suspected Krystal's murderer was getting away? They'd think she was some crazy person or a hoaxer, ask why she thought she was tailing a murderer. No, she wanted to talk to Sid, not the police.

At the bottom of a long slope, the road flattened out. Miles of ranch land stretched ahead with few houses along the way to the city. On impulse, she sped up, passed Sid, and then slowed down and straddled the center of the road. She flipped on her right turn signal and waved her arm out the window to catch Sid's attention. She slowed down even more and moved to the right, hoping he would pull over behind her. Instead, he moved to the left and tried to pass. She aimed for the center again, alternating her right and left turn signals, then put on her emergency flashers. This time when she pulled over, he followed suit.

She counted on him not recognizing her SUV, thinking a motorist needed assistance. As he stopped, she turned off the engine and flipped up her parka's hood, holding it tight to her face with one hand. She ran to the passenger side of Sid's truck, banged on the door but didn't let Sid see her face, then tried the handle. The truck wasn't locked, so she climbed in and pushed her hood down. "Hello, Sid."

"What the heck are you up to, young lady? Driving like a mad hen right in front of me. I could of run smack into you. You could of got us both killed!"

Sid would have made a good Santa Claus with that folksy voice. But it didn't look like he intended to honor that commitment, not with his home in tow.

He opened his mouth to say something more, but before he could get it out, she said, "You stole the pot. You, not Krystal. Rusty brought me some of Krystal's journals this afternoon. I saw what she wrote. 'Sid did it, Sid did it, Sid did it' with a sketch of four pots, not five, along with the sketches of the dresses. She figured it out."

"I don't believe it. Show me." Sid avoided her gaze.

"The journal is safe. You don't think I would have brought it with me, do you? It's evidence of your crime. Who did you sell the pot to, Sid?"

He put a hand to his short beard and rubbed his chin. Then he clamped both hands on the steering wheel and gazed out at the valley landscape. Down here, no snow fell. The red sports sedan sped past them.

Sid's voice sounded far away. "A gentleman walked in and made me an offer. He knew the real McCoy when he saw it. One pot. He had no interest in the others. Said they were fakes. Said I could sell that one to him or tell the owner what the museum had and not make a dime. My choice. Simpler, he said, if we two did business. Who'd be the wiser? He had a private collector all lined up who'd never tell nobody. Gave me time to do a little research on my own before we struck a deal. Do I need a lawyer?"

"That would be a good idea, Sid."

"It had nothing to do with Krystal Decker, nothing at all. Old man Sorrell was getting senile. He'd promise me a bigger paycheck than minimum wage for a few hours a week, but he'd forget he said it. Then he moved to that retirement home, so I knew I'd never get more out of him. I've been caring for the museum like it's my own place. Nobody else would keep it going but me. I deserved a heck of a lot more than he paid me."

"You stole a pot and sold it. And bought the truck and trailer."

"I only got enough for a down payment on this rig. My old cabin wasn't livable no more. David Sudesky bought it off me for a song. He thinks he can fix it up. Well, good luck to him. The roof leaks like a sieve. The snow blows right through the walls. I deserved a snug place, so damn right I sold that pot."

"You sold it before Krystal went missing." He turned to her, and she leaned toward him, her face inches from his. "She found out and blackmailed you. It's all in her journal. You killed her. The ironic thing is that she

225

was going to stop the blackmail after she got serious about Matt."

He didn't flinch at her words. "I never harmed a hair on her head. She never said a thing about the pot."

"When she saw your new truck and trailer, she knew you'd sold the pot."

"Not true! I didn't get them until way after that girl went missing."

"Okay, so you killed her to stop the blackmail and waited to buy them until after the hue and cry about her disappearance settled down."

"Young lady, I waited, sure, 'til things got quiet around here again but not because I did any harm to Krystal. She never asked me for a dime. I liked the girl, liked having her in the museum. She brightened the place up."

"You let me believe she stole the pot. The police have to know *you* did it, Sid. You've got to tell them."

"They'll drag me in and grill me like a fresh trout about that girl's death. To take the heat off your sister's guilty boyfriend!"

"Fiancé," Bethany said. "And he's not guilty."

"The hell he isn't. I may have jumped at the main chance, but I didn't kill nobody. And you can't prove that girl blackmailed me. Would a nice young girl like that, Barbara's girl, do such a thing?"

He glared at her as if rebuffing an enemy. "Now get out. Tomorrow, I'll go see the old man and tell him what I did. He'll probably fire me, thanks to you. And there'll be nobody to keep his museum open. That won't do the town much good, will it, missy? Call the cops if you want. Tell 'em they can find me at the RV park by the new Walmart."

He reached across her to open the truck's door. His rough gray beard brushed against her cheek, sending a chill through her body. Her foot slipped on the running board as she hopped down to ground level. She almost lost her balance on the loose, wet stones on the edge of the pavement. He glared at her again, and in return, she slammed the door in his face. As he drove away, her legs went all wobbly as she wondered if she had been speaking to a murderer, one who had planned to play Santa Claus. Or had he been telling the truth, that Krystal never blackmailed him? Maybe she hadn't acted on what she knew. Sid could be a thief but not a killer. Bethany trudged back to her car, not sure of anything.

Chapter 18

At the lodge, pine boughs draped the doorways, but the atmosphere failed to seem festive. Joni stoked a smoky fire while Matt sat slumped nearby.

"We can't afford it," he said to Joni, ignoring Bethany completely.

Joni gave a log a hard jab with the fireplace poker, setting the logs blazing. "Postpone building the cabins. We'll concentrate on the lodge." She replaced the poker and stood with her arms crossed, watching Bethany wipe her snowy boots. "What's going on? Why did you rush off?"

The fire burned merrily in contrast to the mood in the room. Bethany didn't answer her sister. "What's up with you guys?"

Joni ran a hand through her spiky hair. "The Santa Fe lawyer's fee is going to be off the charts. Matt thinks there's no way we can afford him and new cabins."

Bethany sank into a chair. Her jaw throbbed as she asked, "Do you have to build them?"

Matt sat up straight, his eyes on the fire. "The lodge won't be profitable if we only have a few rooms. The plan from the start has been to put cabins out back. I want to get a local contractor going this summer on six or eight guest cabins. But that'll never happen if I'm facing a murder charge. I'll probably have to sell the lodge."

"No, Matt," Joni said. "Don't think that." She bit a

thumbnail, caught herself doing it, and dropped her hand.

"Joni, why don't you sit down?" Bethany gave her an encouraging smile.

"My lawyer phoned today after talking to the cops," Matt said. "I should expect a call from the state police asking me to go down to the station for more questioning. I told him they'd have to arrest me. I'm not going, at least not until after the party and open house. He said he's going to talk to the cops, mention I'll sue for harassment since they don't have any evidence I murdered Krystal. Unless they have some they're keeping to themselves. I asked if he thinks I'm a killer, but he said he never discusses guilt or innocence with clients. He operates on the 'as if' principle. 'As if' I'm innocent. Good God, what am I going to do?"

"You're not going to be arrested, Matt. It's not going to come to that," Joni insisted again. She turned to Bethany. "Why'd you leave before? You figured something out, didn't you?"

"Hold on. Let me get Krystal's journals," Bethany said. "Then I can show you as well as tell you."

She went up to her room, breathed deeply a few times to calm her nerves, and returned with the four journals and copies of the newspaper articles. She laid them on the coffee table.

"What's all this?" Matt asked.

Bethany explained she had gotten the journals from Rusty. She asked Matt if he'd ever seen them or the arrowhead on the cord. He said no, never.

"Did you ever see her write or sketch in a journal?"

Matt shook his head. "She must have done it in secret. What did she write?" He picked up the oldest journal and fanned its pages. He dropped it on the coffee table and leaned back in his chair.

"Krystal wrote some about you two, Matt. I'm sorry to have read about private things, but she didn't write in much detail. That's not what's important, though."

As succinctly as possible, she explained that she had thought Krystal stole a Mimbres pot but then realized Sid actually took it. She showed them Krystal's sketch of the four pots in a line and where she'd written *sdiditsdiditsdiditsididit.*

Pointing to the five pots in the newspaper photo, Bethany explained, "But now there are only four Mimbres pots in the museum."

She told them about confronting Sid as he headed for the RV park in La Plata. "Or he might be making a run for it, for all I know."

"And you let him get away, didn't phone the cops? I can't believe it! I'm going to call them right now!" Matt jumped up and headed for the office.

"Wait," Bethany said. "Please, stop."

"Why?"

Joni went to his side and put an arm around his waist.

He glared at her. "What?"

"Listen to Bethany," Joni said. "She always makes sense."

Bethany felt Matt size her up. "Sit down, both of you, please. Wait a minute."

She advised Matt to call his attorney but not the police. "Sid Rogers has a motive for killing Krystal if she threatened to turn him in for stealing that pot, or if what her journal implies is true, that she blackmailed him about the theft until she met you, Matt. But he says he didn't kill her, and the more I think about it, I simply don't see him as a murderer. He's an elderly man, not in great shape, probably not someone who even takes walks in the forest. I can't imagine him meeting Krystal there."

"But if the police have another suspect, it'll take the pressure off me."

"I know, and that's why you'll have to talk to your lawyer and let him explain. You can fax the relevant journal pages to him right after you call him. Fax him the newspaper article and photo, too, so he understands how I realized a pot is missing. Let him deal with the police, and let me keep Krystal's journals and go through them with a fine-tooth comb. We need to keep looking for clues about Krystal's killer. I feel in the pit of my stomach that the killer is not Sid Rogers."

For a moment, nobody spoke. "Okay, I'll call my lawyer," Matt said. "But remember this. Krystal died seven years ago. Sid Rogers was a younger man back then, a lot stronger. He had a shack in the forest, the one David bought. Back when Krystal disappeared, Sid lived in that shack. He knows the forest as well as most of the locals. I think you're wrong. He's guilty as hell. I bet Krystal tried to get him to turn himself in to the police for stealing a pot. That's why he killed her."

Matt and Joni went to the office to make the call. Bethany remained by the fire, determined to take another look at every word and sketch of Krystal's. Gloria came down the stairs and saw the materials spread out on the coffee table. "What have you got there?"

Briefly, Bethany explained about acquiring the journals from Rusty and the news clippings from the library.

"Krystal kept journals? Who knew?" A speculative look passed over her face. "Anything useful in them?"

"Maybe. I don't know."

Bethany decided not to mention Sid's theft. Matt and Joni could tell Gloria if they thought she should know. Gloria went to the kitchen and could be heard banging around in the big room.

Matt and Joni came back from the office. "We're in luck," Matt said. "The attorney, John Gibbons, can help us. He wants what Krystal wrote faxed to him ASAP. He'll take a look and call me back. He's all for notifying the police about Sid but not until he's versed in the evidence. Bethany, he wants you to call him as soon as we finish faxing. He can fly to El Paso, rent a car, and be in La Plata tomorrow. But he'll bill me for time and expenses, so I said to wait. If I'm arrested, I'll need him here. If not, he can stay in Santa Fe."

Bethany's conversation with the attorney took no more than ten minutes after he received the faxes. He understood from them how she'd realized Sid stole the pot and congratulated her on her detective work. But he disagreed with her belief that Sid wasn't the killer. "Put Matt back on the phone."

When Matt finished the call, he took the state police detective's business card out of his wallet. "John says to contact the detective. He also says we should copy every journal page and all the newspaper clippings. He expects the detective to ask me to take the journals to him tomorrow, if not tonight, and that I should comply."

"But the journals aren't mine to hand over," Bethany said. "I suppose they belong to Rusty as next of kin."

"I don't know about that. It may complicate things. Anyway, the attorney suggested you go to La Plata with me and get your story on record. The police will probably bring Sid in for questioning, too. If they can find him."

"I'm coming along," Joni insisted. "You're not going to La Plata without me."

"We've got the party tomorrow," Matt said. "You have to stay with Gloria and David to get ready for it."

"There won't be a party if you get arrested, Matt. And if you do, I'll need to be at the station to support you."

Bethany admired her sister's spunk. She was stepping up to the plate as Matt's partner.

"I won't get arrested, not with this evidence against Sid," Matt said. "He did it, all right. I know he did."

Matt left a message for the detective. "Now I guess we wait."

Bethany still thought Matt wrong about Sid having killed Krystal. She sympathized with, but didn't agree with, his wishful thinking as she held the journals and clippings. "I'm going to look over these again. Let me know if the detective calls you back and what he says. We can make copies of the journals later if we need to."

In her room, Bethany felt an adrenaline rush abruptly fizzle. It had taken all of her energy to confront Sid, drive back up the mountain, and talk to Matt and Joni. She could not face the journals until she'd had a rest. She lay on the bed, fully clothed. After a while, she folded half of the quilt over herself and rolled onto her side in a burrito-shaped package. She dozed off and didn't wake until Joni came to tell her Gloria would have dinner on the table in about twenty minutes and that the detective hadn't called back. Joni didn't ask if she'd found any new clues.

Bethany brushed her teeth, washed her face and applied moisturizer, and tugged a comb through her hair.

Realizing she lacked the strength to sit through a meal, she went down to the kitchen and asked if she could eat in her room.

Gloria stood stirring a thick chicken soup, and Joni filled a water glass at the sink. "You're exhausted," Joni said. "One of us will bring you a tray."

But Bethany said she could take it up. With little fuss, Gloria found a bamboo tray and placed on it a steaming bowl of soup, bread, a cookie, and an orange. Bethany refused a glass of wine and thanked the two women. As she carried the meal upstairs, she met Matt coming down. He offered to take the tray to her room, but she said she could manage and not to be late for his own dinner.

She ate hungrily, sitting on the bed propped up by pillows. Then she leaned her head back to think about the journals and all that people had revealed about Krystal, Matt, and themselves. She sat still for an hour, staring into space.

****

Joni poked her head into the bedroom. "Gloria called from the Black Bear to say Crush wants to see you. She wouldn't tell me what it's about, only that it's something he wants to mention. She sounded nervous, like he was listening to the call. Can you go?"

Bethany rubbed a knot in her neck. "Okay. I'll find out what Crush wants. I've been making it plain to everyone that I hope they'll contact me if they think of anything related to Krystal. Maybe he remembers something important."

"You're the best. My best sister ever." Joni hugged her.

It felt like being hugged by a sparrow. "Only sister."

****

Bethany parked across from the Black Bear. For once, it looked to be doing a reasonable business; she couldn't find a free space on its side of Main Street. Inside, Crush occupied his usual spot, a bar rag over his shoulder, his gaze on the muted TV.

"Gloria called," she said. "I didn't talk to her. Joni did. What's going on?"

Two men in ball caps glanced her way, then back at a basketball game on the overhead screen.

Crush waved her to a table. "I'll join you."

He came around from behind the bar and wiped the table before he let her sit down. Gloria moved around the room seeing to customers; the girl went from the lodge to the job here without a break, it seemed. She took Bethany's order of white wine as Crush dropped into a chair that creaked under his weight. The former football player must still work out; his body didn't run to fat. His big hands clenched and flexed until Gloria brought him a beer along with Bethany's drink.

"Thanks," Crush said. "Handle the bar for a few minutes, okay?"

She melted away after darting Bethany a look of thanks.

"Everybody's talking about Sid Rogers," Crush said. "Somebody noticed his trailer and truck are gone. The trailer he lives in by the museum. The museum's locked with no notice or nothing on the door."

He took a swallow of beer, then clamped his hands around the glass so tightly Bethany worried he would break it.

"I know he's gone," she said.

"What else do you know about it? That he's a killer?

I won't tell anybody. A bartender is like a priest, you know. We take vows of silence. In one ear and out the other."

"I bet." She put a measure of amusement into the two words.

Crush frowned. "I mean it. You can trust me."

Bethany considered how much to say. "I don't think Sid killed Krystal. The police will find him and determine he didn't do it."

"Then why'd he take off?"

She ignored his question. "Why did you want to see me, Crush? To tell me what I already know and pump me for information? You got me in here for that?"

As she waited for whatever he needed to get off his chest, she watched an older couple feed coins into the jukebox.

Crush twirled the beer glass around in his hands. "When Dad died of cancer four years ago, Mom moved to Nevada, where my sister and her family live. I don't own this place by myself. It's split three ways. But back when Krystal went missing, I only worked here. Only place I've ever worked, really, except for stocking shelves and pumping gas across the street at the merc."

He leaned in close as, from the jukebox, a singer vowed her eternal love. "I hated my job back then. You got to understand that. Dad made me work long hours with no breaks. Bossed me around like I was a kid and paid me peanuts. I was a mess. On the way to becoming a drunk and a doper."

He took a drink of beer. "Now I don't do drugs, and I drink this stuff in moderation."

"Good for you." *What in the world is he getting at?*

"Yeah, right. Look, Bethany, I want to tell you

something I've only told Gloria, and I don't want you to blab to anybody else, okay? Not your sister, not Matt MacGregor. You have to promise."

"I don't know…"

"Fine, then. Enjoy your drink." His chair screeched as he slid it back.

"Okay, I promise."

"Good. The thing is, one time when Matt was out of town, Krystal came in here. It was a slow night, so we got to talking, and she started complaining about Matt. How he'd gone to Santa Fe on business without her, how she wanted to move there or L.A., but how he dreamed of making a life for them at the lodge. 'We're polar opposites,' she said. Her exact words. Anyway, it got to be closing time, and she was pretty drunk. Me, too, actually. Everybody else had gone home, even my dad…"

He stopped, took a breath, and pushed his rimless glasses higher on his nose. "Krystal and I had sex. Right here in the bar."

"When she was engaged to Matt? Wow." Bethany hadn't touched her wine, but now she drank half of it.

"Yeah. It wasn't even a one-night stand 'cause we didn't even sleep together. We had a quickie in the dark. Something I'm not proud of, okay?" Through the shiny lenses, his eyes locked onto hers.

"She wasn't still working for you by then, right?"

"Not waitressing, no. Like I told you before, when she got engaged to Matt, that stopped. He didn't want her waiting tables. But she'd sing here once in a while."

"She was singing the night you two got together?"

"No, only in here drinking alone. Sitting on a barstool, whispering to me about being mad at Matt. And back then, I was mad, too. At my dad. Sick of the lousy paycheck he doled out, about him leaving me to close up alone most nights. And there was Krystal, all ticked off at her fiancé, babbling on about how unfair her life was, flipping her hair around, and showing a lot of chest. Not acting like the sweet girl I thought I knew."

"Throwing herself at you."

"And listening to me, too. Got me started with her complaints about Matt. I whined about my sorry life right back at her. Until the bar cleared out. And then… Like I said. We got it on."

"Then what happened between the two of you? After that night, I mean."

"Nothing. Never saw her again."

Lorene's information about Krystal going into a man's motel room came to mind. "You never slept with her again? At the Ponderosa Motel, for instance?"

Crush gave her an "Are you out of your mind?" look. "No. We hooked up just the once. Why would we get a room at the Ponderosa? People would find out when we checked in, don't you think?" He rubbed the bridge of his nose, popping his glasses up and down.

"Where were you living?"

"With my dad and mom. Oh, I see, you figure I'd have to go somewhere else for sex than their house. I had lady friends back then occasionally, and we'd always figure something out, go to their place or the forest, you know."

"To the fire tower?"

He resettled his glasses on his face. "You know a lot about Sorrel, don't you? How'd you find out about the tower?"

"I went up there, saw a lot of initials carved in that

little room."

"But not mine with Krystal's. Like I said, we only hooked up once. Here, the last time I saw her. I thought, like everybody did, that she'd left Matt. It's what she told me she aimed to do. 'I have to get out of Sorrel, and I've got a way to do it.' She didn't explain what that meant, and I never found out."

"Wait a minute," Bethany said. "You swore Krystal never told you she planned to leave town. Now you're saying she did? Why change your story?"

"Because I had to get the whole truth off my chest." He sounded defensive. "Gloria said she told you about seeing Matt and Krystal fighting in the street. I up and spilled my guts to her about Krystal and me. Gloria's good people. I asked her not to tell the police, and she promised me she won't. But then she convinced me to be straight with you because you're trying to find out what happened that got Krystal killed. Gloria likes Joni a lot. She came right out and said what I've been thinking, that if Matt found out about me and Krystal, maybe that's why they fought.

"Like I said, maybe I'm the reason she's dead. I bet he killed her after he found out she got it on with me. Couldn't take her betraying him. Then he left Sorrel for years, only came back once in a while to the lodge, never came into the Black Bear on those trips. Only since he got engaged to Joni has he come in for a meal or drinks. And only with Joni, never alone. I think he knew about me and Krystal."

"Maybe you should talk to him about it."

"No way. If I'm wrong and he never knew, I'm sure not going to tell him now."

Gloria swung by their table. "Another round?" Both

of them shook their heads. She picked up Bethany's empty glass, then reached for Crush's, which she almost had to pry out of his hands. "Did you tell her?"

"Yeah, I told the priestess here. Confessed that old sin and don't feel one bit better. It happened so damn many years ago, but it feels like last week. Stupid mistake."

Bethany didn't sympathize with his mournful tone. "You should inform the police."

"No!" Crush jumped up and leaned close to Bethany. "They'll think I had something to do with her death, but I didn't. I only told you because Gloria's convinced you can find out the truth. Look harder at Mr. Matt MacGregor. And Rogers, too. Maybe Sid has something on Matt, and Matt paid him to leave town in a hurry today. Hell, I don't know. I wish I never met Krystal. I better get back to the bar. Your drink's on me."

Gloria clutched the two glasses, her mouth open. "Sorry, Bethany. I didn't expect him to get so riled up. He's not mad at you, not really."

"I know. He's a decent man, isn't he? A lot of guys would have shrugged off what happened, never thought about it again."

Gloria surveyed the other customers. Nobody needed attention, so she sat down. "What do you think about his suspicion of Matt? That Matt found out. That he fought with Krystal on the street and then, well…"

"I don't want to believe it of Matt." *Please don't let him be the worst of Joni's lot.*

"What are you going to do next?" Gloria sounded confident that Bethany would have a plan.

Bethany pressed her fingers to her temples. The jukebox playing in the background suddenly sounded way too loud. "Since Crush has sworn me to secrecy about him and Krystal, I can't talk to Matt about it, can I? But I might find out what Matt and Krystal argued about if you tell Matt you saw them. You shouldn't keep quiet about it any longer, Gloria. You told Crush and me. You need to tell Matt."

"Matt will fire me for sure. What'll I do then?"

"He won't fire you if he has a perfectly good explanation for what you witnessed. I'll do my best to see he doesn't punish you for talking to me."

"And what if he killed Krystal?"

"Then he's dangerous, not somebody you should be working for, not somebody my sister should marry. We have to know the truth. If you won't confront Matt, I will. I'm going back to the lodge right now and do that."

"Okay, I guess I can't stop you. You're a brave woman, Bethany."

A foolish woman, more like, to have gotten involved in this mess. But what else could a big sister do? Bethany rummaged in her daypack. "Thanks for getting Crush to talk to me."

She put a five-dollar bill under the napkin holder. The drink had been on Crush, but Gloria deserved a decent tip. The couple fed the jukebox again; Bethany left to the sound of a classic artist crooning about a lady always on his mind.

Chapter 19

Driving back to the lodge, Bethany wondered what Krystal had meant when she told Crush she had a way to get out of Sorrel. Had she gotten enough money from Sid for a life on her own? Or did she have another source of funds? It was all so confusing to contemplate.

Joni and Matt, both half asleep, sat by the Christmas tree in the enclosed porch. Joni rubbed her eyelids. "You're back late." A bottle of red nail polish sat on a side table. She'd painted her stubby nails and wore a red-and-black plaid wool shirt so large it had to be Matt's.

"Look, you guys, I want to ask something. Matt, it's about an incident Gloria saw. Years ago."

He took his arm from around Joni's shoulder. "Say what?"

"Gloria's afraid to mention it. She didn't want me to either, but you've got to know what she saw. Back when she was a senior in high school. Spring semester, she and some girlfriends cut classes and drove up here one day. Matt, she noticed you and Krystal arguing on the street. Right before Krystal went missing."

Matt pressed his lips together and said nothing. Then, "I can't believe this. Gloria thinks I did something to Krystal?" His jaw jutted out, and he clenched his fists.

Joni placed a hand over his. "Gloria doesn't think that, does she, Bethany?"

She wished she could tell Joni not to worry. "Do you

remember the argument, Matt? Why you argued? Gloria said Krystal called you a bastard. Why would Krystal do that?"

He shook off Joni's hand. "Oh what the hell. I might as well say. Krystal was sick of Sorrel, sick of the lodge—this 'old pile of logs' as she called it.

"According to her, I was a bastard for not supporting her dreams. She had a line on a singing gig in Santa Fe. She wanted to move back there. She thought after she made a name for herself in New Mexico, she could go back to L.A. and become famous. What a dreamer! I told her opening this lodge together was a solid dream. Achievable. She clung to a child's fantasy she should've outgrown. Yeah, we argued on the street. Then disappeared, and like I've said, I assumed she left me. When she never turned up in Santa Fe, I figured she took off for L.A., and when she fell on her face, didn't have the courage to come back to me. How many times do I have to say it, Bethany? I don't know what happened to her."

"You didn't tell the police about the argument."

"Because it had nothing to do with Krystal's death."

"Are you sure about that?"

Joni leaped to her feet. "Stop it, Bethany. Stop harassing Matt."

The plaid shirt fell below her knees. She looked so small, so fragile. "I can see why Matt didn't say anything to the police. It would have made him an even bigger suspect. They might have arrested him."

"They still might if Gloria tells them what she saw," Matt said. "Does she plan to?"

Bethany shook her head. "Joni, sit down, please. No, she doesn't. But she should if you don't, Matt. It's been eating her up inside. She knows I intended to talk to you, and she's sure you'll fire her. And another thing, before she confided in me, she told Crush."

"I *should* fire her."

"You can't!" Joni's eyes widened. "We can't do without her. And how would it look to people if you fire her or she quits? Talk to her. Tell her what you've told us, that you argued but so what? It didn't lead to Krystal's death."

Matt clasped Joni's hands in his. "Right. I'll speak to her tomorrow, tell her everything is fine. But why didn't she ask me? Why talk to Crush and Bethany? I'm not such a scary guy."

"No, you're a teddy bear." She planted a kiss on him. Bethany got out of the way of the lovers.

****

Nobody could go to La Plata today, Matt said in the morning as he gazed out of the kitchen windows. "We've got a full-blown snowstorm on our hands."

He had been alone and in apparent deep contemplation, drinking coffee, when Bethany joined him. Snow covered the trees, the ground, the windowsills.

"I called for a road report," he said. "The police have blocked off the road up to Sorrel, not a big surprise in this weather."

"Isn't there any way out?" Bethany asked. "What if there's an emergency?"

"Let's hope there isn't one. The only alternate route is a roundabout trail through the forest for four-wheel-drives only. For all practical purposes, we're cut off until the road reopens. My attorney called. He can't get a flight because the weather's bad up north, too. He promised to get hold of the detective who interviewed me and explain about Sid and how he took off—to La Plata supposedly. He expects the police will find him. They'll want to question you as well as me again. But we're in luck. We're not going anywhere today."

"What about tonight's party?"

"It's on. Most everybody we invited lives in town. They'll come if they have to use snowshoes."

He wore his black-framed glasses instead of contacts. Worried about facing another interrogation, he couldn't be getting much rest. Deep down, he probably feared he would remain the prime suspect, maybe for the rest of his life.

Bethany helped herself to coffee. "Where's Joni?"

"Still sleeping. I decided not to wake her."

"What needs to be done for the party?"

"Mostly the setup. Both fridges and the freezer are packed with food Gloria made. Plus we ordered some from the merc, and Lorene is going to bring pies. This afternoon, we'll need all hands on deck to set up tables and clear an area for the fiddlers. It won't be complicated."

He stopped talking as Gloria came in, a wary expression on her face. She had a bandanna tied around her head and wore no makeup. She went straight to the coffee pot.

"I told Matt about what you saw," Bethany said. "He's explained to Joni and me."

"I'm not a killer, Gloria," Matt said. "I didn't cheat on Krystal. She called me a bastard and worse because I didn't want to live in Santa Fe anymore. The way she saw it, I stood between her and her dreams. Didn't take her seriously. And I admit it. I didn't. She stood the best shot at a good life here, with me. But she wouldn't face reality. The next time I talk to the cops, I'll tell them that. But first, we have a party to throw. And we've got to get ready for it."

She set down her cup. "I'm not fired?"

He put his hands on her shoulders. "Definitely not. You're essential around here. Joni and I are counting on you."

Gloria examined his face. "You look like a geek in those glasses."

Matt laughed and released her. "Have breakfast and then get to work. As for me, I'll be plowing the parking area. Wish me luck my uncle's tractor starts."

Gloria watched him go. "Bethany, did you mention Crush and Krystal got it on?"

"No. What good would that do? Gloria, you don't think there's any chance Crush killed her?"

"Oh, gosh, no. Crush is a gentle person. He'd never hurt a fly. Anybody can tell that."

Bethany sat nibbling toast that Gloria made. Nobody else seemed to be putting their minds to who murdered Krystal because they wanted to believe the police would arrest Sid. He was a dishonest man, sure. But Bethany would bet the farm, as her father liked to say, that Sid wouldn't physically harm anybody. She felt as sure of Sid as Gloria felt about Crush.

What to do next? She thought of the journals spread out on the desk in her room. She hadn't made copies; she could do that now. She began to clear away her cup and plate, but Gloria stopped her. "It's my job. Thank the Lord I still have one."

****

Upstairs, Bethany set the copies on the desk. She

contemplated the arrowhead. Why had Krystal traced around it? Why did she have the arrowhead in the first place? Why attach it to the cord? Rusty said he didn't know anything about it. Neither did Joni. Who in town might? Jazz. She sold Rusty's creations, other Southwestern jewelry.

Bethany slipped the cord over her head so that the arrowhead hung like a necklace. She stuck her wallet into her jeans pocket. She would leave her daypack behind and walk to town; no sense getting the leather pack wet or driving on the snow-clogged road.

The world outside, a winter wonderland, lifted her spirits. Matt waved to her as he cleared the parking lot. With the snow still coming down, he would have to do it again later today. She didn't stop to say she was headed to town; he could figure that out.

The pines, junipers, and oaks along the roadway sagged under pristine blankets of snow. Making the first fresh tracks except for ones left by a rabbit and some birds, Bethany pictured the steep, twisting mountain road. The highway department had been prudent to close it. In these conditions, driving it would be scary; chasing after Sid on a dry road had been bad enough. What had possessed her? She wasn't a brave person. And what if he had attacked her? At the time, she had given that possibility no thought.

"You're like a terrier when you're after something important," her father once said. "You never give up."

He had been talking about her effort to get the Foundation to fund a daycare center in Joy, New Mexico. The town had so few residents that her father doubted the project had merit. So she had gone door to door in the town and surrounding valley to prove the need for

247

daycare. A one-room center had been built, and since then, a second room had been added as a senior center. The bookmobile stopped twice a month.

"You've given that little town a bright spot," her father had said when he saw her video of elders reading to the kids. "Joy, New Mexico. That town's name is no longer a joke, thanks to you, sweetheart."

Now, she paused at the edge of Sorrel, nervous about approaching Jazz again. She noted the time. Nine-thirty, probably past the shop's opening time. Yes, there was Jazz, talking with a massive man in a winter overall and orange cap with earflaps. Melting snow pooled around his work boots. As the shop bell jangled, the man left with a quick nod in passing to Bethany.

"He clears the streets and shovels the sidewalks," Jazz said. "Sorrel doesn't have a town council, so he relies on us business people to pay him."

Did Bethany imagine it, or did Jazz seem nervous? She was certainly talkative. She hadn't needed to explain the man's presence.

Bethany unzipped her parka and lifted the arrowhead for Jazz to see.

"Where did you get that?"

Ignoring the question, Bethany asked if the arrowhead could be an old, authentic one.

"I wouldn't know. It's stone. It might have been chiseled yesterday by anyone or by a warrior hundreds of years ago. Pretty, isn't it?"

"Do you have anything like this for sale?" Bethany asked. "Or did you ever?"

Jazz took a closer look. "No. It was Krystal's, wasn't it?"

"Yes, that's right. How did you know?" Bethany let

the arrowhead drop against her sweater.

"Why else would you ask me about it? Doesn't Rusty know where it came from?"

"He says not. Has he ever made an arrowhead pendant that you know of?"

Jazz shook her head. "He's an artist. He doesn't bother with ordinary designs. I think of him as a minor Michelangelo. He releases the potential of a stone, finishes shaping it as nature might have done, given time. I don't think he's ever carved a beautiful stone into something as mundane as an arrowhead."

"Or as useful," Bethany said. "For hunting or war."

"True, but these days they're tourist souvenirs. If I were you, I'd check with the Whitneys. The one you've got there might have come from their shop."

Bethany had already thought of going there, but she thanked Jazz all the same. She turned to leave but stopped as Jazz said, "I saw you notice us, David and me. Out of the corner of my eye, when I came to the lodge for a free massage."

Embarrassed, Bethany felt her face redden. *Stop blushing! Jazz should be the ill-at-ease one!*

"You might have heard me the second time, too. I get noisy when my back releases."

A release, all right, Bethany wanted to say. As if Jazz could read her mind, the woman let out a loud, throaty laugh. "You should have David work on you. You're as tense as piano wire. A massage would do you a world of good."

"David gave me one in his chair," Bethany said.

"Well, have him give you the full treatment. I heartily recommend it."

Bethany left the shop grinning. That woman was the

devil! Still on good speaking terms with her ex, Ernie, now she had her sights set on David. Had Krystal actually stolen two rings from Jazz, or had the shopkeeper made that up? Jazz seemed like a woman capable of anything. "Stop it," Bethany said under her breath. There was no reason to disbelieve Jazz. She wouldn't have concocted the story about the rings, right?

The walkway in front of The Treasure Box had been scraped clean of snow once but would need clearing again. Bethany wiped her feet on a mat inside the door and said good morning to the Whitneys.

Tom opened his arms in greeting. "First customer of the day. That entitles you to a free cup of whatever you want. How about a hot chocolate?"

"It'll warm you up," Flora said. "I'd say put color in your cheeks, but you already have a nice, rosy glow." With a hitch in her step, she went to the nearby drinks counter and eased herself onto a stool.

Bethany followed her. "I walked into town."

"I can see that," she said. "You've got white stuff melting on your shoulders. Thank goodness for waterproofing. In my day, girls wore wool coats. We smelled like wet dogs after we'd been out playing in the snow."

Tom busied himself behind the counter making the hot chocolate. "Have a seat. Take a load off."

Flora glanced hopefully toward their merchandise. "Why are you out so early? Christmas shopping?"

Tom set a cup overflowing with whipped cream in front of Bethany. "Or sleuthing?"

What an old-fashioned word. "I did come in to ask you something." She hadn't zipped up her parka at Jazz's, so she simply lifted the arrowhead on its cord.

"Recognize this?"

They glanced at it resting in Bethany's hand and then at each other. "Not really," Tom said.

Flora shifted in her seat. "Don't think so. Why?"

"It was Krystal's." Bethany didn't mention the cord had been wrapped around one of the journals. "Rusty makes pendants, you know, but he didn't recognize this one. I thought maybe it had a special meaning for Krystal."

"I never saw her wear it. What did Matt say about it?" Tom asked.

Flora gave him a sharp look. "Tom, let the girl drink her hot cocoa." To Bethany, she said, "We always used to call it hot cocoa, not hot chocolate."

Bethany took a polite sip. Tom had made it with water and a powdered mix. A nothing-special drink topped with a spritz of artificial whipped cream. The drink fit with the shop's other offerings. Cheap tourist souvenirs, like Jazz had said. But the Whitneys knew their customer base. They probably made as much money as Jazz with her pricier goods.

"I thought maybe you sold arrowheads like this one," Bethany said.

"We used to get some from China from time to time," Flora said. "Some dark ones, some light."

"But not recently," Tom said. "'Course it's years ago you're talking about if Krystal had it. Let me take another look."

Holding out the arrowhead, Bethany leaned over the counter toward Tom. She could smell coffee on his breath. She would have preferred that drink to the too-sweet hot chocolate. After a moment, she eased back on the stool.

"Might have been one we sold," Tom said. "We had a box of them. The Boy Scout troop was always into Indian lore. They made 'em for Old Timers Days. After the festival, we took what they didn't sell off their hands."

Flora tapped her stubby fingers on the counter. "I hate to say this, but maybe Krystal took it from the store, like that box of stationery. She didn't have many things of her own, poor dear. Maybe she slipped the arrowhead into her pocket. We wouldn't have missed it. Can't be worth much."

"Looks like it's got a real sharp point," Tom said. "But it can't be the murder weapon. It would take a bigger hunk of rock to crush a girl's skull."

Bethany dabbed her mouth with a napkin. The townspeople seemed to be well informed about Krystal's injuries. The hikers who found her bones must have come straight back to town and spread the story of what they saw before the deputies arrived and no doubt asked them to keep the information to themselves. She swiveled on the stool toward Flora. "Do arrowheads mean anything special in Sorrel, do you know?" She turned back to Tom. "Anything at all?"

"This was silver mining country," he said. "Now if you showed me a pickax or a lump of silver ore, that would mean something. But an arrowhead? Don't think so."

Bethany thanked the couple for the free drink. To be polite, she asked if they sold holiday cards. "Sure we do," Flora said. "Real cute Western ones. Right over here."

Bethany chose a boxed set that pictured a cowboy on horseback hauling a freshly cut Christmas tree through the snow. The scene made her long for the legendary Old West where town marshals dealt with the bad dudes. Discouraged by her investigation, she realized she couldn't even identify a bad guy in all of Sorrel.

Her mom, an avid Nancy Drew fan a generation or so before Krystal read the books, would likely ask, "What would Nancy do next?" Too bad that Nancy, like her creator Carolyn Keene, had never been real. But that didn't bother Professor Eleanor Jarviss. From the fictional Drew mysteries, written by freelancers, she learned the importance of not quitting when a problem seemed insoluble. A solution might stare you in the face if you're smart enough to see it, Bethany's mother taught her.

Up front, as Bethany paid for her purchase, Flora said, "You look far away, hon. Something the matter?"

"Thinking about my mother."

"Missing her, are you? Seeing her for Christmas?"

"I hope so." *If this murder gets solved.*

She left the shop with her thoughts spinning. Maybe Matt did kill Krystal because she intended to leave Sorrel. Did anyone else care enough to stop her? Barbara, whose foster children moved on? Rusty? Possibly. He loved his sister. And the spilled coffee incident in the mercantile, when Jazz touched him, demonstrated how edgy he could get. Suppose he pushed Krystal into the ravine by accident when she made a move that startled him? But Krystal died from more than a fall; someone hit her with force. Rusty wouldn't have gone down into that ravine and crushed her skull, would he? That seemed way out of character.

As Bethany left the shop, she saw the man who had

been talking to Jazz—having done his first round of hand shoveling—chugging down the street on a noisy tractor, clearing the way for traffic and commerce. The snow fell faster now. How long would it be before the mountain road could be plowed and reopened? She didn't like the idea of being separated from the rest of the world in a town that might still harbor a murderer.

She flipped up her hood and crossed the street, aiming for the Ponderosa Café at a jog. Inside, she stamped her feet to rid her hiking boots of snow. Devoid of customers, the long, narrow porch felt chilly, so she stepped into the main room where tables had been pushed together for a group of women. Over breakfast, they were knitting tiny caps and mittens in red and green. Some flicked their attention toward Bethany and went back to their food or handiwork. Others smiled. One of the unsmiling ones turned to whisper into her neighbor's ear. Bethany guessed the whisperer identified her as Joni's sister, the stranger asking questions about that murder. She chose a table as far from the group as possible, under the deer head festooned with holiday lights.

Lorene appeared with a coffee pot and empty cup.

"Yes, please," Bethany said.

"Glad to see you're not a chamomile drinker. Can't stand the stuff myself." Lorene poured, then gestured with the coffee pot toward the group. "This place always feels happy when the knitters come every month. The caps and mittens are for the newborns in the hospital down in La Plata. Usually, they make them in pastels, but seeing as it's Christmas time…"

"Red and green," Bethany said. "Naturally."

"The babies' parents get a kick out of it."

"Do you have kids, Lorene?"

"Nah, some nieces and nephews in Texas is all."

"What do you do for Christmas?"

"Get together with friends. Close up this place and go for a big meal at Ernie's house. We all bring dishes. I make my pies like I'm doing for the lodge."

"For the locals' party?"

"Sure thing. I baked for hours yesterday. Apple and pumpkin for tonight's soiree." She made *soiree* sound like a joke. "I'm glad of the business as well as being invited. Now, what else can I get you?"

Hungry after only having had toast and a sip or two of Tom's awful hot chocolate, and mindful of pleasing Lorene, she ordered an omelet. It was brunch time, after all.

As Lorene moved toward the kitchen, Bethany asked her to wait a moment. She slipped off her parka and fingered the arrowhead. "Do you recognize this pendant?"

"Not particularly. An arrowhead. Pretty stone. Where'd you get it?"

"Krystal had it. Nobody knows anything about it."

Lorene held the coffee pot close to her apron-covered chest. "Sort of like what Rusty fools with, isn't it?"

"Yes, but not nearly as well crafted."

"Sorry, honey. Never seen it before." She went to offer refills to the knitters. The woman who had whispered to her friend looked toward Bethany and said something to Lorene, who nodded but didn't linger in conversation.

When Lorene brought the omelet, Bethany asked if she had figured out which waitress saw Krystal with a man at the motel.

"I haven't. Been too many years. I can see her face, but her name has gone clean out of my head. You know, I shouldn't have mentioned it. What difference does it make now anyway?"

Bethany swallowed a mouthful of egg and cheese. "This is delicious, Lorene." She dug a fork into the home fries and tried to sound friendly, not pushy. "By any chance, did you get to look through your tax records?"

"Came up empty. That girl might of been a Susan or a Christine. Even if I could remember, she'd be long gone. None of the girls from back then are around anymore. Not a one. None of 'em keep in touch even though I gave some of 'em their first paying job that wasn't babysitting. But like Krystal, they all had their sights on something better, and that meant far away from home. Trudy, the one I have now, is off to college after the New Year. Just when I got her trained. Didn't have her act together to start last fall at New Mexico State, but now she's got a scholarship. I'm back to square one looking for help."

Lorene shrugged. "But that's always the way it is. They come and go, but I stay put. 'Course, this is my place, and they're hired hands. Working for yourself makes all the difference."

Lorene nodded at the mounted deer head. "That moth-eaten fellow and I have been companions for many a year now. The perfect pair, you might say. We're not going anywhere, and we like it like that. Tell Joni I'll be there in plenty of time with my pies. Trudy is coming in later so I can go get dolled up for the party." She beamed at Bethany. "Enjoy your food."

Chapter 20

The only other person Bethany could think of who might know about the arrowhead was Ernie, so after the late breakfast, she walked to the mercantile, treading carefully in the deepening snow. He stood behind the cash register, waiting for customers. She said hello and reintroduced herself as Joni's sister.

He patted his black mustache. "Sure. Beth Annie, right? Rusty's new friend. He's been talking about you."

"Bethany, actually."

"Ah. You know Rusty. He means well. He's here somewhere. Want me to get him?"

"No, I came to see you." She showed him the arrowhead. "Do you recognize this by any chance?"

He furrowed his forehead. "Yeah, maybe. But not recently. I think the Boy Scouts sold those years ago. Not on a string. Loose ones."

"I've heard that from the Whitneys, too."

"There you have it. Why you asking?"

"It was among Krystal Decker's things, but nobody recognizes it as hers. I thought maybe Rusty carved it into an arrowhead shape and put it on this cord for her, but he says not."

"Maybe Krystal bought it from the Scouts."

"Maybe," she said.

"You learn anything to get Matt off the hook?"

"As a suspect in Krystal's death? Sadly, no."

"Sadly. Hmmm. Sad. I almost recall something sad and sort of corny about an arrowhead somebody wore like a necklace. I can't place it. Not a lot of help, am I?"

"That's okay. Maybe it will come to you. If it does, would you let me know?"

"Sure, anything to help 'em at the lodge. I'll be delivering an order for the party tonight and plan to enjoy myself at it. I'll think in the meantime. Hey, how about a sweet roll and a latte? The coffee's brewed. Rusty made it, and the girl's training him to make lattes, too."

Bethany thanked him but said she'd had a hot chocolate at The Treasure Box plus a late breakfast.

"At the Ponderosa, I bet."

She smiled. "An omelet."

"Yeah, well, Lorene and me are sort of competitors, but we're friendly about it. When I added the café to the merc, I thought she'd have a cow. But she said maybe more choices would attract more tourists. Now this snow, though, is going keep them down in the valley.

"See that guy scraping off Main Street? Name of Hank. He got the call from the county before dawn to put up the barricade at the front end of town. It's nothing fancy, two sawhorses with flashing lights. Stowed by the museum. Funny thing, when Hank went to get them, he noticed old Sid Rogers' truck and RV trailer were gone from their spots. That trailer is Sid's home. Strange thing, Sid gassed up here yesterday and didn't say a word about going on a trip. I wonder…"

Bethany tried to look clueless. She didn't need to tell Ernie about Sid's flight. Luckily, she was saved from further discussion as the mercantile's heavy door opened with a whoosh of cold air. Three of the knitters from the café stopped to chat with Ernie, giving Bethany a chance to slip away. *Might as well say hello to Rusty.*

At the café area, he was polishing the counter with such concentration he didn't see her until she stood right in front of him.

"Hey, Beth Annie! What you doing? Want some coffee? I made it myself."

"Thanks, but no. Looks like you're in charge. Isn't that girl working today?"

"Morning off, the lucky duck. Need some groceries? The shelves are real full. I stocked them yesterday. Beans and more beans. Green beans, pork 'n' beans, ranch beans…"

"Thanks again, but I don't need groceries. I wanted to know if Ernie had ever seen this arrowhead." She pointed to it on the cord.

"Krystal's arrowhead. From around her journal. Around and around."

"Right, but Rusty, I haven't told many people that you loaned me Krystal's journals."

"Why not, Beth Annie?"

"I don't know. It feels like it should be our secret. Except from Barbara and Joni and Matt. I'd like you to keep it between us, okay?"

Rusty examined the counter critically, touching an area with his finger and shaking his head. "Sticky. Ernie won't like that." He resumed his polishing.

Bethany stood pondering Ernie's vague memory of something sad and corny. *What in the world could that be?* She couldn't ask Rusty. He knew the meaning of *sad*, but he would think *corny* had to do with grain. He'd direct her to the canned corn next to all those beans. "See you, Rusty."

He stopped his work. "Barbara said we're going to

a party tonight. Are you going?"

"Sure. It's at the lodge. I'll see you there."

He leaned across the counter and gave her a hug. He hugged too hard, but she didn't care; she hugged him back with force to match.

Up front, Ernie waylaid her. "I got a flash of memory. Something about a bear."

"The Black Bear Bar?"

"Could be. Nah, I don't think so. It might come to me yet. And I can't help thinking about Sid Rogers. Why would he leave? He's supposed to play Santa Claus in a few days at the school."

She selected a tin of mints and paid for them. "He'll probably be back, don't you think? I'd better get going."

Outside the mercantile, she considered crossing the street and going to the Black Bear to see Crush again. It troubled her that Crush thought Matt somehow knew about Krystal being unfaithful and killed her because of it. She would do nothing about what he had confided. Let him tell the police if he dared.

She unsealed the tin, popped a mint into her mouth, and blinked at the blast of spearmint. A heavyset man in coveralls glanced her way as he pumped gas. With the mountain road closed, he had to be a local. As she walked past him, he called out, "Where you headed, miss? Need a ride?"

Startled, she said, "Thanks, but no. I'm fine."

His eyes bored into her back as she kept moving. How many townspeople had she not met? The small number she had talked to probably knew nothing about the murder. How naïve to think she could accomplish anything by questioning people up and down Main Street and at the lodge. Small business owners, the victim's foster mother and brother, hardworking Gloria, and kindhearted David. Sid, a thief sure, but not a likely murderer.

No, Krystal's killer most likely had been the mystery man seen with her at the motel. A guy wearing the arrowhead on a cord around his neck. But that was ridiculous. If the arrowhead belonged to the killer, Krystal wouldn't have gotten possession of it. Unless he gave it to her at a previous meeting. Well, maybe he did. But why trace its outline in the journal? Krystal didn't write about being afraid of anyone; she didn't see herself as a potential victim. If she'd been strangled, it might have been with that cord, but no, her head had been battered.

Bethany's own head began to ache, and her thinking grew muddled. She focused on slogging through the deepening snow. Concentrating on her muffled footsteps had a calming effect.

Soon, the lodge's holiday lights beckoned. She would take a break from questioning people. At the party, she would treat everyone simply as Joni's and Matt's neighbors and friends, decent people celebrating the hunting lodge's transformation.

Arrangements for the party were in full swing in the lobby. Joni, on a stepladder, was hanging mistletoe in a doorway, and Matt was stacking logs by the fireplace. A long buffet table had been set up with the lodge's mismatched dinnerware and flatware. Hotplates and serving dishes waited to be loaded with food. Recorded Christmas music played in the background from the porch, where an area had been cleared for a pair of fiddlers to perform.

From her perch, Joni beckoned to Bethany. "I called

Mom and Dad. It didn't go too bad. I told them everything's going to be okay."

"That's great, Joni. It's good you talked to them. By the way, I invited Nathan to come Sunday for the open house. But it's a long drive, and now in this weather…"

"Your cowboy! It'll be good to see him." Joni waved the mistletoe. "Where can I put the rest of this? Goddess, I'm jittery. But in a good way."

Bethany asked what she could do to help. Joni pointed to a feather duster lying on a side table. Flick the duster around the lobby, she suggested, then go upstairs and do the same thing. "Make sure the lounges look decent. It's okay if people go up there. That's all for you to do, really. After that, relax and get ready to party."

This might have been the opening night of a play, with Joni in full take-charge mode. She would have everything to do with the lodge's success. Matt, on the other hand, seemed nervous and disorganized. He asked Joni if they had enough firewood and said maybe he should clear the parking lot again. Calmly, Joni said she needed him more for inside tasks; he could plow again later.

David soon arrived and announced school had let out early, given the snowstorm. He asked how he could make himself useful.

"You can bring in more wood," Matt said.

Behind his back, Joni shook her head.

David grinned. "Joni, it's okay. You can't have too many logs for the fire. I'll get another armload from the shed while I've got my coat on."

He put his hand over Bethany's and tickled her nose with the feather duster, then turned away so fast her playful punch only brushed his arm. Matt watched and visibly relaxed; David's presence seemed to calm him.

Bethany straightened objects and dusted the lobby and the second floor, then went up to the third-floor lounge. What a battered, lived-in place. Joni hadn't worked her design magic here yet. David's massage clients, and anyone else who ventured up this far, would see the lodge as a work in progress.

A faded Western scene on the wall caught her attention. It showed a massive black bear, on its hind legs, confronting a cowboy on horseback. The tense meeting of hunted and hunter didn't indicate what would happen next. The cowboy aimed his shotgun at the bear. Would he shoot? Would his horse bolt? *Wait a minute; what had Ernie said in the mercantile?* Something about a bear being connected to the arrowhead. Bethany touched the pendant she still wore. If the hunter had held a bow and arrow, maybe it would have been worthwhile to look behind this picture for a hidden clue. She did it anyway but found nothing on the back side except dust, which she dutifully brushed off.

Finished with her chores, she could join the others. But no, she would keep to herself for a while, take a short nap. Housework, which she hated, always made her sleepy.

Footsteps sounded on the stairs, and David appeared, lugging his massage chair. He set it down with a thud. "Got to get my room ready for the free massages."

"Anything vital to do downstairs?"

"I think it's all in order. Matt's out shoveling the steps again. Gloria's been telling Joni to relax, but she insists on helping in the kitchen. They're looking up recipes for punch, of all things, at the last minute. Got to have something nonalcoholic besides sodas, even though this will be a mostly beer and wine crowd. Drive themselves crazy, they will."

"You will, too, if you give massages to everybody at the party."

"Future customers. Tonight's my opportunity to show what these magic hands can do." He flexed his long fingers.

She handed him the feather duster. "A magic wand, sir."

He aimed it like a sword at the massage room. "I was about to do a clearing with incense, but I can use this, too. Thanks."

Resting on her bed, she couldn't get comfortable. She considered calling Nathan or her parents, but that could wait until after the party. She would tell them all about it.

****

Hours later, she awoke, realizing how deeply she had slept. Obviously, she had tossed and turned. The pendant's cord pressed against her neck, and the arrowhead poked into the hollow of her throat. It was pitch dark outside, six-thirty already. The party would start at seven; she'd better get moving.

She applied more makeup than usual and changed into a party dress—a short, glistening silver sheath that needed no ironing. She put on treasured squash-blossom earrings, which went well with the pendant, and slipped into the high-heeled sandals she saved for special events.

Downstairs, the fiddlers—teacher friends of David—chatted with him as they tuned up. The buffet table was laden with appetizers, the kitchen packed with local people. Ernie, Rusty, and Lorene had brought the food ordered from the mercantile and café. They watched Joni and Gloria arrange more appetizers on trays.

"Lordy, you look a vision," Lorene said in greeting to Bethany. "That dress sparkles like the fourth of July."

Rusty gazed at the dress in admiration, his mouth slightly open.

"All you ladies look mighty fine," Ernie said.

Lorene wore a red wool pantsuit and Gloria a purple sweater over skinny jeans tucked into polished boots. Joni had changed into a Western shirt with fancy embroidery. Her gold pants matched her nail polish.

"Maybe this dress is all wrong. I should change," Bethany said.

"Honey, if I had that figure of yours, I'd flaunt it," Lorene said. "Don't you change a thing."

Joni agreed. "It's not often I get to see you in a dress. It's perfect."

Bethany asked what still needed doing. Carry a fruit tray to the dining room, Gloria said, while she took one loaded with meat and cheese.

"I've never seen so much food," Bethany said as they made space on the table.

"This isn't even the main course," Gloria said proudly. "That'll be served around eight, with Lorene's pies. Ernie and Rusty are leaving for a while, but Lorene is staying to help out. Nice of her, huh?"

Gloria set down her tray. "Oh no. I put the tablecloth on wrong side up." She flipped up a corner. "It's so old and worn, you can hardly tell. Think anybody'll notice?"

"With all this food covering it? I'd leave it be." As Bethany said it, her heart upped its beat. "Gloria, I have to go to my room for a minute."

"Sure, see you in a bit."

Bethany sped up to the third floor, her heels clicking on the steps. She closed her door and went over to the journals, seeking the two with paper covers presumably made and decorated by Krystal. She slid her index finger under the clear tape that secured the brown paper to the earliest bound book. Trying to remain calm, she removed the cover and flipped it over. Nothing hidden under the paper, nothing written on the back.

That left the other paper-covered journal, the one that ended right before Krystal went missing. Bethany took care not to rip the paper as she removed it. There was writing on the back! Reading the cramped cursive, Bethany realized who had killed Krystal and why she had died. Certain secret knowledge had been Krystal's downfall when she tried to profit from it. Her killer hadn't stood for blackmail.

Bethany's hands quivered as she put the journal covers back in place. The tape didn't stick properly, but that couldn't be helped. And anyway, the police would need to read the truth.

Feeling sick to her stomach, she went downstairs to where the fiddlers played as Matt, Joni, and David watched. She motioned to the three of them with a jerk of her chin. "Come into the kitchen, away from everybody. Now, please, you guys."

"What's up?" Matt asked.

"Please, just do it." Lightheaded with dread, she kept moving, sensing the others behind her.

In the kitchen, Gloria worked at the sink, and Lorene sliced pie beside the butcher's block. The group of four charging into the room startled them.

Bethany, shocked by facing a double murderer, cried to Lorene, "You killed your husband, and Krystal saw you do it! She was hunting for stones for Rusty when she heard your truck crash. She ran to where the trees end, above the road into town, and what did she see down below? You, with Flint's jacket over his head. You'd smothered him. Krystal guessed he was unconscious from the crash and that you finished him off."

Lorene stopped cutting pie. "What in the world are you talking about, honey? I got hurt bad in that crash."

Bethany wouldn't be deterred. "Cuts and bruises, you told me. Later, Krystal hinted that she saw what you did. She tried to blackmail you to get enough money to leave Sorrel. That's why you killed her, too."

"Where in heaven's name did you get all that?"

"From one of Krystal's journals. Just now. I took off the paper cover she made. On the other side, she wrote all the details. How she planned to meet you in the forest by that pine tree with the two tops. That's where you killed her, isn't it? You must have hit her on the head and pushed her down the ravine. I imagine you shoved her body into a crevice and concealed it with rocks. Because of the drought, nobody found where you left her, not until this year when it finally rained hard enough to uncover your crime."

Bethany clamped her mouth shut and stared at the knife Lorene thrust straight at her.

"Krystal Decker shouldn't have tried to profit from my misery," Lorene said, her voice harsh and loud. "Flint could be a mean bastard. He knew where to hit me so nobody'd see the bruises. When he drove off the road, we were fighting about some woman of his, the latest of his truck-stop beauties, as he called them. I saw my chance to get out from under his thumb, and I took it."

Bethany felt Matt strong-arm her aside. The poor

267

guy looked astonished. "You killed Krystal? In cold blood?"

"Not cold. Hot blood gushed from her pretty skull. I didn't get any of it on me, though. Guess I hit her just right."

He lunged at Lorene, his hands inches from her throat. Pies hit the floor with a messy slap.

Lorene jumped back and waved the knife in front of her chest. "Everybody stay put! I've got nothing against any of you."

She backed away from them, out the kitchen door, and into the snowy night.

Bethany ran around Matt and called over her shoulder, "Somebody hold him back!"

Outside, past the corner of the building, she slipped and fell in the snow. When she looked up, Lorene's car careened out of the driveway and turned toward the town. Bethany picked herself up, brushed off her dress, and stamped her feet. *Useless, flimsy shoes!* The soles didn't have a bit of tread; she should have stuck to her boots.

The first of the guests, waiting to be welcomed at the entrance, gaped at Lorene's taillights. Bethany couldn't face them but retraced her steps to the kitchen where only Gloria—on her knees—remained, scooping spilled pie into a wastebasket.

"Matt went to call 911," Gloria said. "Not that the cops can get up here tonight to deal with Lorene. He wanted to go after her, do a citizen's arrest, but David and Joni stopped him."

Bethany got a handful of paper towels and helped wipe up the mess, then slumped into a kitchen chair. "People are showing up."

"Joni can handle them." Gloria put the wastebasket away. From a cupboard, she took a bottle of whiskey and poured a shot for Bethany. "Don't tell the guests. Not enough to go around."

Chapter 21

The whiskey steadied Bethany's nerves. After a while, she went to the lobby, where Matt and Joni mingled with their guests. The fiddlers struck up a Western tune. David introduced Bethany to the school principal and her husband, the senior-center director. Barbara and Rusty arrived in time to join the group circling the buffet table. The lobby and porch filled up with locals Bethany didn't know.

Then Ernie burst into the lodge. His voice boomed. "Somebody spotted Lorene in her car heading out of town. Word is she rammed the barricade and kept going. That barricade has flashing lights. Everybody knows that means the road's closed. She want to commit suicide or what?"

Matt squared his shoulders and moved to where Bethany stood by the fireplace. He raised a hand to the fiddlers. "Stop the music, you guys. Everybody, if you haven't met her, this is Bethany Jarviss, Joni's sister. She found evidence that…" He took a breath. "That Lorene Callender committed some bad acts. Terrible things."

Silence settled over the room except for a shuffling of feet. The crowd parted to let Joni go to Matt and Bethany. Gloria watched from the kitchen doorway.

"Tell them," Joni whispered to Bethany. "We're all friends here."

Under the townspeople's frank stares, she hesitated,

then plunged ahead. "You all know about Krystal Decker's bones being found. Well, Krystal left some journals that I read. She secretly wrote about seeing Mrs. Callender suffocate her husband at the scene of their truck accident."

"Flint," someone said. "Mean-eyed bastard."

Matt turned toward Bethany. "Tell them the rest of it."

"Krystal happened to be in the forest when she heard a crash. She ran to where the ground drops away over the road. She saw what Lorene had done. Then Krystal did something she shouldn't have. She tried to blackmail Lorene. Tonight, right before this party, Lorene admitted she killed Krystal, hit her deliberately. We were in the kitchen and…" Bethany's throat went dry. She swallowed but couldn't continue.

"She had a knife," Joni said in a small, firm voice. "She threatened us with it. Then she drove off."

"She won't make it down the mountain. That's a dead woman for sure," one of the fiddlers said.

A murmur passed through the crowd.

Joni put an arm around Matt's waist. "Now everybody can stop wondering about Matt, thanks to my sister."

"Hear, hear," David said. People applauded, except for Barbara, who stood stock-still at the edge of the crowd.

Rusty patted her shoulder. "It's okay, Barbara. Krystal's in a better place."

People milled around in groups, unsure of what to do. Matt urged the fiddlers to resume playing. When the office phone rang, he went to answer it.

Minutes later, he rejoined Joni and Bethany. "Crush

Dobbs called. He guessed Lorene had been here, so I told him what happened. Her car blasting through the barricade is public knowledge at the bar. Some of the younger men are hiking down to see how far she got. I offered to help, but he said they've got it covered."

"That's right. You need to stay here," Joni said. "It was good of him to call."

Crush had never planned to come to the party, Bethany realized. He must have kept the Black Bear open for anyone not invited to the lodge. He and Matt weren't friends, after all.

More guests arrived, including Tom and Flora Whitney from The Treasure Box, for what seemed more like a wake than a party. Matt worked the crowd for a while, then slipped away to phone Santa Fe. "No need for that expensive attorney now."

Joni urged the fiddlers to play their liveliest numbers and encouraged everyone to help themselves to food and drink. Gloria refilled the punch bowl, kept an eye on the buffet table. People went upstairs to see the guest rooms or enjoy David's chair massages. Eventually, Jazz arrived, fashionably late, in a fur coat and much fancier dress than Bethany's. David took Jazz aside to get her a drink and no doubt tell her about Lorene. They sat talking by the Christmas tree as the crowd thinned.

When the party ended at ten, a couple of hours earlier than planned, Bethany found Gloria in the kitchen staring at the apple and pumpkin pies that hadn't smashed on the floor. "I didn't have the heart to serve them," Gloria said. "Luckily, I made a lot of cake. I told Joni we never needed to order those pies."

It sounded so funny they leaned on each other, laughing. Bethany wiped her eyes with her fingers as the whiskey bottle again materialized in Gloria's hands.

Gloria poured double shots. "We need another dose of this. It's medicine."

"I liked Lorene," Bethany said.

"The whole town did," Gloria said somberly.

Later, Matt and Joni found them still in the kitchen, cleaning up. He reported the searchers had come upon Lorene's dead body in her car, not far from town, where the car had gone off the road and crashed. They would take turns staying at the scene of the accident until the road up the mountain could be cleared for the police and ambulance crews. Crush planned to keep the bar open all night to give the volunteers a place to warm up.

"We've got plenty of leftover food," Joni said. "Let's pack some to take to the Black Bear."

"I'm on it," Gloria said with an unbelievable amount of energy.

Bethany told Joni she wanted to stay behind. "I'll phone the folks and Don to let them know what's happened. Nathan, too. We wouldn't want them to hear it on the news." She watched out a window as the three others left in Matt's SUV. A similar one she didn't recognize remained in the parking lot. Jazz's car, she assumed.

On the third floor, the massage-room door stood ajar. No one occupied the tiny room, but David's bedroom door had a *Do Not Disturb* tag over the knob.

Bethany decided to call Nathan before her parents and brother. She needed to hear her boyfriend's comforting voice most of all. In her room, she took off the arrowhead pendant and looped its cord over the dresser mirror. Why had Krystal traced it in her journal? That remained a mystery.

****

On Saturday, the road connecting Sorrel to the wider world eventually was plowed, the accident scene cleared, and the go-ahead given to remove the sawhorse barricade. People could again drive up and down the mountain. Only then did the locals stop their vigil, Matt reported. The night before, he had sent Joni and Gloria back to the lodge while he stayed with the Black Bear group.

He returned on foot with the news that Lorene's body had been taken by silent ambulance to La Plata. "A detective is coming to get our statements this morning. You'll have to talk to him, Bethany."

In private, she had shown Matt what Krystal wrote on the inside of the journal's paper cover, then made a photocopy.

"Krystal did plan to get out of Sorrel. She didn't love me enough to stay," Matt said. "But that seems like ancient history. Krystal doesn't seem real anymore. Maybe that's what makes a true star, somebody so far above the ordinary, you can't touch them. No sense dwelling on that now, though."

Bethany agreed. She decided not to tell Matt about Krystal supposedly sleeping with a mystery man at the Ponderosa Motel. Lorene must have made him up; Krystal hadn't mentioned him in her journals. But then she made no mention of the impromptu sex with Crush either.

As Bethany placed the last photocopy with the other materials, she paused at the photo of the flowers and stuffed animals left outside the Ponderosa Café after Flint's death. Among them, she noticed what she hadn't before: a teddy bear with an arrowhead at its throat instead of the usual bow. It didn't matter who put the teddy bear there. Krystal must have taken the arrowhead off it. *But why?*

****

The state police detective who came to the lodge was a thin, respectful man. He set his black cowboy hat brim up on the coffee table in the lobby but didn't bother to remove his sheepskin coat. He came alone and took his own notes. Before he questioned Bethany, he spoke to the others in private one by one—first Joni, Gloria, and David briefly, then Matt at length.

When her turn finally came, Bethany found the detective easy to talk to. He asked about her investigation with no hint of disapproval or admiration. She handed over the journals, which he had heard about from Matt's attorney, and showed him what Krystal had written on the back of the handmade cover.

Even though Bethany explained that the journals probably belonged to Rusty, the detective took possession of them. He sealed them in clear plastic envelopes and had her sign a form. "I'll be talking to him and his foster mother as well, don't worry.

"I did some checking up on you, Ms. Jarviss. Heard about your part in getting the SOB responsible for that student's death up north."

He tucked away his notebook. "By the way, Sidney Rogers came into our headquarters. Confessed to stealing that pot Mr. MacGregor's lawyer contacted us about. Says he paid Krystal Decker over time about a thousand dollars to keep quiet before she just up and stopped bleeding him. But in the backpack found with her skeleton, she had about twice that much, a fact we never made public. From what's on that brown paper, the girl meant to meet Mrs. Callender to put the touch on her. Apparently, the woman killed her rather than pay a dime in blackmail. You got any ideas about where the rest of the cash came from?"

Bethany had some ideas. "Her earnings at the bar? And you might talk to Jazz Marcham about two rings she thinks Krystal stole from her shop. If so, Krystal probably pawned them in La Plata. The rings aren't mentioned in her journals."

"Okay, thanks. And about Rogers. Before he turned himself in, he went to see the museum owner in the nursing home. Seems Mr. Sorrel is confused about how many pots he owned. Or how much they were worth or where they used to sit. I doubt he'll want to press charges. Kind of small potatoes compared to murder." He picked up his black hat. "Think I should spend my valuable time investigating that situation?"

Bethany could tell he didn't want to bother. "No, sir. Sid will probably retract his confession, so you'd have to prove where he got some of the money to buy his truck and trailer. They'd be confiscated. An elderly man would be homeless and without wheels and might serve a jail term. The museum would lose its curator. And another thing, Sid plays Santa Claus at the grade school every year. That's only a few days from now."

The detective's mouth widened in a slow smile. "Fine then. Wouldn't want to lock up Santa Claus."

He put on his hat and adjusted it. "We thought Matt MacGregor was guilty. Guess you had faith he wasn't."

"Not really. I don't know Matt very well. I wanted to find out the truth for my sister's sake."

The detective dipped his head in a gentlemanly gesture. After he left, Bethany realized the arrowhead still hung from her bedroom mirror. She had forgotten to mention the photo of the toy bear wearing what looked like the very same object.

****

Early Sunday morning, Ernie and Rusty brought bags of food ordered from the mercantile for the open house. Bethany was helping Joni make breakfast since Gloria had the morning off. They offered to bring in the rest of the order from Ernie's truck, but he said he could handle it.

With a flourish, Rusty handed Joni a Christmas tin. "From Barbara. She said they're not for the general public. You better hide them."

Joni pried off the lid. Inside were sugar cookies shaped like stars and candy canes. She bit into one. "Homemade. I'll go call and thank her."

"Wait a minute," Rusty said. "I've got something for Beth Annie." From his coat pocket, he took the stone he had shown Bethany the day she met him. He had polished parts of it, wrapped it in thin wire, and attached it to a silver chain. "I made it nicer for you. Like I promised. Jazz gave me the chain for free."

"It's a beautiful pendant, Rusty." Bethany took it from him. "Look how it sparkles!"

For some reason, she had felt compelled to wear the arrowhead today. Now she took it off and held both pendants in her palm. "They're the same stone."

Returning, Ernie heard the comment as he plunked down more grocery bags. "They sure are."

"I know what kind," Rusty said. "Flintstone."

"Do you think Krystal knew that?" Bethany asked.

Rusty shrugged. "Sure. She was smart."

"Indeed," Bethany said. She imagined Krystal

seeing a flintstone arrowhead on a teddy bear among the tributes to Flint Callender outside of the café. People who never knew he abused his wife would have placed them there. Krystal must have taken the arrowhead to wear in Lorene's presence as a warning: *Pay, or I'll tell the police you killed your husband.* There could be no knowing for sure, but Bethany guessed she was correct.

Gently, she pressed the arrowhead into Rusty's big hand. "This was Krystal's, you know. You keep it."

Putting on her new pendant, she wanted to say so much but kept it simple. "You're an artist, Rusty. I'll think of you every time I wear this."

Matt poked his head into the kitchen. "Ladies, your dad's on the office phone. He's itching to fly that plane of his now that the weather's clear. Says he and your mom will be here in a couple hours. They've got a rental car waiting at the airfield in La Plata, so they'll make it to the open house. Go talk to him. Bethany, he said something about bringing your boyfriend along for the ride."

"Nathan's coming? All right!" Bethany made a beeline for the office with Joni at her bootheels.

A word about the author...

Rita A. Popp has worked as a newspaper reporter, public relations account executive, university writer and editor, and community college instructor. Her light and twisty short stories have appeared in online magazines and two Sisters in Crime Guppy anthologies. She and her husband divide their time between their home in Colorado and cabin in the New Mexico mountains. Visit Rita's website at: https://ritapopp.com.

Thank you for purchasing
this publication of The Wild Rose Press, Inc.

For questions or more information
contact us at
info@thewildrosepress.com.

The Wild Rose Press, Inc.
www.thewildrosepress.com